Kimberly Jane Oswald was born and raised in Michigan and spent summers with family in Oklahoma. Her writing has appeared in the *Cincinnati Enquirer, Breast Cancer Wellness* and *Today's Christian Women.* She is a two-time cancer survivor and currently lives in Ohio, with her husband. She wants everyone to know she is healthy, happy and hoping her book sells. *Death of the Cosset* is her first novel.

DEATH
OF THE
COSSET

KIMBERLY JANE OSWALD

Matador
9 Priory Business Park,
Wistow Road, Kibworth Beauchamp,
Leicestershire. LE8 0RX
Tel: 0116 279 2299
Email: books@troubador.co.uk
Web: www.troubador.co.uk/matador
Twitter: @matadorbooks

Library of Congress Control Number: 2020907308
Also published, Fairfield, Ohio

ISBN 978 1800460 454

British Library Cataloguing in Publication Data.
A catalogue record for this book is available from the British Library.

Typeset in 11pt Adobe Jenson Pro by Troubador Publishing Ltd, Leicester, UK

Matador is an imprint of Troubador Publishing Ltd

For every parent who has ever lost a child

ONE

A.D. 1988, CINCINNATI, OHIO

She only had a week. The curator of the Kreativ Museum in Cincinnati was sending her, Cassandra Seldon, resident Egyptologist, on an excavation to Egypt, hoping to find any artifacts or evidence supporting if a Dynasty Zero really did exist. This was to be a shared excursion with the Field Museum in Chicago. Field was helping Kreativ pay for the excavation and was sending their resident archaeologist. So whatever they found to either prove or disprove Dynasty Zero would be a joint venture, meaning they would be sharing the much-needed publicity.

The museum world was split on the subject and was looking for more substantial proof to end the debate once and for all. If evidence was found of a king ruling a unified Egypt before 3150 B.C. it would change history. So this was how the five foot four, thirty-two-year-old, blue-eyed, short blond-haired Egyptologist, whom everyone called Cassie, found herself on her way to the airport for her first professional excavation since coming to work for the Kreativ Museum.

The museum was given a German name, for the majority of early settlers to Cincinnati were of German descent. And to this day Cincinnati is known for its German heritage. The word *Kreativ* (pronounced kree-a-tiv), translates to *Creative*. The board had recently met to discuss closing, due to lack of funding and public support. They were in their final weeks and needed something big to keep their doors open.

Thus finding the answer as to whether Upper and Lower Egypt were unified earlier than is historically accepted as true, would be huge. However, several other museums were sending their most notable experts to try to do the same thing. Turin in Italy's Museo Egizio had already sent their Egyptologist on a couple of digs. So had London's British Museum.

Cassie was on her way to the airport, enjoying the music playing on the radio, as she pulled into the nearest gas station. After filling her tank, she ran into the mini-mart to pay and grab a cup of coffee. She noticed a young woman holding a crying baby. She looked to be almost two, rubbing her eyes with the soft fur on the cuff of her pink coat. Her little eyes were red and swollen as if she had been up all night.

Fumbling with her coffee lid, Cassie thought it was far too early for a baby to be out and looked up once more, catching a glimpse of her crying. But then the beat from the music came back into her head, reminding her to hurry. Walking out, she noticed the young woman putting her crying baby into a car seat. She said a quick prayer for the baby as she drove off. This would have to suffice, as the radio started playing her favorite punk rock song, reminding her she was in a hurry.

*

The line to board the plane was long and the aisle was narrow. Cassie had found her seat but was having trouble shoving her bag into the small overhead compartment. "Ma'am, if it won't fit, you are going to have to check your bag. You're holding up the line." Even in heels she was height-challenged, so a little help from the flight attendant would have been nice, but that clearly wasn't going to happen. So she tried again, thankful she had worn a jumpsuit instead of a skirt.

"Let me give you a hand," a man said from behind her. His hand reached over her head, pushing the case back. "There, that should do it." The man had dark hair and green eyes that were magnified by his large-framed glasses. He moved into the row of seats with her, ending the sneering directed toward them.

"Thank you for helping me. The aisle's clear so you can find your seat."

"I know, but I'm standing by my seat." He extended his hand to introduce himself. "Dr. McCormick, from Field Museum. But you can call me Mark, seeing as how we'll be working together."

"Dr. Cassandra Seldon, from Kreativ Museum. But I guess you already knew that." She shook his hand, trying to mask her surprise. She wanted to make a strong impression when they met. "But you can call me Cassie." *Great, now he'll see me as a damsel in distress who needed to be rescued.*

"You look troubled. Are you alright?" he asked.

She hesitated. "Me, yes, it's just… I didn't know we would be flying out on the same plane." She sat, fumbling with her seatbelt.

He smiled at her while fastening his. "Dr. Edmund Ramsey, the head of this excavation, thought we should get to know each other, so I flew here from O'Hare so we could be on the same flight. No one told you?"

"No," she said. "Apparently the curator failed to mention this." She felt her boss should have, seeing she was one of the few women with a Ph.D. employed in the museum world. And the only female on this excavation. The flight attendant did the oxygen drill as the plane taxied before taking flight. Settling in, Cassie just wanted to relax and have a drink. She looked over at Mark. "Would you like to have a cocktail with me?"

He didn't answer. He sat, his back stiff into his seat and kept wiping his face with a handkerchief until the plane was steady in the air. When the flight attendant came around with the cart, Cassie opted for a white wine instead, while he put in his order for a cup of water. "Are you afraid of flying?"

"No, it's just…" He briefly shut his eyes. "It's the cigarette smoke. It makes me nauseous when I fly."

"Probably because of the enclosed space we're in." She pursed her lips together. This was going to be a rough trip for him. After a four-hour layover in Paris, they had to board another plane. His pale face forced a smile as the flight attendant handed them their drinks. He took a sip and then leaned back, closing his eyes. It was just as well. She didn't want to play nursemaid. She sipped her drink and pulled

4

out a small paperback from her purse, preparing for the long flight ahead.

Cassie finally felt as if her work was being noticed. It was tough enough just to be employed as an Egyptologist, much less being one of the few women trying to get some sort of recognition. Everyone always asked her why she wanted to go to the Middle East, with all the turmoil surrounding the region. Or why she, a young, pretty woman, would want to work with old, dead, decayed things. But her personal favorite was, "Museums are so boring. Why do you want to work there?"

She felt good about her underpaid, over-employed, chosen profession, even if no one did understand, because she was doing something she wanted to do. Needed to do. And every time she pulled into the museum's parking lot and parked her car next to the pole reserved with her name on it, she felt a swell of pride.

She still couldn't believe she was on her way to Egypt. *Thank you, Dr. Ramsey.* Anybody who had any connection with the study of ancient civilizations had heard of him. He had studied archaeology at the University of Cambridge, in the United Kingdom, and then earned his Ph.D. in Egyptology at the American University in Cairo, Egypt. He started his career at the Institute of Egyptian Art and Archaeology, and then went on to write and co-author several books on ancient civilizations, many of them being about Egypt, along with his florilegium of anthologies on the subject.

And now he was the head of the antiquity department at the Metropolitan Museum of Art. He even knew Dr. Ahmed Khadry, the head of Egypt's Antiquity Department. Dr.

Ramsey, the man who was as revered as an ancient Egyptian god, had chosen her, in conjunction with the Kreativ Museum curator, to come along on this excavation. She took another sip of her drink, feeling the same amount of anticipation and eagerness about meeting Dr. Edward Ramsey as she did about going to excavate in Egypt.

She looked out the window and then back at Mark. He was dozing and still looked pale. Her eyes drifted to his notes on the tray in front of him. As she drank her wine, she began reading them. Wow! Field Museum did not believe in the new dynasty she and the Kreativ Museum were eager to help create. She wondered how he personally felt about the theory.

She continued reading until she felt the aura of someone. She turned her head to find him staring at her. Swallowing her guilt, she spoke. "I didn't mean to pry, it's just…"

He waved her apology away, pushed his glasses up onto his nose and took a sip of water.

"Are you alright?" she asked.

"I'm better now that we're in the air." He gave a faint smile.

"May I?" Cassie extended her hand and turned his notes closer to her. "It says you want to check the Turin King List. I'm afraid that won't help you. You see, the beginning and the ending of the list of kings is missing. The rest of it… well, it's in over 160 fragmented pieces." She continued reading. After a few seconds, she was laughing.

"You're not serious about this, are you? Your reason for not accepting Dynasty Zero is due to the fact that the earliest rulers were Horus rulers? That doesn't mean they weren't the kings of early Egypt."

Mark grabbed the papers from her view. "You're an Egyptologist. You of all people know that pharaohs have their ruling name and birth name inscribed inside of cartouches." He started sketching in his notebook. "The early rulers had their names written in a *serekh*: A hieroglyphic symbol picturing the palace façade, inscribed inside with the name of the sovereign, surmounted by a falcon, which represented the god Horus." He showed her what he had sketched. "No cartouches. Also, there was more than one center of power. The centers were at Naqada, Hierakonpolis and Thinis. So Egypt was not ruled as a country as of yet; the dynasties start when we have one ruler of everyone in Egypt." His voice was derisive. "A pharaoh."

He had some nerve. "Sarcasm doesn't suit you," said Cassie. "And if that's the way you see it, then we can't have the First, Second or Third Intermediate Period in Ancient Egyptian history. They call them the intermediate periods because Egypt had more than one center of power throughout those times." She watched him shove his notes into his carry-on bag. "My, my, we certainly are close-minded when it comes to discussing the timeline," she added, taking another sip of her drink, feeling satisfied.

"We have a difference of opinion. And now is not the time for the line." He smiled, looking silly, and she couldn't help but laugh. His green eyes seemed to illuminate a type of authenticity from within. Maybe it wouldn't be so bad working with him.

She wondered if she would find any proof to help support the earlier timeline theory. Maybe an inscription, an artifact, a king's name, a date from a predynastic time, anything. Not only was the museum's future on the line… her reputation was as well. If she failed, how long would it be before they hired another female Ph.D.? Or worse, would she still be employed? And the man next to her was hoping for the exact opposite of what she wanted. Was his good nature real, or was it meant to catch her off guard, giving him an advantage? She would need to keep her eye on him.

"Cassie, did you hear me?" asked Mark.

"Sorry." She brushed off her thoughts. "No, the plane's kind of loud."

"I said, the biggest benefactor of our excavation would be Egypt. They will be making money on the digs and permits they're issuing. And any artifacts found, proving or disproving the timeline, would be on a temporary loan to the museum or museums the excavators came from, but then Egypt would keep them. The country is tightening its grip on ancient artifacts."

She sipped her drink. "Well, the main source of their economy is tourism. The more they keep in their country, the more they hope it will go up."

Mark nodded. "Yes, and anyways, as dedicated professionals, what we really want is to bring to light the process of preservation against time, and how it affects our civilization today, to ensure our future."

"Really?" She hesitated. "How long did it take you to come up with that statement?" She didn't wait for an answer. "That was good." She smiled. And now he had the upper hand in this journey. She didn't feel like talking anymore. "Enjoy your flight, Dr. McCormick. You probably want to rest. We'll talk again in Egypt." She turned, staring out the window.

He smirked. "No, we'll talk in Paris first."

But she didn't hear him, for the clouds looked soft and comfortable. Like she could crawl up into one. And they hypnotized her into a tranquil state of slumber.

TWO

Mark took out the handkerchief he kept in his left pant pocket and began wiping his brow. He felt hot. He ran his hand through his dark hair and straightened his glasses. Pretending to watch the movie on the big screen at the front of the plane's cabin, he started dissecting his life. He deserved to be here. He had a doctorate in archaeology and had worked his backside off to attain it, despite his family. His father thought his goals were ridiculous and often ridiculed him for working meager jobs throughout his twenties while he attended school fulltime, often reminding him that most of his cousins and friends had well-paying jobs and a wad of cash in their pockets, while he was still living at home. After receiving his master's degree, he could finally afford to rent a house by the campus, but his father resented that it took him so long to move out.

Growing up, his father had constantly compared him to his brother who played sports. As a kid, he would rather have been digging in the dirt and analyzing his finds. And by the time he was twelve, he had a rather extensive collection of bottles. All sorts of them—old, new, green-colored; he even had some depression glass. He often reflected on why he had chosen the path that he had. Some of it traced back to his uncle who showed some interest in his bottles. Whenever he came over, he would ask him where he had acquired his latest find. Mark's treasures were magnetic. He would get just as excited telling his uncle how he acquired them as he did when he actually found them. His finds made him feel important. But his uncle had two children of his own, so his interest in Mark was kept to a minimum.

Only his mother showed the slightest degree of happiness when he finally attained his doctorate and became an archaeologist. He graduated from the University of Chicago and began working immediately for Field Museum. Now, four years and five excavations later, any chance he got to travel, he did, keeping his family at a comfortable distance.

Recently, the curator of Field Museum in Chicago had put in a good word about him, based on his prior work. And this was what had led to Dr. Ramsey asking him to go on this excavation to Egypt. The timeline theory had piqued his curiosity. He had read Dr. Cassandra Seldon's research, resident Egyptologist at the Kreativ Museum, since this was going to be a joint excavation. He saw this as a perfect opportunity to meet the respected Dr. Ramsey and to debunk this Dynasty Zero theory, which made no sense to him.

The original Egyptian timeline, that was the nucleus of his research, and disproving any other theories would secure his place as a respected archaeologist. It would give him the validation he was seeking, since digging seemed to be his purpose in life. And the museum that could provide the answer would have several artifacts on loan to them, helping them bring in much-needed revenue.

His belief stemmed from Manetho's *Notes About Egypt*. Manetho divided Egyptian history into ruling houses, and historians recognize thirty of them, starting with the unification of the two lands, Upper and Lower Egypt. The dates of the ruling houses were arrived at by Manetho from early regnal dates or sequences and by working backwards from known astronomical dates. Manetho's theory made sense to him. He took a drink of water, adjusted his seat and closed his eyes, trying to find some relief from the ruminations causing his headache.

He didn't realize he had dozed off until he heard the flight attendant telling everyone to fasten their seatbelts. He squinted his eyes before opening them. Paris was seven hours ahead of the Central Standard Time he was used to, and daylight was erupting through the window, as well as his nausea. He yawned, relieved to have slept through most of the flight as the plane made its descent. He glanced at Cassie, feeling the only thing they had in common was that they both dealt with ancient artifacts and worked in a museum.

*

After stopping at the men's room, Mark slowly proceeded toward the gate. His focus was on the excavation. Cassie was already there and so were the people who were to continue to Egypt as part of the group. Dr. Ramsey was informing everyone they were to meet back here in three hours. He suggested everyone should go eat some breakfast, and then try to nap. The flight to Egypt would be four and a half hours, and it would be mid-afternoon when they landed. Upon arrival, everyone was expected to check in at the hotel, get settled and meet for a group dinner to hear the agenda for the excavation.

He heard some mumbling from the group but didn't pay attention. He just wanted to find something to eat, in the hopes it would settle his stomach. He turned when he felt someone tapping him on the shoulder. A hand was extended toward him.

"Mark McCormick, right? I'm Ian Richards."

Mark shook his hand. "You're the papyrologist on this excavation?" asked Mark. "I heard you speak once regarding the preservation of papyri. Good speech."

Ian nodded. "Thank you. Do you want to grab a bite to eat?"

"Sure." He was not in the mood for another debate with Cassandra Seldon.

THREE

Cassie did a U-turn and bumped into the art historian who dropped by the museum from time to time. "Excuse me… I'm so sorry." He nodded. Embarrassed, she abruptly left, walking toward the restrooms and found a row of payphones. She exhanged some money for franc coins because she had to call her mother. She hadn't told her she was going to Egypt and she was already in France. She waited to call because she never knew how her mother would react to things. Sometimes their conversations went well and at other times her mother would be argumentative, withdrawn or only talking about the past. Nobody needed to hear that.

She plopped her purse on the shelf beneath the phone and scooted her luggage up against the wall with her foot. Digging through her purse, she took out every last coin and laid them on the shelf, thinking about the father she had never known. She didn't even know his name. As a child, her mother always said it didn't matter; he was never going to call or visit, so what difference would it make in her life? And her mother didn't have any other relatives. She always let Cassie know it was just the two of them in the world, and they were a family of two. When Cassie became older and wanted, needed, more answers about her father, the more she craved knowledge, the more her mother went into hysteria. This eventually led her mother to psychotherapy, and when that failed, an entire list of prescribed medications ensued.

This wasn't a phone call Cassie wanted to make, but she had no choice and she knew her mother stayed up most of the night. She picked up the receiver and inserted coin after coin, after coin. After a few moments, she began to dial the long-distance number. She held the phone to her ear. One ring. Her mother was functionally unstable. She could get through the day, but her daydreaming often took over reality. Two rings. A man walked up to the payphone next to hers. Three rings, still waiting. After a couple more, her mother picked up. Cassie felt herself stiffening; she took a deep breath before speaking. "Hi, Mom, I've got something to—"

"Cassie! Finally. Why haven't you been by to see me lately?"

She sighed. She called every week. She felt it was her duty as a daughter. She tried to change the subject. "I need you to listen, Mom. I don't have much time."

"I've been feeling ill; I don't know if it's the weather or—"

Cassie interrupted. "Mom, I'm in Paris."

"Paris! As in France…" Her mother's voice teetered off.

"You're cutting out, Mom," she sighed. "It's business. I'm only on a layover in Paris, just for a few hours. I'm on my way to Egypt."

"Egypt! Oh, Cassie, now I won't be able to sleep until I know you're back in Ohio."

She turned, eyeing the man at the phone next to hers. Drawing in a deep breath, she steadied herself. Her mother had a way of throwing her off-balance. "Mom, listen—"

Her mother interrupted. "You're going to get yourself killed."

That was the way all their conversations went. Cassie would try to say something, and her mother would go off on a tangent. But right now, she was out of patience. "Mom! I've been chosen to go on an excavation to explore some of the ancient ruins, to try to find something to back up the theory on Dynasty Zero. Remember, Mom, my research?" The man at the phone next to hers smiled. She turned her back to him, hoping he hadn't heard any of her conversation.

"Oh, Cassie, you're never gonna find a man if you keep on arguing with all of them."

Oh God, not the 'you need to find a man' speech. She stared at the numbers on the phone. "Mother, this is 1988. I'm arguing with women too." She shook her head.

"I don't know why you want to work in that stuffy old museum."

"Mom, this is an all-expenses-paid trip to Egypt which will further my job and reputation."

"What kind of reputation? That isn't what a good girl wants."

"A reputation as an expert in my field." She cupped the phone receiver with her other hand. Oh, how she longed for a good ole-fashioned phone booth. Her frustration was mounting as she tried to keep her cool. "This theory is starting to gather some merit in the museum world. The head of the antiquities department at New York's Metropolitan Museum of Art recommended me."

Clunk! "Mom?" Cassie let out a long exhale; her breathing was off. "Mom?" Silence. She knew the call was over. Well, her mother knew where she was in case something happened. She jiggled the coin return, but the payphone kept all her money.

*

Susan was in her rocking chair facing the picture window in her living room looking at her reflection. Her blondish brown hair, speckled with gray, was covering one of her eyes. Back and forth, back and forth, was the rhythm of the rocker. Glaring into the night, she was hypnotized into a trance-like state, never wondering how her life had gotten to this point. She felt worn out. She had been rocking for hours. It was the middle of the night, but she didn't notice. Her thoughts, dreams, and how she envisioned herself, it was all mid-sixties.

She lived off the government, because she was declared a manic-depressive who was considered to be temperamental and unstable. And she had plenty of medication to prove it. None of which did much good. It was much easier to stay in bed all day and watch television. On the days she could get up, she would put in an old cassette tape with music from the seventies and sit in her rocker. Ironically, a song was playing about a woman who never left her room.

Susan had rocked back and forth in her chair so often, her movements had worn the old faded carpet. She didn't seem to notice, or if she did, she didn't care. She couldn't afford to replace it, so why care? She didn't own a pet, not even a plant. Her meals, when she ate, consisted of microwave popcorn or a bowl of cereal. Once in a while, she splurged on a candy bar. When Susan was in one of her trance-like states, sometimes she ate nothing for a day or two. She liked hot tea, water and sometimes only a cup of hot water with no tea in it at all.

Back and forth, back and forth, the steady rocking soothed her. The seconds ticked into minutes, and the minutes rocked into hours. Finally, the sheer boredom of the steadiness her life had for the moment gave her the energy to get out of her rocker, take a few pills and go to bed—the bed she planned to stay in until she spoke with Cassie again.

FOUR

Cassie was walking through the airport trying to find a place to eat when she spotted a boutique. Not just any boutique, but one that sold lingerie. The leopard teddy the mannequin was wearing caught her eye and it enticed her enough to go inside.

She loved lingerie. Some women have a fetish for shoes, others for purses, but with her, it was the look and touch of the silky fabric. It made her feel like an adult. A *sophisticated* adult. A *sexy, sophisticated* adult. When you buy lingerie, no one will ask you why you bought it, nor will they say, *Do you really think you should have spent so much?* Like they do when a woman buys yet another pair of shoes. Because no one knows you bought it; with lingerie, it's private and personal. Your own little secret.

You don't buy lingerie because your friend told you to. You usually don't even have anyone with you when you do buy it. You don't buy it to show it off; you either buy it to wear for that certain someone or you buy it for you. No one will tell you they don't like the color or it's too revealing. They won't say, *It's just not you,* because the majority of people you know, even pretty well, don't know you buy it. No one knows what you have on underneath your clothes. And that's why Cassie had a closet full of lingerie. No one, not even her mother, could judge her. It was a part of herself she shared with no one, and it made her feel special.

She went into the store, and within five minutes, she had three pieces to try on in the dressing room. The deep purple camisole was her favorite. It looked gorgeous on her skin tone, and the satin felt luxurious, unlike the lace one she previously tried on, which pricked and itched.

Turning, she pulled out her compact and held it up to the mirror for a back view. Then she looked again from the front. She liked the way the halter strap held up her breasts and the empire waist hid any tummy flaws. She slid her hands down the front of the cami over her breasts. She breathed deeply as her hands glided across her stomach, feeling the richness of the satin.

As she left the dressing room, she decided she would look for a purple garter belt. She already owned several pairs of black thigh highs. Put this all together and she had yet another sophisticated, sexy, adult outfit to wear underneath her clothing.

She found a matching panty to accompany the ensemble, paid for everything and looked at her watch. Between talking to her mother and shopping, she had just enough time to get something to eat. She wouldn't have time to sleep, but it didn't matter. She felt satisfied and would sleep on the plane. On the way out, she stopped again to look at the leopard teddy. She smiled at the mannequin who knew her secret and left, wondering why Mark had popped into her mind.

FIVE

A.D. 1988, CAIRO, EGYPT

Finally settled in her hotel room, Cassie was dressing for the meet-and-greet party Dr. Ramsey had planned for this evening, an array of hors d'oeuvres, cocktails and acquaintances. Everyone who was on this excavation would be attending. She gave herself one long glance in the mirror. Then she put on her black thigh highs, which accentuated the purple garter and panties she had on, not to mention the purple camisole, which was nothing less than gorgeous.

She tucked the cami into her black knee-length skirt and put on the matching blazer. She felt pretty. And sexy. She put on her four-inch sultry black pumps with the cross strap and pointed toes, finishing the outfit. Now for the jewelry. She chose a pair of silver dangle earrings and her watch, because it had a white gold band and looked like a bracelet. With one last look in the mirror, she fluffed the back of her hair. Only she knew her fetish for lingerie, and her reflection shared her sensuality with no one.

Studying the reflection looking back at her brought up past memories. There had been no one special in her life since Chad Westin, her high-school boyfriend. He was slender built, with blond hair and blue eyes. His family had just moved to Cincinnati, and he had fallen for her when they first met on the school bus. His father was a Methodist minister, and his mother a homemaker. She remembered the nice dinners she had been invited to at Chad's home. She had to admit she fell in love with the Westin family before she fell in love with Chad. She liked the feeling of being part of a close-knit family.

This was a far cry from her family, which consisted of an absentee father she had never met, and a half out of her mind mother, who often needed mothering. She remembered being embarrassed as she told Chad about Susan's times of being in and out of coherency, how they lived on welfare, and if anyone tracked the time of day in her household, it was Cassie. She made sure Chad never saw her mother when she was in her hypnotized trance state, or depressed. She knew her mother's cycle after years of taking care of her, and only invited him into the house when her mother was on one of her manic highs. She was larger than life at these times. Even then one would be able to tell, at the very least, she was a little off her rocker.

But Chad always played his role. Eating the cereal she served after inviting him over for dinner, or her endless babbling about the past when Cassie was little. Cassie would not have made it through her teen years without him. But now as an adult, she had dated men, even slept with a few, but she had not been in love since Chad. And he'd become a distant memory. One she buried, so she could cope.

Her body began to shake, and a sudden wave of nausea rushed into her stomach. She stumbled as she made her way to the bathroom. She managed to open her toiletry bag, grabbing a syringe and clenching it in her teeth as she pulled off the cap. Her hands were shaking as she took out a vial. Somehow she was able to tip it upside down and fill the syringe before her shaking became violent. She sat on the toilet, pulled up her skirt and started injecting the drug into her left thigh directly above her nylons. Her shaking was so bad, it caused her to jab the needle forcefully into her skin.

Her tongue slipped between her lips. She tasted blood. She had bitten her lip. She pursed them together waiting for the bleeding to stop. Leaning back on the toilet, resting her head against the back of the tank, she closed her eyes. She felt anesthetized. Peace had arrived and she began to fade from the room. Her breathing was faint and undulant.

She didn't know how much time had passed when her shaking subsided. The fading-away feeling stopped, and her breathing resumed as normal. She was okay. She exhaled, releasing any remaining anxiety, and then reapplied her deodorant before looking at herself in the mirror. Not too bad, considering. She brushed her hair and powdered her nose for the second time. She searched her toiletry bag for her lipstick, reapplying it to her lips. She pinched her left nylon at the ankle and continued pulling it up, tightening it to the garter, and then did the same to the right leg. She was finally ready to go to the meet and greet… again.

SIX

ANCIENT EGYPT,
DYNASTY SIX, SAQQARA,
INSIDE THE PYRAMID OF QUEEN IPUT

The queen and her companion entered the tomb. The torches illuminated the rooms where the queen would one day live for all eternity. It was a small pyramid, for it was not for a king. The niches glowed with golden statues, adding splendor to the already magnificent walls, which were painted and carved with pictures of the queen, amongst the gods and goddesses. The corridor had carvings of long-stemmed lotuses along the Nile. The blue in the lotus flowers was the same color as the sky at sunrise. And the blue of the Nile was as dark as dusk. If she inhaled, she could almost smell the hyacinth scent of the flower.

"How lovely. The lotus flower is my rebirth."

They reached a narrow opening leading to the burial chamber. She looked on as he inhaled deeply, taking in the fresh smell of cedar. Her companion asked, "Do you see your cedar coffin?"

"Yes! And a sarcophagus made out of limestone. You truly do love me."

Her companion spoke. "Nothing but the best for you."

Queen Iput touched the canopic vessels, which would one day hold her organs, with the same gentleness she used to use when touching his sidelock of hair. She stopped to examine the headrest.

"Have you seen the red pottery pieces that you so do love?"

She gasped. "Look how brightly polished they are. Oh, and my rock crystal cup." She placed her hand upon her heart.

"Layers upon layers of the finest treasures. Just for you. It's all for you. Let's sit." He pointed to the two chairs with a small table placed between them. "Along with your favorite pottery and statues, I had the servants also bring in your favorite wine." He smiled. "But first I have one last thing to show you." He handed her a small basket.

She opened it and pulled out the statue of the miniature cosset. It was the statue her *abi* had given her when she was a small child. It had the markings *Sefekhu Shenet* on its belly. Next she pulled out a shard—a small piece of engraved pottery, also from her *abi*. She placed the items into one of the niches.

"How did you get… oh, it doesn't matter." She wiped the corner of her eyes with her hands. This love she felt absolved the choices she had made before the gods throughout her life. "I also brought something to place in my tomb." She pulled from her bosom a small gold bracelet and placed it next to the other items, muttering a prayer to the gods under her breath.

"What did you say?" he asked.

"Nothing, I just asked the gods to never let you forget the sacrifices made for you. That's all." She sat down.

"Please take a sip. It is your favorite." He handed her the wine in her rock crystal cup.

"Are you still haunted by night terrors?" She took a sip of wine.

Her companion grinned. "No, I haven't had any since I finished your tomb. The gods must be pleased with what I did for you. Did you see the images of the goddess Maat? The goddess of truth and justice. Remember, life is short, but death is long. You want to be judged fairly, don't you? I had her statue placed and her image carved in your tomb, because your *abi* also had her in his tomb. I thought it would please you."

She took another sip of wine. "It does please me, very much. You have made it so I will long be remembered in the afterlife." She placed her hand upon her stomach, her head tilted back, then, suddenly but slowly, she slid off her chair, falling upon the tomb's floor. He picked her up and laid her upon the slab of rock in the burial chamber. "I feel... ill... maybe the wine has gone bad."

He placed the headrest on the slab and gingerly lifted her head onto it. "Just rest as the goddess Maat judges you for truth and justice. For you see, I only finished what you started. What you did to secure your future and lineage! So now your wine has been poisoned with opium and hemlock, and mixed with the sweetness of *shedeh*, to secure my future and lineage, for no one can know the tale you have weaved.

"And with your death I have secured the dynasty. There is no enemy I cannot defeat, for I am my own worst enemy. My poor little cosset. It is time for your secret to be buried along with you. You are my sacrificial lamb."

The queen whispered, "For the betterment of Egypt?" She tried to lift her head.

"Don't try to get up. You know one taste of the poison makes you ill. It is time for you to make your final supplication to the gods and goddesses." Her eyes began moving rapidly from left to right. "You look pale and tired, so I will do it for you as Maat takes you into the afterlife." He gazed upwards. "You do not fear the darkness that is rising to claim you, in fact you welcome it." She watched him until all the images in the room intertwined, too close to death to be able to do anything, and then closed her eyes.

She heard him breathe deeply before speaking. "May the curse of Maat, daughter of Ra, follow you into the underworld. Your public and ritual life was not in harmony with the cosmic rhythms of the universe. Since you have disturbed the harmony, you must suffer the consequences. Your indestructible nature will follow you out of this natural world. Your life in the underworld will be chaotic and violent, for you opposed the right order expressed by Maat. Should you ask for forgiveness and accept Ra's judgment of the wider order of the universe, only then will your *ka* and *ba* be forgiven. And with the help of your *akhu*, your descent from the underworld will cease and your ascent to the afterlife will begin. Accepting Ra's judgment is the only way to cosmic harmony." He leaned in closer. "Hurry, the god of death, Anubis is near. Do you ask for forgiveness?"

Queen Iput nodded, and then her body went limp. Her *akhu* drifted skyward toward the gods, her rebirth now complete. She had already departed when he picked up the jug of poisoned wine and the rock crystal cup, placing them into the basket he carried before leaving her tomb.

SEVEN

A.D. 1988, CITY OF THE DEAD

Cassie stared out the window, smiling. She wanted to absorb every minute, every second, of this experience. She tightened the bandana around her neck, straightened her straw cowboy hat and adjusted the string underneath. She was now confident it would stay on when she bent low inside the pyramids. They all wore a similar uniform: a pair of brown khaki pants and a tan shirt. But most everyone else's heads were topped off with a baseball cap. Amongst the chatter of the similar-dressed people, she noticed the bus was kicking up dust from the road as they approached the first capital of ancient Egypt: Memphis. As the dust cleared, so did her thoughts, and she focused on getting her bearings.

She knew it was located twenty-four kilometers or fifteen miles south of Cairo, and was the resting place of many Old Kingdom pharaohs. She remembered from her college research that it contained the necropolis Saqqara, a Greek word meaning 'City of the Dead,' located west of the Nile River, close to the point where the Nile splits and then flows into the Mediterranean Sea. Looking out the window, she took pride in being able to jog her memory of her college research.

She recalled reading that the cemetery was nine square kilometers, with Giza seventeen kilometers to the north and Dashur ten kilometers to its south. And the modern capital of Egypt, Cairo, being forty kilometers to the northeast. She already knew there were two parts to Saqqara. The north, called Saqqara north, contained several smaller cemeteries grouped around larger monuments. And in between the archaic tombs were the oldest-known funerary monuments, also known as mastabas. It was here the buildings of Sekhenkhet were located, which to this day are not finished. The south, called Saqqara south, was between the pyramids of Pepi I and Shepseskaf.

She felt a sudden fluttering in her heart as they entered the City of the Dead. If they were going to find anything to predate Dynasty One, it might be here, among the oldest of all funerary monuments. If their exploration led them to anything of which the earliest dynasties considered ancient, they may just find artifacts predating Dynasty One. The main focus of the royals buried here was to prepare for their death.

She stood up to exit the bus. Her ankles and knees felt like they were made of rubber. She worried her legs would buckle underneath the weight of her body. So she sat back down, letting everyone file off before her. She heard one of the local guides, a woman, telling everyone the pyramid's shape was to resemble the sun's rays in reference to the sun god, and how people had died climbing them. When Cassie finally did exit, she carefully proceeded down the aisle, and with each movement, her body wavered ever so slightly. She hoped this wouldn't cause her to bounce off the steps and hit the ground.

Dr. Edmund Ramsey was standing near the bus looking at his map. He was tall and sixtyish, with grey temples showing underneath his Buffalo Nickel hat. His face was leathery, probably due to too much time in the sun on his excavations. He motioned everyone to come together for a huddle. She observed that at this moment he looked as if his world only consisted of the necropolis at Saqqara. And he spoke as if his agenda was the only thing going on in the world.

"Because everyone here knows about Pharaoh Djoser, he will be our focal point, so that no one gets lost in the endless wind of sand once the bus leaves the desert. Ignore the tourists who will be here shortly, as they do not have access to what we will be exploring. They will be admiring the first pyramid ever built. The famous Step Pyramid of King Djoser, designed by his architect, Imhotep. You may also meet amateur explorers, since it has become popular to try to find where Imhotep was buried. Please do not help them in their exploration; remember, ours is to prove or disprove Dynasty Zero. We will be exploring the mastabas and pyramids, of which only we have been given sole access to, due to my close professional relationship with Dr. Ahmed Khadry, the head of Egypt's antiquities department. He has helped me secure the authorization needed for this excavation and the permits to do the archaeological digs in these tombs."

Dr. Ramsey took a deep breath. "And in case any of you are wondering why we aren't excavating in Hierakonpolis, the place where a lot of predynastic rulers have been buried, it is because Dr. Ahmed Khadry has a team exploring in that region. However, we are here at Saqqara because of his recommendation. Pharaohs from the Old Kingdom collected a lot of predynastic artifacts, because even in their time they were considered ancient. We are hoping they buried some of these artifacts in their tombs." Looking down, he referred to the paper in his hand, never missing a beat. "Dr. Tom Granite and myself will be on team one exploring the tomb of Teti I, who, as you know, was the first pharaoh of Dynasty Six. His pyramid is a few hundred meters northwest of Djoser's Step Pyramid.

"Dr. Roger Barrington will be on team two, exploring Kagemni's mastaba with one of the local guides, located just north of King Teti." He looked up. "Kagemni's tomb is of importance because of his influence, not only on the pharaoh Teti, but also on the last pharaoh of Dynasty Five, King Unas. He was the vizier to both of these kings. And his mastaba is located near both pharaohs."

Edmund cleared his throat and continued reading. "Dr. Mark McCormick and Dr. Ian Richards will be on team three, which will be exploring King Unas's pyramid, located directly south of Djoser's Step Pyramid, in the southwest corner of the Step Pyramid complex.

"And Dr. Cassandra Seldon will be on team four with one of the local guides. She will be examining Queen Iput's tomb. Most queens were buried in the Valley of the Queens, except for Iput, wife of the pharaoh Teti. She is also buried here in Saqqara, in her own pyramid, which is near his."

Cassie's heart once again fluttered. A queen buried in Saqqara amongst kings. This was a sign of good fortune. In the distance she heard Dr. Ramsey say something about who was exploring King Teti's son, Pepi I's tomb, second king of Dynasty Six. She thought she heard Dr. Ramsey saying his pyramid was about two kilometers, or about one and a quarter miles south of the Step Pyramid. But what he was saying was unclear; she was too excited since being assigned to Queen Iput's tomb.

She refocused on what Dr. Ramsey was saying. "We will be exploring Pharaoh Djoser's tomb on our last day here in Egypt as a sightseeing tour, just for the pure enjoyment of seeing ancient Egypt, since his pyramid is the centerpiece of Saqqara." He continued. "Since there is public access to Djoser's tomb, I firmly believe we will not find anything to help our exploration. The odds are somebody would have found something by now in regard to an earlier dynasty." Dr. Ramsey returned to looking at his map, and with that, his speech was over and each group began heading toward their assigned tomb.

EIGHT

Dr. Edmund Ramsey and geologist Dr. Tom Granite walked up to a hill of rubble. King Teti's tomb. Edmund bent down on one knee, letting the granules sift between his fingers as if the sand could turn back the hourglass. "I knew at one time this area was a quarry, but I imagined King Teti's pyramid to be a little more preserved than this."

He looked on as Tom bent down to examine and take measurements of the limestone blocks on the east side of the hill, before proceeding to the pyramid's north side. It was there he made an abrupt stop.

"Dr. Ramsey… come to the north side."

Edmund began walking around the hill to where Tom was standing, wiping his hand on his pants. "Well, well, we have an opening."

"Actually, it's just a large hole."

"Well, it's an entrance into this hill of rubble," said Edmund.

Tom extended his left hand and tipped his hat. "After you, Dr. Ramsey."

Edmund turned on his lantern, bent low and walked through the portal. The light illuminated the reliefs on the wall. He studied them for a while before speaking. "These are depicting an offering. Maybe we'll find the pyramid's chapel."

"Look!" said Tom. "Another opening."

He pulled himself away from the relief. "This is a descending passage." The thought of being able to proceed farther underground into Teti's tomb had Edmund's heart beating as if it would pop through his shirt. He started walking through the passageway with his lantern, leaving Tom behind in the darkness.

"Wait! Wherever we're going under this heap of rubble, we need to do it together." Slowly they walked through the low passageway. "These walls are granite-lined."

"Well, Dr. Granite, you should know." They bent lower and lower as they progressed, their bodies almost buckling in half, only stopping when they came upon a horizontal corridor. Off to the side was a portcullis slab.

Tom touched the slab. "This is also made of granite."

"Granite walls by Dr. Granite." Edmund was tittering as the words came out of his mouth. "I guess your last name predestined you to become a geologist."

"A great geologist." Tom smiled.

Dr. Ramsey chuckled. "Moving on, I remember Dr. Ahmed Khadry saying, Teti's pyramid used to have three granite portcullis slabs on the outside of the antechamber." He stepped through the corridor and entered the vestibule, relieved to be able to finally stand up, easing the strain on his lower back.

"We're in the antechamber?" Tom's mouth hung open.

"Yes," he said. "That's why we can stand, because we're under the center of the pyramid."

"These blocks are made of limestone," said Tom, as he touched them.

Edmund's entire being was taking in the feel of the room. "The antechamber, like most tombs of this period, has a vaulted ceiling made up of huge blocks…" His voice trailed off. "…which should continue into the next room." His eyes were navigating around this second room. He could see it as it once had been in all its splendor and glory. They had entered King Teti's burial chamber. On the east side of the room were three niches, which he visualized as probably having ornate statues in them at one point in time. They had entered the room along the west wall's entrance. "As it should be." He spoke under his breath.

"As it should what?" said Tom.

"Nothing," he said. "I just figured this room should be the burial chamber, and it is. Look, the entrance has been sealed more than once." The seal was partially cracked, then broken. "Someone has re-entered the tomb. Notice there is a second and third seal. And the picture on this one is different."

"These walls are also made of limestone," said Tom.

Edmund wasn't listening. His eyes were beholding a most extraordinary sight. "The Places of Teti Endure," he muttered.

"Did you say something?" Tom's voice was resounding through the small burial chamber.

He turned. "The Places of Teti Endure is the name given to this tomb. And on this wall are Pharaoh Teti's Pyramid Texts." He turned his right hand palm side up, as if he was modeling the wall for Tom to see the texts. "The texts describe the king's journey starting from the Land of the Living and ending with life in the Netherworld. On the walls are spells intended to guide the pharaoh to eternal life with the gods."

He ran his hand along the wall, touching every impression of each column, feeling the elegance of the carved texts. "They're beautiful," he whispered. He stepped back when he saw the cartouche. Then the texts stopped. There were some blank spaces, and then the walls were painted with stylized reliefs to resemble the palace façade.

"Look at the stars." Tom was turning, staring at the ceiling. "*Ouch!*"

Edmund heard a thud and then saw Tom flat on his back. "Jesus, are you alright?"

"Yeah, from the view I have, you look really tall."

He extended his hand. Dr. Granite was short and stout, and Edmund groaned as he helped him back onto his feet. Tom was wiping the dust from his knees and pant legs, when Edmund noticed a grey object. He bent down on one knee to observe. "Come closer, look at this."

"You're killing me."

"What you tripped over was a portion of Teti's sarcophagus lid." On the other side of the room was a grey basalt sarcophagus. "Dr. Granite, please take some photographs." Edmund continued examining the lid. "Look, you can still see the hieroglyphic impressions." He then proceeded to study the sarcophagus. "From what I can make out, this is a single band portion of the Pyramid Texts. It's not finished, but most sarcophaguses were not decorated in the Old Kingdom."

"Look," said Tom. "At the base by where you're standing, at the foot end of the sarcophagus. There's a deep impression in the floor." He pointed at the dusty indentation.

Edmund looked down. "Pharaohs were known to keep their canopic chests at the foot end of their sarcophaguses. These chests contained canopic jars, which held the king's organs, his stomach, intestines, liver and lungs. It was believed all of these organs would be needed in the afterlife." He looked at Tom, then back at the tomb's floor. "This impression is about the size and shape of a chest." Then he looked back at the sarcophagus, mesmerized by the single band of the Pyramid Texts.

Tom's voice echoed. "Agh… Dr. Ramsey, I think you need to come over here."

He was starting to become a little annoyed with Dr. Granite's stars, ouches and aghs. "I'm busy. What do you see?" He did not look at him nor make a move.

"Part of an arm… I think? Well, the bone of one."

Edmund looked up, abandoning the sarcophagus, and advanced toward him, shouting, "*Don't touch it!*"

NINE

Mark and Ian came up to the southwestern corner of the enclosure wall, which surrounded the complex of King Djoser. They rested a moment so Mark could rearrange his lights and backpack. "Right there." He pointed. They were only a short distance from Pharaoh Unas's pyramid. "He was the last King of Dynasty Five," said Mark. "His pyramid is called 'Beautiful are the Places of Unas.' It also has a mortuary temple accompanying it, and the walls inside his tomb were the first to contain the Pyramid Texts." They continued walking, only stopping when they reached the rubble core pyramid located at the edge of the desert. "Wow." His tone was solemn. "This really is an ancient ruin."

Ian began setting up the portable table for his equipment. "This seems like a good place to do the architectural mapping."

"Okay," said Mark. "I'll start taking pictures of the surrounding area."

Ian set his green square box with the knobs on the side onto the portable table. "This radar equipment is a powerful machine that will send sound beams into the sand or rock to search for hidden underground spaces." Mark stared directly at him, causing him to pause. "Then this gradiometer," Ian picked it up, "will identify hidden structures beneath the surface. It will send magnetic pulses through the ground. If it finds anything, it will give us the precise measurements of each corridor. How long it is and where it leads. This way you don't excavate where you wouldn't find anything." He began walking up one side and down the other of King Unas's rubble core pyramid, pointing the gradiometer toward the ground.

Mark furrowed his brow. "I thought you were a papyrologist?"

"I am. But I also minored in archaeology. I received my doctorate from Duke University, in Durham, North Carolina."

"Expensive hobby?"

"I come from money, but I've also made my own." Ian shrugged. "That's why I think I was chosen. The excavation sort of gets a two for one with me."

Well, that explains his impeccable taste in clothes. "Ian! Your equipment is making a noise."

"Good!" he said. "It's showing me that something is buried under the sand in these two spots." He summoned some of the Egyptian locals Dr. Ramsey had hired, showing them where to dig. "It's telling me that this is disturbed sand."

"No kidding." Mark's tone was sarcastic. "You have two Egyptians digging in it. I could have told you that."

"No!" said Ian. "The top sand is mixed with some sub sand, indicating that something is buried here. Undisturbed sand has a different feel to it than disturbed sand. Disturbed sand is softer." He yelled to the locals. "What does the sand feel like?" The locals just smiled back; one of them even waved.

"I could have told you that, without any of this equipment," said Mark. "Undisturbed sand or even soil is packed hard, while disturbed sand or again soil is not as firmly packed. A kid building a sandcastle even knows that."

"Yes, but can a kid tell you if something is buried underneath his sandcastle?" One of the local's shovels made a clanking sound as he tried to push it into the sand, causing the others to start yelling. Ian and Mark ran over to where they were and kneeled into the sand, digging around the object with their hands. The local guide pulled up a good-size stone.

"It's just a stone." Mark's tone was bland. "Let the guides continue to dig. We need to get going." They began walking down the long causeway consisting of macadam. The causeway had a bend in it, and as they walked they could see something leading up to the east face of the mortuary temple. "There, an entrance." He pointed.

As they approached, they noticed parts of the causeway had been restored. They looked up at the top of the walls and noticed the roof had a couple of slits through it in which light entered, reflecting the carved reliefs on the walls. The pictures were of ships in full sail, a marketplace and hunting. There were pictures of servants with baskets of produce, jars of beer and loaves of bread. The reliefs still had small amounts of color in them. Strangely enough, there were scenes of famine, which must have happened during the reign of King Unas.

After several moments taking it all in, their attention was drawn to the south side of the causeway. There were two stone-lined boat pits. Mark knew this wasn't just symbolic for the pharaoh's afterlife. They were large enough for a real boat to have actually fit into the pit.

"These pits are big enough for a real boat!" exclaimed Ian.

Mark smiled. "You read my mind." He turned on his lantern before proceeding through an entrance, stopping when he spotted an inscription.

Ian came up beside him. "Do you know what it says?"

He studied the hieroglyph for a moment. "This is an inscription recording the restoration of this pyramid. If I remember correctly, it had fallen into ruins and a high priest from Memphis in Dynasty Nineteen restored Pharaoh Unas's tomb." He read the name. "Khaemwaset. He was one of the sons of Ramesses II, the pharaoh of Egypt in Moses's time." He remembered the name from his grad-school days, when he had decided to become an archaeologist. "Khaemwaset was often described as the first archaeologist of conservation."

"And what do you know about King Unas?"

"Well, I know he did not have a male heir," said Mark. "This led to a minor period of instability. However, this ended when Pharaoh Teti came upon the throne, becoming the first ruler of Dynasty Six."

"How did that happen?" asked Ian.

"You see, King Unas did leave a female heir—his daughter Iput." He cocked his head. "But in the Old Kingdom, women did not rule. That did not happen until Queen Sobekneferu, of the Middle Kingdom. Then not again until Queen Hatshepsut and Twosret, two women rulers of the New Kingdom."

"And don't forget about Cleopatra."

He laughed when Ian mentioned the most famous queen in Egyptian history. "Getting back on topic. King Unas's heir was his daughter Iput, who ended up marrying King Teti. But since the bloodline from the male's side was not of the same royal blood as King Unas, it created a new dynasty."

"Hey, King Teti is where Dr. Ramsey is excavating." Ian smiled. After a brief moment of silence, Mark felt the two of them had connected as they ventured deeper into King Unas's tomb.

TEN

The amber orb was beginning to rise. Its rays were emblazed upon the tombs and blended well with the sand. A cool breeze was coming off the desert and the air was filled with peace. Cassie walked a few paces ahead of her young guide—a local villager and his camel. The lumpy macadam roadway slowed them down, its gradual erosion giving way to the desert. The camel was loaded with supplies they might need on site.

"Miss Cassie, Miss Cassie."

She stopped and turned. "Yes, Simo." She liked the simplicity of his name.

"Did you know this is the best time of the day to visit the pyramids? Just after sunrise, while the tourists are having their breakfast."

She smiled and continued walking. "Good to know, Simo." She wasn't worried. Queen Iput's tomb was off limits to the tourists. After walking a short distance she stopped again, taking in what was now in front of her and was stunned. Queen Iput's tomb. Her body faintly quivered. She wanted to pinch herself to be sure this was all real. Instead she took off her hat and sunglasses and took a few photographs. She was well aware once she crossed through this Egyptian pylon, her life would be changed forever.

This was what she had worked so hard for. What it had always been about. Her shirt rippled as a cool breeze swayed across the desert. She continued unhurried but steady. This was the reason for all the sacrifices and choices she had made in her life. With a serene touch, she felt the outside of the pyramid and grains of sand sieved through her fingertips.

"Let me lead the way. I have the lantern," said Simo.

She was glad it was only the two of them. She could hardly breathe, much less speak. It took all of her emotions and strength to comprehend what she was seeing.

They entered a portico and walked through a rough-hewn passage, followed by several rooms, all empty. Simo walked ahead of her down a long corridor and then disappeared, leaving only a trail of light. "Miss Cassie." He reappeared as fast as he had disappeared. "Look over here to your right." She entered another small, empty room.

"Former excavators must have looked around and left," said Simo. "It looks like this wall connects to the back wall, but if you actually run your hand…" He waited until she was right behind him. "See, the wall ends. Now we have a narrow passageway." He pulled out a tape measure from his backpack. "Forty-six centimeters, so from a distance it looks like it's just a small, square room, but this wall has… how do Americans say… ah yes, inches. It has an opening of eighteen inches, which veers to the left. Lucky for you, Miss Cassie, you are not a big woman. We'll have to go through sideways."

She knew Queen Iput's tomb had been altered from a mastaba to this small pyramid. The reason why was still unknown. Iput's pyramid at one time was thought to contain a chapel, but no one had ever found an entrance into it.

"Here, you go in first and take the lantern," said Simo. "I have my high-powered flashlight."

She walked slow, veering to the left. If it wasn't for the light, they would have plunged into Stygian darkness; she said a quick prayer, thanking God she was not claustrophobic.

It was small and narrow, but it was an opening. She wanted to turn and make sure Simo was still behind her, but the passage was too narrow. She stopped and felt his breath on the back of her neck. Lucky for him, he wasn't a big man. Cassie had to duck to enter, but there it was, another room. *Could it be?* "I think we may have just found Queen Iput's chapel." She noticed Simo's eyes widening with fascination as he looked at the room, and then her.

They walked in from the east side of the pyramid and at first glance she saw an *ankh*, the symbol for life, engraved in the pyramid's wall. Looking around, the room felt ethereal. Her dreams were coming true in this tomb. Ever since she had first thought of becoming an Egyptologist, she had envisioned seeing rooms filled with gold. Glittering gold so shimmering it blinded your vision. Lapis so blue, it pierced through your soul. Onyx so deep, it penetrated down to your bones. And aventurine and carnelian so luminous, it warmed your flesh. Layers upon layers of the world's finest treasures.

She shivered at the thought of such wealth being buried. She continued looking around the room when a glimmering object caught her eye. She moved in closer, crouching down to the fragment partially uncovered on the tomb's earthen floor. Setting the lantern down, she reached into her knapsack, pulling out a pair of latex gloves and a miniature brush. After putting on the gloves, she began brushing the gilded fragment, uncovering a tiny gold bracelet.

Since only royals wore jewelry in the Old Kingdom, this bracelet was for a young royal. Queen Iput had two babies. Sons. One died when he was around a year old, and the other baby became Pharaoh Teti's heir to the throne, Pepi I.

Cassie stood still, focusing on the bracelet, then she stumbled on something under her right foot. She crouched down to the earthen floor again and pulled out a plastic airtight baggie from her knapsack to put the bracelet in. Then, with the miniature brush, she slowly began uncovering the mound, which had caused her to trip. Bit by bit she uncovered a stone statue of a lamb. With a sacred touch, she picked it up. The lamb was small, about three inches wide and two inches high. Perhaps it was also for a baby, or maybe it was just a statue, but for whatever reason it had special meaning to Queen Iput, because she had made sure this small, insignificant artifact had found its place inside her tomb.

She heard Simo calling. "Miss Cassie, Miss Cassie, come here. I have found something I think you will find very interesting."

She took a deep breath. His voice was distant. She knew he had found another room. "Okay, give me a few minutes," she yelled. Her mind was circling. She couldn't believe she had literally stumbled upon these treasures.

"Just go through the door and follow the trail of light."

"I'm coming," she said, taking a closer look at the lamb. It had an inscription on its belly. The carving was crude and rudimentary. *Sefekhu Shenet.* She recognized it as the written form of seven hundred. But of what—seven hundred lambs? Seven hundred years? Seven hundred statues? She turned the lamb around. It had withstood the test of time. She placed the lamb into its own airtight baggie and pulled out the baggie with the bracelet. She sat on the floor of the tomb cross-legged looking at her finds, still in wonderment that she was in an ancient Egyptian pyramid.

*

Cassie became pregnant, probably on her sixteenth birthday, since that was the first time she and her boyfriend, Chad Westin, made love. A few months before she turned seventeen, she gave birth to her baby girl. Chad's parents wanted them to marry before the birth, but her mother, Susan, wouldn't have any part of it. Susan was determined Cassie was going to finish high school while she watched the baby. Susan had the high school part right, only Chad's mom watched the baby.

Cassie named her Cassandra, which was her real name. She always had a secret longing to be called by her given name, but the nurse at the hospital where she was born had told her mother Cassandra was just too big a name for such a little baby. And that everyone would shorten it with a nickname anyway, so they should just start calling her Cassie. She thought when she became an adult people would start calling her by her full name, but that didn't happen. So she named her baby after the name she had always wanted to be called—Cassandra. She was a healthy and beautiful baby… Simo's voice brought her back to the present.

"Miss Cassie, Miss Cassie, please come here." This time he was yelling. "Go through the door." She put the two plastic bags back into the front pocket of her knapsack to keep them safe. She would mark and catalogue her findings once she got back to the lab. Leaving her gloves on, she followed the trail of light.

Simo pointed as soon as he saw her. "Look."

She was in the burial chamber. The room had three niches within the walls and each niche contained pieces of pottery. On the western wall there was a limestone false door. It had an inscription on it in hieroglyphs: "The queen. Mother of Pepi I." She looked back at Simo with widened eyes.

"Over there." Simo pointed to the far side of the room.

A slab of stone was built into the wall. On the table was a large clay jar with a thin piece of linen hanging out over the top. She took off her gloves, reached into her knapsack and put on a new pair, handing another pair to Simo. "Here, put these on. I want you to hold the jar steady while I try to pull out the linen." He nodded.

She tipped the jar ever so slightly and tenderly took the linen out of the jar. It was wrapped around a rod. She started unwrapping it, then stopped. She couldn't believe what she was seeing. She tried to form the words, but nothing came out. She found herself staring at a rolled papyrus... utterly speechless.

ELEVEN

Edmund took the gloves from his back pocket, pulled out a small tool that resembled a miniature paintbrush from his shirt pocket and bent down by the bone. "This is a significant find. It looks like a humerus."

"I wonder why it was just lying here?" said Tom. "Prior excavations must have missed this since it was partially buried." He shined the light on the object.

"I remember reading about King Teti's tomb containing the mummies of Meri and Bebty. They were Teti's son Pepi I's teachers. The bodies were mummified and interred in their pharaoh's tomb. Maybe this bone was left from their disinterment?" He looked puzzled, trying to recall the story, and began dusting what looked like an arm.

"Dr. Ramsey, I wouldn't do that if I were you." Tom bent down beside him. "As a geologist, I want to remind you that the dust on the arm can help determine what era it might be from. There's a difference between contemporary and historical dust. If it's historical dust, there will be microfossils. We need to examine the arm's dust for particles, to determine the time frame of the contaminates."

"Of course, you're right," said Edmund. "I need to leave this untouched." He went back into deep thought, wondering if this bone was from a slave, a servant or if it was one of Pepi I's teachers.

"Poor guy or gal. Being buried with your pharaoh doesn't sound like something I'd want to ever have happen to me. I mean, wouldn't you want to be buried by your family?" Hearing Tom's voice brought him back to the present. Good thing; he needed to stay focused before he dusted away any more of the past.

"On the contrary," he said. "It was considered an honor back then. If you were a slave of a royal, it wasn't unheard of to be buried alive when your master died. You were to live out the rest of your days in the tomb. But you wouldn't have lasted too much longer than the dead royal. The slave's job was to ensure the pharaoh had his rituals performed and his food prepared to guide him into the afterlife. Which probably ended with the slave eating the food, and with every breath taken, dying from his own carbon dioxide." He shuddered at the thought.

"Well, I wouldn't have volunteered for the honor," said Tom.

Edmund was placing the bone into an airtight bag when he spotted another object covered in dust. He began brushing it to expose more of what it was with his miniature paintbrush, only stopping when he revealed another piece of a human body. He looked up at Tom, then the object, then back at Tom. "Oh boy," he blurted. "This looks like an ulna bone from the arm of a small child or baby." He ever so gingerly picked up the tiny bone as if it was a newborn baby and placed it into a plastic bag, sealing it.

"Excuse me, Dr. Ramsey, but will these bones help in proving if Dynasty Zero existed?"

"You never know, but they're coming back to the lab where we can photograph and catalogue them." He handed Tom the baggie with the smaller arm bone, and then picked up the bag with the larger bone, holding it out as if it was on a tray. "Lead us out of King Teti's tomb, Dr. Granite. The head of antiquities probably already knows about the sarcophagus, but we need to turn these findings in to the proper authorities."

TWELVE

The west wall of the antechamber. That's where Mark and Ian first came upon the Pyramid Texts. Mark explained, "These are spells and incantations designed to help the deceased on their journey into the afterlife. Unas's pyramid was discovered in 1881. He was the first pharaoh to have the texts engraved within the walls of his tomb, a practice that continued until the Middle Kingdom." He noticed Unas's cartouche in the left- and right-hand columns, and looked on, captivated. "I wish I could have seen the completed texts in their original state. But I have read there are 283 of them inscribed in these walls, to help the pharaoh sail from this world into the next."

"Really, you know the exact number?" Ian asked as he touched the wall.

"Yes, and they look preserved enough for us to read."

"To read?" asked Ian. "We're going to be here a while."

Mark held up the lantern. "Look, this one is short. Spell number 258 reads, 'King Unas goes upward...' I think it speaks of him going toward our version of heaven." Mark paused. "Or something of that sort. However, some of these spells are really long. I do better decoding the short ones."

They continued walking farther into the pyramid. King Unas's tomb contained several funerary writings once believed to help attain eternal life. Mark noticed the writings told the story of Ra and began to read aloud, feeling the texts as he spoke. "'Ra, the sun god, was purified each morning together with the deceased king'... then it speaks of the sky goddess Nut, who invites Unas to take his throne among the stars, which many think equates to heaven. Um, it says thereafter the pharaoh is an indestructible spirit, or he is godlike. King Unas identifies himself with Osiris, who was the god of the afterlife." He quit reading and looked at Ian. "His followers believed as the sun set each evening, it traveled through the underworld, which Osiris ruled, and was reborn each morning on the opposite side of the Nile." He felt proud remembering this from his college days.

"Good job," said Ian.

*

They had been in King Unas's tomb for a few hours reading some of the Pyramid Texts, when they walked into the burial chamber facing the south wall. Now Ian was holding up the light while Mark scanned more texts, looking for anything that might be a clue or a glimpse of some sort of history which would be ancient even for a Dynasty Five pharaoh.

"You're pulling on your lower lip. What's on your mind?" asked Ian.

Mark grinned. "I was actually thinking where we could go to sit on the floor and take a break." Then, what seemed like out of nowhere, his eye caught the adducing of the Sed

Festival and the crown. "Ian look! In spell 220 and 221, the hieroglyphs tell of a priest announcing the coming of the divine king to the crown, 'O Great in Magic.' This spell mentions the festival hall and the stone markers."

Incredible. He felt flushed. He might have just found something to support his view of the timeline. "Dr. Richards, these were fundamental elements of the Sed Festival, which was held in the Late Predynastic Period, through the Ptolemaic Period. The festival represented a king's right to rule.

"It also cites a king wearing a *Deshret* crown and having a Ritual of Valor ceremony, at the Sed Festival with the red crown, where his royal powers would be renewed. This may be some proof." Mark paused, tilting his head. "The mentioning of the festival hall and stone markers proved there was a Sed Festival. The wall mentions only a *Deshret*, or red crown, not a *Hedjet*, or white crown. Nor does it mention a double crown. The mentioning of only the red crown for the Ritual of Valor ceremony could mean in predynastic times, it did not represent a certain region of Egypt."

He relaxed a bit. This was a start, an indication to him that he was on the right track of trying to disprove Dynasty Zero. The text mentioned only the red crown. He decided to photograph several pictures of the exact hieroglyphic wording of the utterances. Then he would take his findings back to Dr. Ramsey and see how he perceived this information. If anything, it would show everyone that he had found some sort of support for his view of the timeline theory.

He wondered if anyone else had found anything in their assigned tombs. Hopefully not; the less evidence found to contradict him, the better. He knew he shouldn't take this personally, but he did. He needed approval in the professional world to make him feel like he belonged. Although he already knew he did, he needed more. Time and time again all his insecurities seemed to resurface from his childhood. Hearing Ian snapping his fingers cleared his thoughts.

"You okay? I thought I lost you there. It's like you were looking beyond the Pyramid Texts."

Mark flinched. "Did you know that eighty pyramids were built in a span of one hundred years?"

Ian responded, "Did you know the earliest Egyptians were buried into pits in the sand, with a mound of dirt thrown on the top?"

"Hey, do you think you could keep the light steady while I take some pictures?" Mark got out his camera.

"I'll try. Are you sure you know how your camera works or should we use mine?"

Mark guffawed, enjoying the bantering. He photographed the spells on the east wall, at every angle, and took numerous pictures of the tomb. Its various inscriptions, hieroglyphs and carved wall reliefs told a story, and he tried to imagine the activities of daily life. Stepping back, he took a deep breath. He was mesmerized by it all.

THIRTEEN

"Don't touch the papyrus. It needs to be handled with special care. We don't want it to break apart," said Cassie. "Leave all the equipment here with me and find Dr. Ian Richards. He's on team three exploring King Unas's pyramid. Do you know where that is?"

"Yes, Miss Cassie. What do you want me to say to him?"

"Tell him we found a rolled papyrus in Queen Iput's tomb. When he hears that, he'll follow you back. Whatever legend, tale or story is written inside that old rolled-up papyrus is sure to be interesting. Tell him you'll bring him back on a camel. That way you'll be back sooner and it will be a good reason for Dr. Richards to come alone. I personally would really appreciate that. Oh, and make sure Dr. McCormick has a guide with him before you leave with Dr. Richards."

Simo nodded. "Are you sure you'll feel safe?"

Cassie looked at her watch. "That depends. How long do you think it will take until you return?"

"Not long once I find Dr. Richards. But, Miss Cassie, the pyramids do not know of daytime; it is always nighttime and of long ago inside a tomb."

"I'll be fine. I have the lantern, plus these treasures to keep me busy. Take the flashlight and go. The sooner you leave, the sooner you'll be back." She patted Simo on the back before he left.

Her walk along the walls was slow and intense. With gloved hands, she traced each etching of the hieroglyphs embedded into the wall. She spent time examining and photographing every niche, wondering if anyone had ever made it back to these last two rooms. The question lingered in her thoughts until she found a pottery shard laying in one of the niches. She could tell by the way the shard lay that it was in situ. There were figures on the piece, and it looked as if it had been placed there after it had broken.

She picked it up. It was rather big for a broken piece, about four by four inches, with two tiny men looking at each other, holding lotus stalks and a *serekh*. Next to that was a hieroglyph. It was one word. Then another picture of a man wearing a crown, a *Pschent*. Which meant he was the king. The crown was a combination of the *Hedjet*, white crown of Upper Egypt, and the *Deshret*, red crown of Lower Egypt. She pulled out another baggie from her knapsack. This piece was definitely going back to the lab with the bracelet, lamb and papyrus. She wanted these objects to be labeled, photographed, recorded and analyzed. They each held a story within them.

*

She wasn't sure how much time had passed, but she felt she needed to sit for a while. She set down her knapsack and looked around the tomb. The place had an eldritch feel to it, which made her feel a little skittish, as well as excited. She propped herself against one of the tomb walls. It felt good to sit. She pulled out the baggie, which contained the lamb, and opened it. She was drawn to this little object, looking at it from all angles. The aesthetics of this statue were extraordinary.

She found this interesting because generally lambs were not important to ancient Egyptians. There were no gods that were lambs. They only herded them before the dynasties, when the land had shepherd kings. In predynastic time it was considered a noble profession. They were well respected and each shepherd king was in charge of a territory. And they were the authority over their territory, which was about as royal as you got back then.

Then, once Egypt was ruled by dynasties, Egyptians considered themselves to be agriculturalists. They were into farming, and sheep and goats meant death to their crops. Later Egyptian art and historical records portrayed shepherds in a negative fashion. Pharaohs' clean-shaven courts looked down on the ruggedness of shepherds. Lambs were even disregarded for food. Yet many early ancient Egyptians thought the god Osiris was once a human, and because of his crook and flail, some thought he was a shepherd, only ascending to become a god upon his death. Even though shepherds and sheep were disregarded, the signature crook and flail had stayed with royalty, and Egyptian pharaohs had their sarcophagi carved and painted with images of themselves holding these items.

She rubbed the statue. It was rough, but it reminded her of the stuffed animal she had given her daughter, Cassandra, to hold while she read to her at bedtime. "Dr. Seldon!" Simo yelled. She gasped and felt pain. He had startled her. She straightened up, burying the memories of her daughter when she heard Dr. Richards. "We're coming. I just have to suck in my stomach so I can fit through the passage. We'll be right in."

"Great." She laughed through her pain. "Can't wait to see you." She looked down and saw blood on her left hand. She had held the lamb so tight, the roughness of the statue had sliced through her latex glove and cut her left hand between her thumb and forefinger. She tore off the glove and brought her hand to her mouth, sucking off the blood, then wiped her hand on her pant leg. She started to cough. With her gloved right hand, she put the statue back into the baggie, and throwing her senses into the dust, she shoved it into her front pant pocket. Then she took off the bandana from her neck and wrapped it around her left hand.

"What happened?" They were both watching her wrap her hand.

She slowly stood. "It's nothing, a scrape. Turn around and look." She pointed to the slab of stone with the rolled papyrus and saw Dr. Richards' eyes getting larger than life.

"Whew baby, what a find!" he shouted.

FOURTEEN

A.D. 1988, CAIRO, EGYPT

Cassie and Ian were in the basement of the Cairo Museum, in its state-of-the-art laboratory. Cat scans and the new D.N.A. testing on mummies were done here, and next door was the mummy storage room. A room full of mummies; Cassie was stoked. She looked around the room at the white walls, the cupboards, the shelves lined with skulls, along with papers and replicas of artifacts from prior tomb excavations. There were four lab tables, each accompanied by four stools. On each table was a microscope. In the corner was a skeleton hanging on a pole. One wall had a large window overlooking a smaller adjacent room containing a C.T. scan for scanning mummies.

"The lab is kind of small for the type of work we're doing. Don't you think?" she said.

"It's sort of what I'm used to." Ian shrugged.

She looked on as Ian photographed the papyrus. He took pictures from all angles. He measured the width, height and thickness of the roll, before examining it under a microscope. Its suede-like finish proved it was ancient. He gingerly placed the papyrus into the dehumidification chamber. After a few minutes, the roll was starting to relax. "Ah, look at it," said Cassie.

"Turn off the lights before I take it out of the chamber," he said. "Deterioration begins when it is exposed to any type of light, even natural light, after being in the dark for so long. Every minute we work with the papyrus, it's deteriorating." He handed her a pair of soft white gloves similar to the ones he was wearing. "Here, put these on."

She did as he said, waiting by his side for further instructions.

"As I start to unroll the papyrus onto the acid-free blotter, I want you to lightly touch the corners to hold it down. I'm going to photograph it bit by bit as we unroll it."

"And then what?" Cassie was getting a first-hand look at a process she had only read about.

"When we're done, I'll process the pictures. Then I'll view the images one at a time by enlarging each fragment. This way our research will not be done from the actual papyrus."

"Whatever you say." She smiled. "This is your subject of expertise."

He continued. "After we take the photographs, we're going to carefully place the papyrus on top of another acid-free blotter. I'm going to have to change the blotters every hour or two. When it's dry, I'll assign it an inventory number and date. Then I'll note the data, place and subject matter with a brief description. Next I'll record the size, color, consistency, type of ink used and condition. And hopefully this will help us determine how old it is. Then I'll house it in between a glass frame made of polycarbonate plates. Oh, and I must record the direction of the fiber in the papyrus."

She was excited. "When you're done, Dr. Ramsey probably wants this turned over to the head of the Egyptian antiquities."

"Yes, I think so too," said Ian. She knew he was in his element.

"What's this about the minister of Egyptian antiquities?" Edmund's voice boomed as he entered the room. "We just left him. He gave us this metal box for our tomb findings. Look what we have." He took off the lid.

She peered inside. The metal box was padded with some sort of red material, protecting another box made out of stiff cardboard. "Well, don't just stare," Dr. Ramsey announced to everyone. "Help me lift it."

"Ah, ya, sure," said Ian.

Inside the cardboard box was balled-up tissue paper. As Dr. Ramsey and Dr. Granite removed all of the crumbled paper, Cassie gasped! "You found these in Teti's pyramid?" Inside was a human arm bone on top of a sheet of cloth. Next to it was another very small arm bone.

"Yes." Tom nodded. "We did."

She looked at Dr. Granite and then back inside the box, before taking her hand away from her mouth.

"I need to take pictures with my high-resolution camera, before I measure the bones and record the details. And a C.T. scan will be done when the radiologist arrives." Dr. Ramsey gazed back at the box. "Maybe these bones will tell us their story."

"Well," said Tom. "Examining the dust on them should help too."

"Oh, speaking of dust, I would also like you to examine the patina from a baby's bracelet and pottery shard I found in

Queen Iput's tomb." She felt her pant pocket. The statue of the lamb was still inside.

"Well, well, look who finally arrived," said Ian.

"Am I the last one back?" asked Mark.

Cassie noticed he entered the lab with a sheepish smile on his face. It was clear he was excited about something he had discovered. She felt a lump in her throat. She wanted to speak but decided against it. She wasn't ready to hear if he had found something to discredit her theory.

"Yes, you are," said Edmund. "Did you find anything to sustain your view of the timeline?"

Mark was looking humble. "I found a spell which mentions the Ritual of Valor ceremony and the pharaoh wearing only one crown."

"One crown? Who was the pharaoh?" she asked.

Mark put up his hand. "Not so fast, I haven't gotten that far. I photographed the spells, but I haven't fully deciphered them yet, seeing how my new friend needed to go…" Mark smiled at Ian, "…and help you, Dr. Seldon."

*

Darkness approached through the lab window; however, the Ph.D.s in the room did not notice. Everyone helped to catalogue all the artifacts, before they began their own research. Dr. Granite was busy with the magnifier, analyzing dust particles from the pottery shard. Dr. Seldon was with Dr. Richards, placing the papyrus on top of yet another acid-free blotter. Dr. McCormick was busy deciphering the hieroglyphs from his photographs. And Dr. Ramsey was in the smaller room analyzing the findings on the two arm bones. The museum had sent a radiologist from another lab within the building, to do the scanning. She shot beams of X-rays onto the two bones without damaging them and then did an Accelerated Mass Spectrometry Analysis, known as an A.M.S., before leaving.

With gloved hands, Edmund ever so carefully, and with the most intricate of movement, delicately scraped off the dust on each arm with a small pick, placing it onto a slide for Dr. Granite to examine. Next, he re-examined each bone through a magnifier before taking his own measurements on the humerus and ulna. He then viewed the pictures he had taken of the bones from every angle. The adult bone was in good condition—thick and porous—considering how old it was. By the diaphyseal length, he could almost say with certainty that this was a woman's arm. However, the scan would confirm his answer.

Last, he examined the photos alongside the C.T. scan and A.M.S. analysis results, hoping to get some answers as to how old these bones were, to give some indication of when these people had lived. They were not from a royal. Of that he was certain. The lack of proper preservation confirmed this. He continued staring at the monitor. Due to the thickness of the smaller bone, the ulna had been determined to be that of a boy baby.

The larger bone appeared white due to its absorption of energy. And the soft tissue appeared gray. The cross-sectioned images appeared onto the screen, looking like negatives from photographs. On the right side of the monitor was a graph of the humerus, breaking it down to the minutest dimensions. More results scrolled onto the screen.

He read the results aloud. "Sex… female. Projected height… around one point six meters or just less than five foot three inches tall, determined by the length of the humerus. Age… nineteen to twenty years old." He paused. "The isotopic ratios of both arm bones are true to type, making them approximately 4,365 years old." He looked up. *Dynasty Five or Six*, he thought, estimating by the results the C.T. scan was showing. He continued reading aloud. "Bone deterioration… none, probably too young."

So he now knew the smaller bone, the ulna, was definitely from a baby boy, maybe a year old, and the larger bone, the humerus, was from a young female adult. He just had to wait to see if the radiocarbon and D.N.A. results would tell him anything new. He needed to let the others know of his findings. He left the scanning room, walking into the main part of the lab, only stopping when he saw Dr. Granite analyzing the dust particles from the pottery shard with the scanning electron microscope known as S.E.M.

Dr. Granite spoke. "I am now studying the inner layer of dust. I do not see anything that would indicate this to be from a later era, saying the nineteenth or twentieth centuries. There are no anthropogenic aerosols found in ancient dust. I do not find lead, brome or nickel. There seems to be no man-made particles found in this dust. No calcareous microfossils and foraminifera or coccolithophorids, which are found in airborne dust. There are levels of the nutrients, K, P, S, and NH4 along with other organic materials. And there is carbonate, quartz and clay." He looked at Edmund. "Based on these findings and the carbon-14 dating, I would say you have yourself some ancient dust."

"How ancient?" Edmund waited.

Tom cleared his throat. "Very ancient, because of the high degree of organic materials and nutrients. I conclude this dust is approximately five thousand years old, making the actual pottery shard a bit older... by one or two hundred years."

"Thank you, Dr. Granite," said Edmund.

"Marvelous," said Cassie.

Dr. Granite had moved on to examining the patina on the baby's bracelet with the scanning electron microscope while everyone waited.

"Why did the Egyptians stop building pyramids?" asked Dr. Richards.

Edmund noticed Dr. McCormick was about to speak, but Dr. Seldon wasted no time in answering. "Egyptologists like me seem to think it might have something to do with the Valley of the Kings. On the burial grounds is a pyramid-shaped hillside. You can only see it when you are in the Valley of the Kings. Most of us think it served a symbolic purpose for the worshipers of the solar cult in Egypt. When the sun glistened on the pyramid-shaped hillside, its rays reached up toward the sun god. It served the same purpose as the man-made pyramids, but was there in the valley for every person, not just for the few who could afford to build pyramids. Maybe you should have become an Egyptologist like I did." *One point for Dr. Seldon*, thought Edmund.

"Well," said Mark. "Dr. Richards told me that he minored in archaeology. Which enables one, like myself, to excavate other ancient cultures such as the ancient Romans and Greeks." Edmund smirked to himself. *And one point for Dr. McCormick.*

"But even though they were Greek, the Ptolemys ruled Egypt during that time." *And another point for Dr. Seldon.* Edmund knew he should say something.

"Which leads you back to the Egyptian culture. That's why I became both. Some say, 'All ancient roads lead to Egypt.'" He smiled.

"Ancient layers," said Dr. Granite, putting an end to the conversation. "But, according to the carbon-14 dating, not as ancient as the patina on the pottery shard. From what I can conclude from this dust, it is approximately four thousand years old. Making the shard about a century older than the bracelet."

Dr. Richards interrupted. "The papyrus has been fully scanned."

Cassie and Mark shot over to the table where he was sitting. "I can read hieroglyphs," said Mark.

"But I'm faster at deciphering them," said Cassie.

"How do you know you're faster?"

"Because I'm an Egyptologist and you're not."

They faced each other, clearly ready to jump into battle, but then Dr. Granite burst with such a robust cackle it caused everyone to laugh, breaking the tension. "Wait!" said Dr. Ramsey. "I have the results of the C.T. scans on the two arm bones." Everyone stopped and stared. Silence had consumed the lab. You could even hear some breathing, and Edmund had everyone's undivided attention. Which was just what he wanted.

FIFTEEN

While everyone was working, the desert began kicking up a dust storm. Whether it was God, the ancient Egyptian deities or just the weather, the land was indurate to the fact that one of its visitors had taken a piece out of it and had kept it for themselves.

Cassie felt the outline of the lamb statue in the pocket of her pants. She felt the need to have it close to her. She knew she should bring it out to be examined, but she wasn't ready. She just couldn't seem to part with this ancient artifact. It brought up memories for her. She had her own history with lambs.

Dr. Granite and Dr. Ramsey were examining the dust scrapings from the two bones. Dr. McCormick was hovering over Dr. Richards, who was trying to determine the age of the scanned papyrus. Everyone else was at one of the lab tables, logging their findings of today's excavation.

"Dr. Seldon," said Ian. "Sit down and look at the monitor. It's time for me to change the blotters on the actual papyrus."

"Oh, thank you."

"It sort of reads like a story," said Cassie.

"Or a journal," said Mark. "Queen Iput entered the temple to ask the priest Kagemni, to give her a blessing. It says here she also had her infant son with her and was showing him to the priest, for her purification had just ended since giving birth. She was finally welcomed inside the temple."

Cassie added, "I take it as she wasn't so much showing her infant son to the priest in as much as she was asking him to take the baby and introduce him to the gods and have them bless the newborn's *ka* and *ba*."

"His what?" asked Ian.

"His *ka* and *ba*," said Cassie. "The *ka* is the person's spirit. Or what we would call the person's soul. Ancient Egyptians believed when a person died, the *ka* stayed in the tomb and had to be sustained with offerings of food and drink. The *ba* is the energy created at birth and would go with the person when they died. It's the person's personality. The *ba* made the journey through the underworld, waiting for judgment of the person's earthly life. Only then could it be reunited with the *ka*. The deceased would then be transformed into an *akhu*. You know, a transfigured spirit."

Mark agreed. "That makes more sense. Ancient Egyptians brought their newborns to the temple to do just that— introduce them to the gods and get their blessing. And it was done when the mother's purification had ended."

"Wait," said Ian. "When Dr. Ramsey was assigning tombs, he said Kagemni was the pharaoh's vizier?"

"He was both." Dr. Barrington joined the conversation to explain. "In the Old Kingdom a priest was a part-time occupation, and most priests held other positions." Dr. Barrington gave an authoritative look before continuing. "As you know, I was assigned to Kagemni's mastaba. But since it had been excavated several times previously, it didn't yield any new results."

Cassie vaguely heard him. His voice faded to the back of her mind. She was recalling a vivid memory of taking her baby over to Chad's parents. Cassandra was having her first birthday and had yet to be christened. Chad's father, who was a minister, wanted his first grandchild to be baptized. She had no problem with that and was grateful Chad's parents were taking an interest in Cassandra. She remembered the little stuffed lamb she had wrapped up in the blanket with her baby. Reverend and Mrs. Westin were delighted to see her and the baby. While she, Chad and his father talked about the birthday baptism, Chad's mother held Cassandra, showing her the little lamb. She remembered how enchanted her baby seemed to be.

"Dr. Seldon, please go back to the last set of scans," asked Ian. She sat up, pushing down the memory as she scrolled to the last set of pictures. Ian pointed. "See, this long piece comes before the part Dr. McCormick was just trying to decipher."

Mark adjusted his stool and leaned in to the screen. "It is written Queen Iput became involved when she heard her handmaiden Anhui—"

"It's pronounced Anhai," said Cassie. "It says she was in love with a priest."

"A priest?" asked Mark.

"Was it Kagemni?" asked Ian.

Cassie glanced around the room. From everyone's expressions, they seemed just as fascinated by the elements she and Dr. McCormick were unfolding. "Well, go on," said Ian. "Figure out what else it says."

SIXTEEN

2350 B.C., ANCIENT EGYPT

The high priest Kagemni looked unusually dark against his white *schenti* kilt. He was clean and had no hair, which gave his sable eyes a mystic quality. His head, face, chest and arms were shaven to show purity to the gods. He was on his priest rotation and living in the temple, the most pious and quiet of places, the home to the gods and goddesses.

He looked out from the open portion of the temple wall when he heard children making noise. He noticed Anhai, favorite handmaiden to Princess Iput, running past the children playing in the streets as she approached. Two giant obelisks were on each side of the temple's façade. She ran up the steps, only stopping when she reached the temple's massive doors. Non-royals were not permitted to enter the temple except on festival days, so he wondered what she was doing here.

She had on her finest *kalasiris*. It was held up with shoulder straps, which extended just below her exposed breasts. The sheath ended just above her ankles. It was made from simple white linen. Her dark hair fell just below her shoulders and the ringlets on each side of her face complimented her dark brown eyes. The way she wore her hair showed her youth. He watched as she wrapped her shawl over her shoulders and around her neck, covering her breasts before entering the temple. Kagemni sighed. She was the most beautiful woman in Egypt.

He waited as she walked past the colorful decorated pylons and raised wall reliefs, carved with epithets to the gods Osiris, Ra and the goddess Hathor. Silently, he approached her from behind. "What are you doing here? You're not allowed in the temple."

She jumped, her shawl slipping. "Forgive me." She lowered her eyes as she spoke. "But you know I am Princess Iput's favorite handmaiden."

His eyes strayed. She should be royalty. She was that beautiful. "Come with me." He touched her lightly on the back. She began walking with him. "I will take you to my inner post before anyone notices you." Her sandals slipped as they crossed the tile floor, but the pressure of his hand on her back kept her moving forward. Light was streaming in from the temple's roof windows as they continued down the hallway. Entering another doorway, he guided her into a dark chamber. The floor began to slant upwards while the ceiling gradually hung lower. This was the most sacred place inside the temple. She bowed as he opened the cedar wood doors which housed the gods and goddesses. He lit some incense, and she bowed again before the syenite stone statue of the goddess Hathor. The sweet smell of myrrh encircled the room.

After showing their respect to the stone statues, they proceeded to a room lit by candles. This was where Kagemni did all his planning for festivals and other temple functions as high priest for the king of Egypt, King Unas. He shut the door then hugged her tight before kissing her lips. "You shouldn't have come here."

She pulled away. "I had to," she whispered. "There has been talk among some of the men who serve the future King Teti. They say he wants you to resign so he can put his son-in-law Mereruka into your position as vizier to the king. This cannot be. You have been the vizier for years to the great King Unas as well as the future king. And now because his daughter Seshseshet has married, he feels the need to elevate her husband's position?"

He straightened his stance as if at command. "Who told you this?"

"Some servants were in the kitchen eating and they did not see me enter. When I heard them mention your name I stopped and stood ever so still." Anhai delicately touched Kagemni's arm. "You know Princess Seshseshet is the future King Teti's favorite daughter, having been named to honor Teti's mother, Queen Sesheshet. If this is true, this news I bring you, it is also not good for Princess Iput. Teti has not picked which wife will become his queen when he rules Egypt. Her father, the great King Unas, is ill, and if he dies and the future king has not picked a queen…" She paused. "Then the princess's chances are next to nothing with Mereruka seeing to his affairs, as Mereruka would side with his wife's mother, Khuit, to be chosen queen."

He let out a sigh and walked behind the table, pouring Anhai and himself a cup of *henqet*. He tipped his head back and drank it all at once. She took a sip. "Let's sit." Together they both sat down on the rug covering the floor and propped several pillows against the wall for comfort. He spoke softly. "While I was at the palace yesterday, Teti told me of his plans in front of all of his advisors. He even had Userkare, the head of the *Khenty She*, standing next to him. As if I would try to harm the future king in any way."

She held his hand. "Go on, tell me."

"I said, 'Your Highness, I do not understand. You wish me to retire? Are you displeased with the way I am governing Egypt? Are we not in agreement with the policies of our land?'"

"And what did he say?" Anhai brought her cup of *henqet* to her lips.

"'I am indebted to you, Kagemni, you have been a great vizier, but I feel the time is near for you to step down. Egypt needs fresh blood and a young spirit to govern its people.' Then that was the end of it." He stood, pouring himself another drink.

"What did you do, my love?"

He turned to face her. "I bowed before my king, the *nesu* I helped create." He paused, finishing his cup in one swallow.

"Go on." Her voice was troubled.

His eyes burned with anger and his jaw tightened. He sank onto the floor, keeping his back straight, trying to remain calm. "I asked him if we could talk in his private chambers or in the temple. He said no, he would not be changing his mind. He said he had chosen his son-in-law Mereruka and the official ceremony would be happening soon. He told me I had been a great friend and advisor, but this was for the betterment of Egypt." Kagemni sighed. "He also said when

Mereruka was in charge we would sit down to a great feast and talk. Then he waved his palm. You know when the palm is raised, you have been dismissed."

He stared deep into Anhai's eyes before continuing. "I left before anyone could ask me any questions. I was disgraced, for the betterment of Egypt. Or for the betterment of Teti?" He made a fist. "My fury for him burns bright. After all I have done for him and his wife Khuit."

"Please, I beg of you," said Anhai, "lean back upon the pillows. Let me help to ease your anger."

"You cannot." His voice was bitter. She recoiled, and for a moment he felt bad, but then his anger surged. "Don't you understand? This is the end of my ambitions, my position in life. Otherwise he would have summoned me into his private rooms. Instead he told me in public view, so I would not have to be dealt with." He leaned back upon the pillows. "I need the gods to help me fall back into the king's grace. I need to win back my position and power."

"Does your wife know?" Her voice was soft.

Kagemni nodded. "No. How can I tell her I am no longer in good standing and that I have no power with the future *nesu*?" He gazed downward. His marriage was a union of position and wealth, but what he had with Anhai was real. Silence echoed throughout the room. He slipped the shawl off of her shoulders revealing her full, hennaed breasts. He lowered his head and kissed them one at a time before laying her back onto the rug. Then he kissed her neck with such a serene touch it made her sigh with longing.

His tongue was slow to touch hers. His hands lifted her airy linen *kalasiris* to her waist. Then he took off his loin skirt and penetrated her in a single thrust. Her hands gripped into his flesh as she moaned, and he touched her lips with his fingers to silence their love. He didn't want anyone to know, he not only desired Anhai, he needed her.

SEVENTEEN

2350 B.C., ANCIENT EGYPT

K agemni walked through every room of the temple, placing the terra cotta bowls on the floor along the walls. Each bowl contained a slender piece of linen. When he was done, he went back and filled the bowls with oil and threw in a pinch of salt, so when the linen was lit, the oil would not smoke. He needed to keep his loin skirt white, as he was considered purified while serving in the temple. It was dusk when he returned with his wooden torch of fire and slowly made his way to each room, his papyrus sandals clicking on the slanting floor as he lit the temple for the evening.

When he was done, he blew out his torch and carried one of the terra cotta bowls into the innermost sanctuary. He opened the cedar wood doors and entered the room, which housed the gods and goddesses. He bowed before the god Ra, a gilded wooden statue of a man with a falcon head. Upon the statue's head was a round disk made of gold. The eyes were inlaid with the semi-precious stone aventurine. The color was so intense, he could feel the god's *ka* within him, and it made him shiver.

He prayed Ra would forgive him for lying with Anhai in the temple, but it was the only place they could meet in secret. He was married and she worked in the palace for the *nesu's* daughter Princess Iput, who was also the second wife of the future King Teti. He thought back upon their first meeting. It had been at the celebration of the Opening of the Year Festival, which all the royals attended. It was held every year when the Nile flooded. It represented another year of fertile farmlands.

At this festival, Princess Iput had brought her favorite handmaiden to assist her with her offerings to the gods. One of the priestesses had told him Anhai had many questions. It seemed she was an Egyptian woman with a mission. She did not want to be a servant forever. She wanted to become a high priestess for the temple. This common interest made them close and he felt he could be himself with her.

He stood up and offered incense to Ra's *ka*, the god's spirit. Other than his relations with Anhai, he performed his priest duties to perfection. He did not eat meat or fish. Bread was baked for him daily with the sacred corn, and he was given goose flesh to eat and wine made from the purest of grapes. He did not wear sheep's wool or any other animal. He was circumcised and shaved his entire body every other day so no lice would adhere to him.

He bathed twice, once in the morning and once at night in the temple's purification pool. He gave food to the statues of the gods and clothed them to satisfy their *ba*, the god's personality. He was the one who sealed the temple's chamber in the late evening. Being the chief priest within these walls, the other priests and priestesses referred to him as 'The Pure One.'

Not only did he serve as a priest, he was also the vizier to the future King Teti as well as the great, but ill, King Unas. He was their political advisor. He reported daily to the *nesu* on all of the activities of the palace, along with the finances of the government. He was chief overseer of all decisions the *nesu* made. No document was binding without his seal. He was a diplomat to the royals and was in charge of collecting taxes from the people of Egypt. He had governors under him and scribes who kept all the records, along with overseers who supervised the farming of the land and the peasants. Religion and government were inseparable, and Kagemni was most trusted to the great King Unas and the future King Teti.

*

Kagemni had known Teti since before his manhood. He remembered the day his horse had galloped into the square of the marketplace, kicking up dust from its hooves. The swirling sand and the smell of dampness foretold of the approaching desert storm. On that day, Kagemni had been a young man. He had grabbed the cloth tucked into his belt and dipped it into the communal fountain to wipe his eyes. They burned with bits of sand and he was trying to soothe them with his cloth. When his vision was somewhat better, he began to see people running from the market square. The sand was wicked as it kicked anxiously to greet the storm.

His attention turned to a boy, who was not yet quite a man, riding on a magnificent creature, a horse rearing up onto its hindquarters. The boy was losing control of the reins. He watched him fall off the horse and hit the ground with a thud.

In seconds, he was by the boy's side. He rolled him over, not sure if he was dead. "Wake up!" The sand swirled and hissed, drowning out his words as it encircled them. "Wake up!" He put his ear near the boy's mouth to see if he could hear or feel any breath of life. He heard a shallow breath and placed the cloth he had dampened onto the boy's forehead and tapped his cheeks.

He was sweating. He didn't know what he should do. "Wake up!" Kagemni pleaded with the unconscious boy. He looked over each of his shoulders but saw no one through the dust of the desert. He looked back, pleading again with the boy, and thought he saw some movement. He waited, watching. And then the boy curled his fingers and stretched them back, revealing a signet ring. He was a royal. The boy moaned, rolling onto his side, coughing. His eyes were now opened, showing fear.

Relief set in. He was alive. The boy breathed deeply and began coughing again; he was taking in sand from the windstorm. Kagemni lifted the boy's shoulders and pulled him into the crook of his arm. "Shh, don't try to talk." He cradled him for a bit, until the wind started to encircle them. "I need to move you. Behind us is some shelter." Kagemni pointed. "We have to go inside. Can you hear me?" The boy barely nodded, but it was all he needed. He laid him onto the sand, walked behind him and placed his hands under the boy's armpits, lifting his shoulders and head off the ground, dragging him into the building. He left him lying on the floor and sat beside the boy to wait out the storm. "What is your name?"

"Teti. My name is Teti. My mother is Queen Sesheshet. I live in one of the royal palaces. I want to thank you. It was my first ride on the horse. It was a gift."

"Well, someone needs to show you how to ride your gift." He gave the boy a faint smile. "Your horse is still outside. It can't see to go anywhere in this sandstorm." Little did Kagemni know in his future days to come, he would be this boy's link to the world outside of the palace.

*

Staring at the god Ra, he became angry. He didn't like feeling ignominious. Teti was an esteemed friend. And this was how it was all to end, with him being cast aside for Mereruka, just because he had married Teti's daughter. Kagemni bowed again before the statue, picked up the terra cotta bowl and left the innermost sanctuary of the temple. He walked through each room until he reached the sacred pool, symbolic of the waters of Nu, the cosmic ocean, the beginning of creation. This pool washed away all evil. He took off his clothes and gradually crept into the water. After his purifying bath, he sprinkled himself with oil and dressed in a fresh white linen loin skirt. He was once again pure, so he began his fast to appease the gods and to help his future.

EIGHTEEN

2350 B.C., ANCIENT EGYPT

There was no other structure in all of Egypt to match the royal palace. Opulence would be an understatement. To live among the royal colors of aventurine, lapis and carnelian, these semi-precious stones were inlaid and entwined into the columns made of gold. Mosaic scenes of royal life adorned the walls and the floors were made of glazed tiles. Princess Iput breathed in the smell of wealth. To live within these walls was an honor few Egyptians would ever attain.

The princess was in her bedchamber. The far wall opened up to a courtyard full of greenery. Azure lotus flowers floated in the fountain, its mist creating a rainbow of colors, and a fresh breeze penetrated throughout the room.

Where could her handmaiden Anhai be? Late again, and she needed her help to get dressed for tonight's royal banquet. The future King Teti was going to announce who would be his chief wife, the future queen. His elder wife, Khuit, had given him daughters, but one, Idut, had died in infancy, and there were no sons. She, Princess Iput, was his royal wife, being a royal by birth. Her father was the great King Unas, who had helped Teti come into succession to become the next *nesu*, because Unas himself had no legitimate male heirs. But she had not yet produced any sons for the future king.

And Teti was also about to marry Weret-Imtes. Iput was unnerved by the idea of another wife, especially one who was barely out of childhood and still a virgin. She did not trust her husband, for fear he would make his decision based on loyalty to his elder wife, or lust for his up-and-coming new wife. Her position was secure due to her husband's alliance with her father, but she was of royal birth, destined from the gods and goddesses to be queen, or so she thought.

She looked up when Anhai entered the room. "Forgive me." She bowed. "I am feeling ill. I'm sorry." Anhai stood, grabbing her forehead. "Everything is spinning." She steadied herself, leaning up against one of the engraved bed columns, covering her eyes.

"You are late again," said the princess. "I should not let you eat today. But that would be useless, since you are always sick and can't even hold down a bit of grain." She sighed. "Are you sure you're going to be able to help me get dressed?"

"Yes, the scents of the lotus flowers are helping me to steady." Anhai grabbed her stomach.

Princess Iput held the small polished copper disc, which showed her reflection. Trying to line her eyes with kohl, her slender fingers delicately embraced the handle, a carved naked girl holding a bird, which represented beauty. "Here, help me." She handed Anhai the stick of kohl. "When you are done, line my lips with ochre."

Anhai bowed again and started applying makeup to the princess's eyes. "I am truly sorry, I have not been right the past *senuj* full moons. Even the gods spare me no relief." Then she applied the ochre onto the princess's lips. "Do you know what jewelry you would like me to put on you tonight?"

Iput pressed her lips together, thinking, and then pointed over to the chest beside her chair. "Grab the gold and carnelian necklace. It will help to brighten my eyes. And take some charms out of the chest. I want you to apply them to my wig." The princess was pleased with the gleam from the polished copper as she examined her makeup.

Anhai walked over, placing the necklace on the bed, along with the wig. It was made from the human hair of slaves and was one of the princess's favorites. She dipped her hands into the softened beeswax and applied it around Princess Iput's head. Then she rinsed her hands in the basin filled with water, before positioning the black wig onto her head. The beeswax would help secure it in place. She weaved the charms into the wig and then picked up the necklace, putting it around the princess's neck. "What is that smell?"

"Ah yes, it is the smell of boiled pig and goat, along with roasted duck. There is also going to be the heart of a plucked goose with a twist of onions, along with cakes, grapes and baskets of figs. And Teti, our future king, has brought out the date wine. He has spared no expense for tonight's banquet." Princess Iput noticed Anhai had stopped adjusting the wig. She saw her bend over, grabbing her stomach.

"Excuse me, my lady." Anhai ran over to the chamber pot by the bed, hovered over it and became ill.

The princess stood. "What, sick again?"

Anhai wiped her mouth with the back of her hand before bowing. "I'm so sorry…" Her pale body was swaying.

The princess yelled for her guard, who was standing near the door of her chambers. "Come here and help. Lay her down onto the reed mat. The one on the floor next to the bed." He did as commanded. "Thank you, you may leave us now." She lifted up her calf-length pleated cloak, kicked off her reed sandals and laid across the foot of her bed, looking down at Anhai, who was on her back.

Anhai moaned. "The fog in my head is weaving all the colors of the room together and I can barely see."

Princess Iput pursed her lips together, thinking. "If I did not know better, I would say you are with seed."

Anhai rolled into the fetal position, shaking her head, crying. "Will the goddess Isis and Hathor ever forgive me?"

The princess hopped off the bed and helped her to sit up. "How? With who? I want to know everything. You know I am not much older, and I am having trouble giving the future King Teti a son." She grabbed her shoulders. "Which of the gods helped you conceive?" Waiting for her answer, Iput walked over to the basin filled with water, soaked a cloth and handed it to her favorite handmaiden. She felt slightly bad for being harsh with her. She sat back down beside her on the reed mat.

Anhai began wiping her tears. "This cloth, it is so soft. Thank you." She got up on her knees and began to bow.

The princess stopped her. "Now, now, sit down. We do not want you to feel unclear again. Spare me no details. Start talking. Whose baby is it?"

"Agh." Anhai began weeping again. "I cannot say—I like working for you, Princess Iput. I do not want trouble."

"It's too late for that; you are already in trouble. How can I help you if you do not tell me anything? So start talking. Now!"

Anhai sniffled. "It has been *senuj* full moons since I have seen Kagemni. It is the vizier's baby. He is the only one I have ever lain with."

"My father's and my husband's vizier? How did you ever meet him? He is never in my chambers. Whenever he is within the walls of this palace he is doing business with King Unas or the future King Teti."

"I first met him at the Opening of the Year Festival. I aspire to be a priestess one day. I prayed to the goddess Hathor, heavenly mistress and daughter of Ra, who told me to talk to the priestesses. Then they sent me to meet with 'The Pure One.' It was Kagemni." She paused. "Please forgive me, Princess Iput, but I did not know how long you would want me as your handmaiden.

"We started with long talks on what it meant to be a priest and priestess. Then one time he took me into his room inside the temple, where he does his planning for rituals and festivals…" Anhai looked up. "He offered me some wine. Oh, Princess Iput, I had never drunk wine before. We were alone and…" She began sobbing again.

"Only the one time, and you carry his seed?" asked the princess.

"No." Anhai shook her head and sniffled.

"No? How long have you been lying with him?"

"Many full moons now."

"Do you not know he's married?"

Anhai nodded her head up and down. "Yes. Every time I thought it would be the last, but I have fallen in love with him and now I am with child."

"But prior to the last *senuj* moons, you have seen him? Lain with him? Tell me," said the princess.

"Yes, but I see him more often when he has his priest duties, for we have a place to lie in secret."

"Does he know?"

"No." Anhai's voice was barely audible.

"Well, I do not think he has abandoned you. My father, the great King Unas, has sent him to some of our territories to ensure they are paying their taxes to their *nesu*."

"Or to keep him away from the palace," muttered Anhai.

Iput grabbed her shoulders. "What do you mean? Speak your tongue."

She sniffed again, wiping her nose with the cloth rag. "The last time I had lain with Kagemni, he was upset. Your husband, the future *nesu*, told him he was going to be replaced soon by his son-in-law Mereruka."

"Seshseshet's husband, his daughter by Khuit?" The princess put her hand over her mouth.

Anhai bowed her head in a gesture of respect. "Yes, my princess. You did not know of this?"

"No, I did not know of this. What of my father, does he know?"

"According to Kagemni, the great King Unas knows of the future King Teti's choice. I thought because I had not seen Kagemni, maybe he was already replaced and had left in disgrace."

"No, he has not yet been replaced." The princess put her hand over her heart. "This is hard for me too." She turned and leaned her back against the bed, taking in a deep breath. "This may have happened because he plans on making Khuit his chief wife. This move helps her greatly. I have been worried he would make his future wife Weret-Imtes chief wife, for she is young and virginal. But no, he is going with loyalty, and I am left out in the cold."

"If that is the case, why would the great King Unas approve this?" asked Anhai.

"He has no choice. He has no sons." Iput got up and sat on the bed, motioning to the cupbearer. He brought a tray over and placed it on the table by the bed. He handed her the cups filled with wine and bowed. She dismissed him, before handing Anhai a cup. "Come, sit."

"I can't. I am your servant."

"And my friend, take the cup. I have an idea."

Anhai sipped while Iput took a big swallow from her cup. "You have a baby you cannot keep. I need a baby and I am not yet with seed. I will go to the future King Teti and tell him my womb is filled. This will stop any decision about who will be his chief wife until after the baby is born." She took another drink. "If this child is a son, I will have security. He will have to by law make me his queen, for I have given him his firstborn son. It will make no difference whether he marries again or not."

"And if the child is not a son?" Anhai's voice was scarcely a whisper.

"It gives me time to bear my own seed," said the princess. "And we will give offerings to the gods and goddesses daily. I am a princess. They will bless me, and you for helping me. There has not been a royal birth in many years, and whether it is a boy or girl, it puts to rest the rumors of the future *nesu* not being able to produce any more seeds." She became unswerving. "Once my husband knows I will bear his child, he will be overjoyed. He will do anything I ask. I will become upset and plead with him that he does not move so quickly with Mereruka. I will ask him to wait until my father's death, as Kagemni has been my father's vizier for such a long time. Out of respect for the great King Unas, of course." She drank more wine. "This will work."

"Excuse me, Princess Iput, but what about me? How will you hide me? What will become of me?"

"Kagemni will help with that. He is to return before tonight's banquet. You will tell him of our plan and I will have him place you with the priestesses, where you will learn their ways until after your baby is born. Kagemni's wife will never know, and then you and he will have two secret places to lie with each other."

"And you, what will you do these next *sefekhu* moons?"

"I will find new servants and only keep them for a few sunrises. I suspect I will have an awful time. I will make myself sick like you have been, pad my stomach with belts of cloth and keep to my chambers. Then, when my time is near, I will find a stupid girl and make her my servant." She paused. "Then, after the baby is born, I will say I tire of my servant girl, for she is too stupid to help with a baby. I will dismiss her, and then bring you back."

"This may work," said Anhai.

The princess reassured her handmaiden. "Don't worry. I will bring you back as my handmaiden and wet nurse," she said. "The priestesses will allow that since we will say you have just lost your baby and have milk in your bosom. Everybody wins. The future King Teti gets a son and I get the position I was born for—to be queen. Kagemni will get to stay as vizier for a bit longer, and you get to fulfill your ambition as high priestess. That's a big step up for a servant."

Anhai bowed. "Forgive me, Princess Iput, but am I sacrificing my baby for ambition?"

"What sacrifice? Your son will be raised as royalty. That's a far better life than you could have given the child. As long as you keep your mouth shut, you will live here with me when you are not doing your priestess duties. I can make you caregiver of the child." She grabbed Anhai by her shoulders. "It's just, the baby can never know… as he grows, he can never know. Do you understand?" She was ready to slap some sense into her.

Anhai looked up. "Yes, I understand. But what if Kagemni won't hear of this?"

Princess Iput lowered her hand. "Oh, he will hear of this; he will have to go along with my plan, for when he gets back it will already have been started. I have to tell the future King Teti tonight so he does not announce Khuit as his queen." She gave Anhai a puzzling look. "Kagemni won't care. He is a man. A married man, and I have just secured his position as vizier. You must know of men and their ambitions—they always come first."

"Forgive me, Princess, but I have one last question. Where do we get a dead baby for the one I have lost?"

Princess Iput ignored the question and walked over to her shrine of the goddess Meskhenet. This was the goddess of childbirth and newborn babies. She had been praying to her for many sunrises and sunsets. She was also the goddess of fate. She could determine a person's destiny. She was sure the goddess had answered everyone's prayers. Meskhenet would protect this baby.

She waved her hand for Anhai to join her. They kneeled together before the table. And as the opaque shades of dust entered the room, she lit the oil, which illuminated the shrine of the goddess. Her eyes made of aragonite and obsidian stared back at them as they lit the incense. Together they held up their hands, while looking at a tabletop statue of a woman wearing the headdress of a cow's uterus and began to chant.

*

Beyond the archway in the courtyard was the young scribe Hezi. He sat cross-legged, breathing in the aroma of frankincense, his papyrus scroll on his knees. And with his reed pen, recorded everything he had just heard from the bedchamber of the princess.

NINETEEN

Mark leaned back, pinching the space between his eyebrows. Staring at the monitor had given him a headache. "It says the future King Teti had this enormous banquet. The people thought it was to announce who the future queen of Egypt would be, so everyone was in attendance. But to their surprise, he held a banquet to announce his second wife, Princess Iput, who was also the pharaoh's daughter, was expecting." He looked up, and then continued. "This greatly pleased Pharaoh Unas, as there had not been a royal birth in a very long time."

"I'm sure King Teti was overjoyed," said Cassie. "Since history has recorded that there were some rumors about his ability to conceive a royal heir to the throne. He had three daughters by his first wife—one had died and the other two reached adulthood before Princess Iput had even given birth to her two sons. So there was a lot of pressure on King Teti to produce an heir."

Mark chimed in. "So the banquet wasn't only to announce Princess Iput's pregnancy, but also to squelch any rumors of infertility, as this would lead to instability."

"Oh," said Ian. "You mean King Teti was facing an unstable reign and he hadn't even yet become pharaoh."

Mark's eyes were at half-mast. The light in the lab was too bright and he couldn't think about this anymore. He needed time to process the day and everything that had happened. "I don't know about anyone else, but I'm tired and hungry."

"Yes, I agree. We have been very productive for our first day in Egypt," said Edmund.

"You're not kidding." Ian looked at his watch. "We spent the morning and most of the afternoon inside the pyramids. Now it's midnight and nobody's had dinner yet."

"It's time to put this away for the night. Let's give ourselves the morning off and meet back here at the lab, or rather the bus…" Dr. Ramsey looked at his watch, "…around noon, Eastern European time. Has everyone adjusted their watches to EET?"

There was nodding and faint agreement from all the Ph.D.s. It seemed Mark wasn't alone. They were too tired for any further conversation. Dr. Ramsey was the first one to exit the lab, stopping at the door. "Whoever's last, hit the lights."

Mark was leaning on the door to keep it open. "After you, Dr. Richards. We need to get going. The bus is waiting." Then he hit the switch.

*

Mark was in his shorts leaning against the headboard of the bed in his hotel room. His dinner, a sandwich along with a bag of chips and a can of soda, came from the vending machine down the hallway. He was tempted to turn on the TV, but wasn't sure if anything would be on, much less in English. His room was modern. It looked like it could have been located in any large city hotel back in the States. He took a bite of his sandwich, washing it down with soda, wishing it was beer.

It reminded him of the times he and his older brother had had sandwiches for dinner. When their parents weren't home, they would each make a sandwich and finish an entire bag of chips. And that was when a bag of chips was a full bag.

Although his brother was the family favorite, they were close. After all, it wasn't his brother's fault he was the favorite. Their dad related more to his brother because he was into sports, especially baseball, while Mark was into digging in the dirt and finding glass bottles. Mark was always the more responsible one once they became teenagers, but that didn't seem to matter to his parents; they were closer to his brother. And now that he traveled often for his job, it was probably better.

Anyways, it no longer mattered. The lack of bonding Mark felt with his parents was what fueled his ability to travel—no strings attached. He had seen a great deal of the world for someone barely into his thirties. And it was all for his job, so he was paid to travel. It doesn't get any better than that, but lately he felt empty. He missed the friendship he had had with his brother growing up, and although he was a loner, he missed the bantering they had with each other.

He took another bite of his sandwich before throwing it out. It was stale. He would have to make do with the bag of chips. He was gulping the last of his soda when he heard a resounding knock at the door. "Who is it?"

"Ian. Open up. I have pizza and beer."

TWENTY

"Where did you get pizza in Egypt?" Mark asked as they settled at the small round table by the bed.

"Don't forget about the beer." Ian set the pizza and the growler on the table.

"You know, Egyptians invented beer," said Mark.

"Yeah, and the bar's still open. I asked for a growler of beer, because we don't have to be back at the lab, or rather the bus, until noon. I figure we don't have to get up until eleven-thirty." Ian gave a big smile, grabbing two glasses on the tray next to the bucket of ice.

"And the pizza?"

"At the bar. They say Egyptians have been eating pizza since ancient times. Do you believe that?" Ian flipped open the box and grabbed a piece.

"I feel honored," he said. "Seeing how you had a dinner invitation from the radiologist. She was quick to read the scans, but before she left, you apparently caught her eye."

"You mean Megan?"

Mark shook his head while he was eating. "Oh, first-name basis, I see. Does she know you're gay?"

"Everyone knows I'm gay as soon as they meet me. Anyways,

it doesn't matter." He poured more beer into the glass. "What about you and Cassie? Seems you've caught her eye."

Mark began choking and had to take a drink of his beer. "Not interested. She's obstinate," he coughed. "And close-minded."

"Hmm, sounds like somebody I'm eating pizza with," said Ian.

Mark raised his glass. "To bachelorhood."

Ian raised his also. "To bachelorhood. Now, tell me what is going on between you and Cassie. You said you sat by each other on the plane. Then she took off at the airport in Paris, and you two completely ignored each other on the flight to Egypt. But then you two were talking at the lab. I don't get it?"

"There's nothing to get. We were trying to decipher the hieroglyphs." He took a swig of his beer.

Ian sighed. "Well, not to change the subject, but... I don't know how everyone feels about my latest equipment? I think some of them, including you, think it really doesn't help much."

"The explorers who have been in the field a long time, well... they just don't like being told there's a new way to do things." Mark set his glass down. "I know we need your equipment, but you caught me and some of the others off guard. We didn't know you minored in archaeology. Anyways, my main concern is to prove the existing timeline is the correct theory. I feel my reputation with my coworkers is on the line." They ate in silence for a while, enjoying the food and each other's company.

"You can have the last piece." Ian shoved the box toward Mark. "And I wouldn't worry. You have nothing to prove.

The existing timeline is what stands today. It's Cassie who believes in Dynasty Zero. She's the one trying to change the way we currently view the ancient Egyptian dynasties. It's her reputation that's on the line. So grow yourself a bigger pair, my friend, and get rid of... or at least hide your insecurities." Ian chugged his beer, then put his feet up on the bed, stretching his legs.

"But if she can prove Dynasty Zero, the Kreativ Museum will surely benefit, considering it's on the verge of closing." He took another bite of his pizza.

"Now that I'm relaxed," said Ian, "tell me what you believe."

Mark gathered his thoughts. "I believe in Manetho's writings. He was an Egyptian priest and historian. He lived in Egypt around 200 B.C. and was highly educated. He even spoke Greek. But by that time, Egypt's history was lost, so he made it his life's work to write down the history of Egypt.

"Manetho researched and wrote *Notes About Egypt*. It claimed King Menes, who was from Thinis, which was north of Abydos in Upper Egypt, was the one who unified Upper and Lower Egypt. He was the beginning of the dynasties, which was divided by Manetho into thirty ruling houses." He put down his pizza. "Manetho's ruling houses started with the pure bloodline of Egyptian kings. Which is why we only have thirty dynasties. What would have been Dynasty Thirty-One and Dynasty Thirty-Two are called the Second Persian Period and the Ptolemaic Dynasty, because of the Greek and Roman bloodlines within the kings." He wiped his mouth with his napkin, before continuing.

"His research was so well respected even in C. A.D. 220 times, Sextus Julius Africanus, a Christian chronographer, and Bishop Eusebius of Caesarea both believed in Manetho's research, along with the Byzantine monk Patriarch Tarasios, who also chronicled Egypt's timeline." He emptied the growler into each glass, taking a drink before continuing. "Now the opposing side says because Manetho himself was half Greek he didn't want Egypt's history to be longer than Greece's history. And he figured his timeline by working backwards from astronomical dates."

"Astronomical dates?" Ian gave a quizzical look. "Don't you find that odd?"

"No, not for the time he lived in." Mark was adamant. "Besides, the Royal List of Karnak has Menses as the first king of Egypt. Not to mention when we were in Pharaoh Unas's Pyramid, spell 220 and 221 of the Pyramid Texts told of a Sed Festival. And the Ritual of Valor ceremony was held during the Sed Festival. The texts mentions the king only wearing the red crown, not the white or a double crown, to represent a unified Egypt." He finished his beer.

"Yeah, but he figured his timeline out from the stars."

Mark just stared; although frustrated, he was glad he had found a friend in Egypt.

TWENTY-ONE

Cassie stepped out of the shower in her hotel room. Being in the pyramid had made her feel gritty and musty. She wrapped a towel around herself and tucked the edges into her bosom. She used another one to blot her wet hair, noticing the pictures on the wall. They were all photographs of either pyramids or the sphinx. The umber brown wall color was very calming.

She had not eaten anything that night, so she decided to order room service. While she waited for someone to pick up the phone, she contemplated if she wanted to paint her bedroom at home this color. It was really growing on her. Room service told her all they could give her was cereal and a muffin. She agreed, also ordering a cup of black tea.

After placing the order, she rifled through her suitcase and pulled out a tiffany blue baby doll satin nightie. It had a halter neckline and was trimmed in white fur. She caressed the fur before dropping her towel and slipping the teddy over her head. She felt the smoothness of the fabric. She loved the feel of satin. After putting on the white fur trim slipper shoes, she looked at her reflection in the mirror. She felt sexy. She knew she spent too much money on lingerie, but it was the one choice in her life where no one else had a say. Lingerie was her confidence-builder. It made her feel good that she could not only wear it, but also look good in it.

Cassie smiled at her reflection, remembering the first piece of lingerie she had bought. It had been a bra. A big bra. A big, sexy bra. It had started when she became pregnant. As she became bigger, she wore Chad's T-shirts and just didn't zip her pants. Finally, Chad's mother gave her two pair of her pants, the ones with the elastic waistband. Those, along with Chad's T-shirts, took her through the next two trimesters. You don't gain much weight when you're trying to hide a pregnancy.

And that was how she got into lingerie. By needing a bigger bra. The only piece of clothing she couldn't borrow from someone. Her boobs were too big. In private, she could take pleasure in her developing body. In private, she was happy and confident.

She sifted through her suitcase a second time, looking for the long, matching robe. She wanted it handy when room service arrived. And then she saw it. The one item she kept close to her, even when she traveled. Cassandra's baby blanket. It was made of soft blue flannel. Covering the front were fluffy pink lambs and surrounding the edges was white sateen trim. She brought it up to her nose and inhaled its aroma. It smelled like motherhood. She laid the blanket on the bed and began tracing each lamb with her fingertips, closing her eyes as she committed them to memory.

Her baby, her precious baby, would have been sixteen in a few days. She would have been the same age Cassie was when she gave birth. No one knew what caused her baby's death.

The crib was kept next to her bed. One morning Cassie was awoken by silence. There was no happy babbling baby talk coming from the crib.

The memory of the next few minutes was branded into her brain. She recalled opening her eyes, yawning, stretching and feeling refreshed. Still lying in bed, she turned her head toward the crib. Fully awake now, she sprang up, hopped out of bed and bent down to pick up Cassandra.

What she saw was the most peaceful expression on her baby's face, yet she knew instantly something was wrong. She could sense that the soul had left her baby's body. Cassandra had an eerie type of listlessness. Her life force had ascended. Her baby looked like a mannequin.

Even till this day, what happened next remained a blur. She couldn't remember if she picked up her baby, then screamed, or screamed and then picked up her baby. When her mother ran into the room, Cassie was cradling the blue fluffy lamb blanket with her baby inside, covering her with her tears. She couldn't recollect speaking to her mother. She only remembered that her mother knew. Time stood still. She did not recall if it was two minutes or two hours, but she continued cradling her baby on the edge of the bed, rocking her back and forth, until the paramedics, ever so gently, removed Cassandra from her arms. No C.P.R. was needed. It was obvious to them her baby was already dead when they arrived. When her hands no longer held her baby, she felt as if they had ripped out her heart, and she was inconsolable.

Finally instinct kicked in and told her to call Chad. The funeral was the saddest service anyone had ever been to, or so everyone said. Chad's family took care of all the arrangements;

it was all too overwhelming for Cassie and her mother to handle, and until she graduated from college, she never visited her baby's grave. But now, once a year, on Cassandra's birthday, she goes and visits her grave and kneeling at the headstone with the engraving of a baby lamb at the top, she prays.

She had poured her whole body and entire soul into motherhood. At least she could say she was a better mother than her mother was. She often wondered if the craziness her mother was afflicted with was heredity. She was in fear not only for her mother, but also for herself. And so she decided she didn't want any more children. Ever.

She folded the baby blanket. She brought the left side to the middle, then the right, smoothing out all the wrinkles. She then brought the two ends together, folding it again, caressing it with the palm of her hand, before delicately placing it back in the suitcase and pulling out her robe. No one knew this blanket traveled with her wherever she went. It had become a comfort. A touchstone to the one person who'd meant the world to her, and always would. A remembrance she had buried deep in the tomb of her heart. She put on the robe covering herself. Room service was knocking at the door.

Eating her cereal and muffin, she drifted back into her thoughts. She had given birth at sixteen, shortly after Chad Westin turned eighteen, and the scandal it caused at school and home was unbearable. It never seemed right to her that Chad, who was only sixteen months older and the only saving grace in her life, was presented as the bad guy or, as her mother put it, the molester. She didn't know how her mother could even say this, since her mother had also been an unmarried teenager when she had had her. She was nineteen, not sixteen, but so what? The rest of her circumstances were the same.

Like mother like daughter... runs in the family... these were some of the innuendos people said about her situation. But out of all of them, her mother was the worst. And as the months passed, the more disgrace Chad felt he had brought to his family and his father's ministry. He chose a Sunday... that's when Chad killed himself. Since his father was the minister, his parents left for church earlier than he did, so that's when he performed the action.

No note, nothing. He pulled his car into the garage, shut the door, and kept the engine running. He rolled up the windows, opened the vents and locked the doors. He had a full tank of gas, so the car ran long enough to do the dirty deed. Asphyxiation. She lost the two biggest loves of her life to lack of air.

She didn't realize how hungry she was. The cereal and muffin went down rather quickly and her thoughts once again drifted as she drank her tea. When she had graduated from college she had stopped by to show Chad's family her diploma and to tell them goodbye. Reverend Westin was transferred to a Methodist church in upstate New York. He acknowledged this was best for everyone. It seemed strange, but she understood that not seeing Chad's family would ease everyone's pain. She told them about furthering her education to become an Egyptologist and they wished her luck.

Chad's mother asked how she was handling the loss of her baby and suggested to her she should adopt a child through a Christian sponsorship program. So she did, and every few years she added another child. Now that she was thirty-two, she had four children she wrote to, and she displayed their pictures proudly in her condo. Her goal was to sponsor sixteen children throughout her life. Four at a time, four sets of four. It seemed logical, since Cassandra had died at sixteen months, as well as the only way to help her with the guilt of having a child at sixteen.

Cassie had never experienced grief as dark or as deep as the loss of a child. Her child. Unless you have experienced this loss, you cannot perceive its magnitude. There is a never-ending black hole in your heart, and if you cannot come to terms with your loss, the black hole becomes bigger, and deeper. It will then permeate not only your heart, but also your mind and, eventually, your soul.

You can never mend your black hole. It is a void that will be with you for eternity; you even take it with you, onward toward the heavens. And this black hole can also drive you to insanity. She knew, she knew all too well, for this was the one black hole that sent her mother, who lived on the edge, over the edge, to the point of no return.

You can't patch it. The only way out of your depth of the darkness of despair is to fill your hole. And that's what Cassie did. She filled her hole. She filled it with her career, her adopted Christian sponsorship children and her lingerie. It helped. It kept her sane. But she knew she needed to fill her hole with peace, and until that day came, she hurt.

She continued sipping her tea. It had a tranquilizing effect on her and when she was serene, she could process all the thoughts clogging her brain. As she sipped, her mind began flowing again. She began thinking about the baby's bone found in King Teti's tomb.

Did the child's bone match the adult's bone? This would make them related. Or was it two unrelated incidents? Most tombs had been opened and resealed several times. Since these bones were from the same time frame as the baby's bracelet, was it this baby's bracelet? And if so, why was the bracelet in Iput's tomb?

She finished her tea and yawned. She had to move on with her findings. She needed to find out what the picture carved into the pottery shard represented. And the lamb, it had *Sefekhu Shenet* written on its belly. That was the written form of seven hundred. Seven hundred what?

She yawned again and stared at the statue of the baby lamb on the nightstand next to her bed. She should have left it at the lab. When she went back tomorrow she would try to get the answers consuming her brain. Maybe then she would be able to part with it.

She walked into the bathroom and rummaged through her toiletry bag until she found the drug she needed. She held the bottle upside down, filling the syringe. Then, tapping it with her fingers, she relieved the air bubbles. Leaning against the sink, she injected the drug into her upper arm. When she came out of the bathroom, she finally wasn't just tired, she was sleepy.

She turned off the light and settled herself into bed, rubbing her hand along the fur of her teddy. She shut her eyes and plunged into unconsciousness.

TWENTY-TWO

A.D. 1988, CINCINNATI, OHIO

Susan couldn't understand why her daughter wanted to work in the Middle East. It wasn't safe. Hell, it wasn't even safe outside her window in her own neighborhood, much less halfway around the world. She had already lost her only grandchild. She didn't want to lose her only child too. Cassie was the only family she had.

Her own mother was dead and Susan had been estranged from her father for over thirty years. She had had an affair with a married college professor and had become pregnant. And that had been it. Her father had disowned her. It had happened during her sophomore year of college when she was in the university's work-study program. She was an aide to a history professor who taught undergrads. She never had him as one of her professors. If she had, the affair probably would have never happened. But being his aide, she helped him grade papers, set up slide presentations and organize his field trips.

Susan forgot how the affair got started. Her memories about him were all entwined. It didn't matter. She loved him down to the core of her being. When he was with her, which was most weekday evenings, they seemed married in every way. They took long walks across the campus, hand in hand. He showered her with attention, putting a sparkle in her eyes. He loved the way her blondish brown hair cascaded down her neck. And he brought brandy to their fireside chats, which always seemed to become intimate. She would end up wearing nothing but a blanket and her long vintage earrings.

She loved how sophisticated he made her feel. It was a year of bliss—well, a school year of bliss—until she finally had to tell him she was pregnant. That's when the clouds descended and it began to rain on their relationship. She told him on one of their campus walks.

"How did this happen?" He'd stopped in his tracks, his eyes blazing with fury.

She backed away. Gentle mists of raindrops started surrounding them. "What do you mean how did it happen? You were there."

He grabbed her shoulders, forcing her to look into his eyes. "I thought you were being careful?"

She felt all her insecurities come to the surface. "I was... I guess... I'm not sure. Maybe I forgot—why is this all on me, anyways?"

He shook her shoulders. "I'm married. You knew that." He let her go. "This cannot be happening."

She shouted at him. "But you love me!"

He inched closer to her face. "I lust for you, but I love my wife. There's a difference." He took his hands off her shoulders and rubbed his forehead, letting out a long exhale.

Her insides went hollow, as if the wind blew right through her. "But we're perfect together. You spend all your time with me." Her voice was shaky.

"That's because I spend all my time at work." He raised his voice.

"So you were never going to leave your wife?"

He shook his head. "No." She wiped the tears from the corner of her eyes, sniffling. He lowered his voice. "How many weeks?"

"Months. Almost three months. But I've only known for a few weeks."

His face burned red. "And you didn't think I needed to know?"

"I don't know. I needed time to figure out how, or when, I was going to tell you."

His raised his voice again. "How about every day we were alone?" He started to walk ahead of her.

Susan had to almost run to catch up. "Slow down! Where are you going? We need to figure this out."

He stopped. "Figure what out? You're nineteen, with no family and no education. What's there to figure out?"

"No." She shook her head. "Don't say that. You and this baby will be my family."

"No, Susan." He pointed to her stomach. "We're not a family." He stepped closer to her, whispering into her ear.

She gave him a long stare and then slowly started walking backwards, heading in the opposite direction. "Don't ask me to do this."

"I know people who know people." His tone was authoritative. "It makes sense. Meet me here the day after tomorrow." She turned, picking up her pace. "Did you hear me? The day after tomorrow!" He had to shout. She continued walking, running her hand along her stomach. This baby was her family.

*

Susan's eyes telegraphed the sadness in her heart. It all seemed like it had happened in another lifetime. She knew what he wanted her to do, so she never met him in the park. When word would spread about her becoming pregnant by one of the professors, she knew the ridicule would be something she was not strong enough to bear, so she quit school and moved back home. But this was the beginning of the end of her relationship with her father. After Cassie was born, she moved out and went on government assistance.

She really tried to be a good mother, but the long, isolated hours alone with a baby took a toll on her mental health. It led to drinking. The drinking led to depression. The depression led to antidepressants. And the antidepressants lent their hand, allowing her bipolar tendencies to crawl up to the surface of her life. By the time Cassie was in school, Susan was barely able to just function, to make it through another day.

As time went on, nothing seemed to help. Especially when the couple of people she did keep in touch with, finally told her that her lover had left the university for bigger and better prospects. They heard he had become a department head at another university. But they did not know where. It didn't matter. They did know that he never left his wife. Susan was of ignoble birth and was the star of no one's life. Not even her own.

TWENTY-THREE

A.D. 1988, CAIRO, EGYPT

Mark hit the switch. Ian was right behind him along with the others. Dr. Ramsey was the last person to enter the lab.

"Let's get to work," said Edmund. "We have much to do and our time here is limited."

Mark stifled a yawn. *How does Dr. Ramsey look so refreshed when he's the oldest person in the room? He must sleep like a baby.*

"Okay, about the baby." Edmund looked directly at him. "I'm sorry, Dr. McCormick, did I wake you? I just thought we would start with the bone of the younger person. We established the bone was from a baby. And what did we determine was the time frame on the bracelet? Was it from the same time frame as the bone of the baby?"

Dr. Seldon spoke. "Yes, Dr. Ramsey, we did establish the bone was from a small male child who was probably around a year old." She added, "I do believe the baby's bracelet and the bone of the baby were from the same time period because Dr. Granite had told us the bracelet was approximately four thousand years old."

"Yes, Dr. Seldon is correct," said Dr. Granite, smiling at Cassie. "However, the pottery shard is over five thousand years old, due to its organic materials and nutrients."

"Thank you for your input, Dr. Granite," said Dr. Seldon. "We definitely established the pottery shard was from a much older time frame. This means it could be from before the Old Kingdom. If this is true, the pottery shard now becomes very relevant in the theory of the dynasties existing much earlier than what we had previously known and makes the picture on the shard of greater relevance."

Mark looked over at Dr. Ramsey before interjecting. He'd give more than a penny to know his thoughts. "Okay, well I have another take on this due to the reading of the Pyramid Texts, in King Unas's tomb." They all turned, including Dr. Seldon. "In spells 220 and 221, the texts speak of the coming of the divine king to the crown, 'O Great in Magic.' They state the festival hall and stone markers are elements of the Sed Festival. This festival was held in predynastic times through the Ptolemaic Period. The spells mention the king wearing a red crown at the Sed Festival. The texts say the red crown was for the Ritual of Valor."

"I understand," said Dr. Richards. "Seeing it was worn for the Ritual of Valor, means possibly, at one time, the red crown did not symbolize a certain region of Egypt. It did not represent Lower Egypt as previously thought. However, to further back our findings, we would have to investigate what the white crown symbolized at that point in time, since it would not be the representation for Upper Egypt. Once we establish this, I do believe Dr. McCormick's findings, which are the way the dynasties are currently represented, would be correct. Starting with Dynasty One being the first dynasty of a unified Egypt."

Mark breathed a sigh of relief, knowing Ian agreed with his side of the timeline theory. He looked at Edmund for his approval, but then Dr. Barrington spoke, so he couldn't tell. "Please tell me again. What was the picture on the pottery shard?"

"In a minute." Cassie held up her index finger. "Dr. Richards, I thought you believed in my theory of the timeline? It has been stated that Manetho's timeline was wrong, because he probably wanted Egypt's timeline to be in line with the Greek's, since he was half Greek himself." Mark observed Cassie glaring at Ian. "And what about the Palermo Stone, Egypt's oldest history book?" Her tone was desperate.

Dr. Ramsey answered. "The Palermo Stone is just as inconclusive as Manetho's timeline because each of them has only been preserved in fragments. They do not exist in their entirety."

Mark could tell she was upset now that he had won Ian and perhaps Dr. Ramsey over to his side. "Anybody want to tell me what the picture is on the pottery shard?" Dr. Barrington asked again.

Edmund intercepted. "The shard has a small picture of two men holding lotus stalks entwined with papyrus looking at each other. There is an etching of a *serekh*, and next to it a man wearing two crowns. What this means, Dr. Barrington, is if, and I mean if, the shard comes from predynastic times, it is proof that Egypt was united." He cleared his throat. "Because the man is wearing what ancient Egyptians referred to as the *Sekhemti* crown, or what we call today the *Pschent* crown. We all know this crown symbolized the unification of

Egypt. It was a combination of the *Hedjet*, the white crown, and the *Deshret*, the red crown."

"Wait." Mark held up his hand. "As I stated earlier, the red crown may not have represented Lower Egypt, like it did when the dynasties started. It did, however, represent the Ritual of Valor."

"Well," said Dr. Granite. "Until we find out what the white crown symbolized during that time, I'm afraid I have to agree with Dr. Seldon."

"This is why we are here," said Dr. Ramsey. "To try to end this debate." He paused. "Dr. McCormick didn't you photograph the spells you're talking about?"

"Yes, I did." He swallowed hard, pushing down his nervousness. He saw Dr. Seldon forcing a smile.

"May I see them?" She looked pretty, but he couldn't let this deter him from his cause.

"Over there." He pointed. He saw Ian at the far table looking at the monitor. He could tell he was having trouble. He knew Ian didn't know all the different determinatives when reading hieroglyphs. He didn't want to leave Cassie, but he knew he was needed, so he joined Dr. Richards. "May I have a look?"

"Glad to see you could pull yourself away. Be my guest."

"Sometimes a drawing represents a letter. Sometimes it represents a phrase. And sometimes it represents what was drawn. So we have established a banquet was held to honor one of Pharaoh Teti's wives. Everyone assumed he would announce his queen. But instead, it ended up being held for Princess Iput to announce her pregnancy, since it would put to rest any instability questions about King Teti's reign." Mark felt warm air on his neck. He nervously turned. Cassie was standing behind him, trying to read the hieroglyphs. "That was quick. You're already done examining my photographs of the Pyramid Texts?"

"I didn't look at them yet. I started, but I'm much more interested in trying to read the story within this papyrus." She moved closer to them. "I'll look at them after we've helped Dr. Richards."

"We?" said Mark. "Okay, if you can play nice."

"Ah hum." Ian cleared his throat. "Excuse me, it's my… well, take my seat, so you two can share. I'll leave the deciphering to both of you and I'll go examine the real papyrus. I'm still trying to determine how old it is." He put on his gloves.

"Thank you, Dr. Richards," Cassie said. "And I assure you, Dr. McCormick," she was staring directly at him, "I can play nice." Mark scrolled up a bit so she could take a closer look. "From what I can decipher," she said, "Anhai is telling Kagemni that she is pregnant. It also says she is telling him that she will be giving the newborn to Princess Iput, to raise as her own." She looked up at him. "Why would she do that?"

Mark was standing so close to Cassie their arms were brushing up against each other. "Because she was not Kagemni's wife. He already had one. And if Princess Iput couldn't get pregnant, then she would have had to fake a pregnancy—"

She interrupted him. "To be made queen. This pregnancy secured her future as queen, even if it was fake!" She bent lower to take a closer look and he noticed her hand was swollen.

TWENTY-FOUR

2350 B.C., ANCIENT EGYPT

Princess Iput took off her sandals and placed them outside the door of the king's bedchamber. It was a sign of respect. She would wait outside his door until a bodyguard, a member of the *Khenty She*, gestured for her to enter. Since childhood, she had known the protocol of order and she respected it because it brought her closer to him, the great *nesu*. She smiled at the guard. This was the first time she had ever been in the *nesu's* bedchamber. She had been in Teti's, but never in her father's. She had thought it would be bigger, brighter and magnificent in some way, but it was more somber than she had expected.

He had summoned her, and as was the order of things, she could not see her father, ever, unless he sent for her, so when he did she always had much to tell him. When she had been younger, she would sit on his lap and tell him about what she had learned in school. It was the only time she had had his full attention. He would then tell her great stories of ancient times and about the early shepherd kings.

She remembered in her youth running down the corridor of the palace, gliding her hand along the carved impressions on the wall, stopping only when she reached the guard, waiting for his nod before entering. Then, grabbing each side of her linen sheath, she would practically tiptoe through the room.

Upon approaching the king, she had bowed, her long tress of sidelock touching the floor. Only after he had waved his hand did she run up the two steps to his royal chair and climb into his lap. The leather *schenti* kilt against his bare chest made him look fierce and strong. She never forgot—king first, father second. And she was smart enough to remember all the protocols of the household. Country before family, the queen before the king's mother, major wives before minor wives, and mistresses and concubines before children, and boy children before girl children, even though her *abi* didn't have any, because they were possible future kings. This was why she was the *nesu*'s favorite child.

She squeezed her *abi* tight. He leaned over and kissed the top of her head. His dark brown eyes revealed his love for her. The height of his *Sekhemti* crown displayed power and strength. His *wesekh*, a beaded collar he wore made of electrum with blue semi-precious stones and faience, exhibited wealth and security. Suddenly, a servant wearing only a loincloth scurried up, bowing before the king, handing him an object and scampering away as fast as he approached. He took her hand and placed a small statue onto her palm. Seeing it, her eyes lit up.

"A cosset! It's beautiful." She turned the statue of the lamb around and then upside down. She noticed the markings on the belly. *Sefekhu Shenet*. It was the written form of seven hundred.

Her *nesu* spoke. "This statue represents when we took control over Lower Egypt from the shepherd kings." Out of nowhere the servant returned, bowing again before the *nesu*, and handed him a second object.

"And what is that in your other hand, great king and *abi?*" She pointed her small finger toward her father's closed hand.

"A piece of pottery from ancient times; it was once part of a wine jar. Our ancestors drank out of it in celebration after they defeated the shepherd kings."

She looked at the tiny pictures on the pottery shard. There were two tiny men looking at each other, holding lotus stalks entwined with papyrus. Next to them was a *serekh*. Inside was the name Narmer. Curiosity made her look again. Next to the word Narmer was a picture of a man wearing two crowns. She knew he was a king, and the two crowns represented Upper and Lower Egypt.

She wiped the shard on her linen sheath, as if by doing this, the tiny picture would appear clearer. She grabbed both objects, her small gold bangle bracelet clinking against them as she held them tight. Again out of nowhere the servant appeared, lifting her off of her father's lap and onto the floor. She remembered bowing, clutching the objects close to her body, giggling at her *abi*. And with a wave of his hand he dismissed her. She gently walked toward the door, and only after she left the room would she run down the corridor of the palace, delighted with her new treasures.

Princess Iput wiped a tear out of the corner of her eye, also wiping away the memory. She needed to focus. To be convoked was an honor, even if you were the *nesu*'s daughter, but she wondered why now, when everyone was getting ready for the great feast in the banquet hall. She bowed, catching a glimpse of her father. He was in his bed.

A woman servant was covering him with a second animal skin. He was shivering and looked pale. When King Unas saw her, he dismissed the servant after she set down his cup of warm *shedeh*. "Wait. Bring a second cup for the princess." Princess Iput shook her head no and with a wave of her hand dismissed her a second time. "Ah, my little princess, but you are not so little anymore." His voice had a rasp tone. "You are so tall, come closer. Let me look at your beauty." Inhaling his next breath, he coughed.

He looked weak and faded. Lying there in his bed, his body so frail, he didn't look like a king. He just looked old. She wasn't used to seeing him without his *Sekhemti* crown, or his *wesekh* worn around his neck, and this made her nervous. How sick was her beloved *abi*? The woman servant came back with another cup of warm *shedeh*. It seemed to her the servant only followed the *nesu*'s orders. She then went to help the king sit up, but Iput stopped her.

"No, I'll do that." When she touched him, she felt only bones. She handed him his cup, then pulled up the animal skin to just under his chin. "May I sit?" She pointed to the wooden chair.

"No, come sit by me on the bed. This way I can hear you better." He patted the bed in slow motion.

She sat down looking around the room so he would not see the mist in her eyes. There was a table by his bed. He had already placed his cup onto it. At the end of his bed was a bench with another animal skin laid upon it. On the other side of the bed was the beautiful carved wooden chair, with the legs resembling a lion's paw. And there were colorful mats all over the floor.

"I suppose you're wondering why I called you here before tonight's banquet." He spoke slowly, his speech languid. She leaned in closer to hear him better. "I am not going to be able to attend tonight." He tried to clear his throat. She wanted to stop him from talking. Stop him from saying whatever was next. But he spoke and all she could do was listen. "I am ill, my little princess. I feel as if I am slowly dying with each passing day." He placed his hands over his stomach. "The pain—it is constant, it never goes away."

Her eyes turned glassy. What was he telling her? She knew he hadn't felt well, but he couldn't be dying? He was just sick. She forgot protocol and hugged him without asking. "Do not worry. We will bring in the best examiners and the women who know the herbs and how to heal with them. And the gods, we will all pray to the gods for your good health."

"Out of all of my children, I do believe you truly love me just as your *abi*. Not because I am *nesu* of a wealthy land. This is why you are now here. King Teti's future draws nearer. I have asked him to proclaim a queen, and he will reveal his answer tonight. My body has failed me; I cannot ensure you are the chosen one. The decision is his. I have no living wives and no legitimate male heirs to my throne. And his mother Queen Sesheshet and I made peace between our warring royal families when I proclaimed Teti to be my heir." His voice was growing more hoarse and raspy with each word.

She tried to smile. "All is well and good, for I have the future *nesu's* baby in my belly." Iput was using one of the

121

oldest canards women have been engaging in throughout the ages, but she had no choice.

"Whaat?" His breathing was deep. "How long have you… Does Teti know?" he whispered.

"No, not yet. Out of respect for you, I was waiting for you to send for me. The *nesu* should always know first what is coming forth in his kingdom." Her eyes were glazed and damp. She didn't know if it was because of his health or her lie. She had to tell Teti before tonight's banquet. She was just going to stop him before they entered the great hall and whisper it into his ear. It was just by chance her *abi* had sent for her.

"Oh, my little Iput. You have always been smart for a woman. If only you were born a man—now go." With the last of his strength he pointed toward the archway. "Go to your husband and persuade the future *nesu* to make you his queen."

"And tell me, how can I do that? I have not been summoned."

"Go get the guard, for I am unable to yell." He had a weak but stern tone. "Bring him to my bedside." She went to the door, motioning for the guard to enter. Then King Unas whispered something into his ear.

Her father, the great *nesu*, had one more move in him. She couldn't help but smile. "Is there still a chance?" She saw the iridescence of his love for her come through. He might be frail, but his eyes radiated warmth and she was reminded of her *abi* and great kings of long ago.

"I am still *nesu*." Again his voice had a rasp tone. "I have summoned your husband to come see me, now, before the feast. I will tell him you have urgent news and you need to talk to him before the banquet." Again, he cleared his throat. "At my request he will see you—be prepared. You will be convoked once more. Now go, he cannot find you here." He coughed, the effort ravaging his body. He laid his head back onto his pillow and closed his eyes, drifting into somnolence.

Her instinct was to kiss his cheek. So she did, again breaking protocol. Then she slowly began walking backwards to the door, never taking her gaze off him. She bowed the way the slaves and servants did, down onto her knees, with her lips kissing the floor. Only then did she leave his room. As she walked down the corridor, she grazed her hand along the carvings on the wall. It was too late to turn back now. Her and Anhai's plan was already in motion. It had been a generation since a royal birth had taken place in the palace, and she was going to be at the center of it.

Teti's elder wife, Khuit, had daughters by him, who were already full-grown and only a few years younger than herself. *When King Teti's mother finds out I am with child, she will persuade her son to make me his queen. It won't matter that Khuit named a daughter in honor of her. After all, my husband is very close to his mother, but the mother of the future* nesu *will favor me, for I was also born of royal blood like she, Sesheshet.*

TWENTY-FIVE

2350 B.C., ANCIENT EGYPT

Kagemni was tired as he rode his horse through the courtyard of the palace. The living taxes he had collected were a few hours behind him. The *nesu's* armies were bringing in the animals. He had collected thousands of cattle, pigs, wheat and slaves from the Egyptian people to pay homage to King Unas. Making people pay taxes when they barely had enough for their families seemed to be going against the gods.

Nevertheless, he was a good *nesu*. He stored the wheat paid to him and opened the granaries when the gods did not bless Egypt with a good flooding of the Nile. By doing this in the lean years, he had prevented famine for his country. The people did not grow prosperous under his rule, but they also did not starve. It could be worse. Much worse. Kagemni had recorded his collections, so as far as he was concerned, his job was done.

He already missed King Unas and he wasn't even dead. He would dread that day. King Unas was the one who had elevated him to vizier. He was like a respected family elder to Kagemni. But yet he knew what the future King Teti had done, and had approved it, or at least had not contested his decision. And Teti was like a younger brother to him. He had looked out for him since boyhood, which is probably why he was elevated to position of vizier. Yet even though he knew soon this position would no longer be his, he still went throughout the land and collected the king's taxes.

He dismounted. A servant of the palace came out to greet him and tend to his horse. He entered the palace with his tax book. He would show his collections to King Unas, not King Teti. He walked along the corridor, heading toward the great hall. The smell of foul keened his senses. Hunger plagued him. He had stopped to inhale the aroma of the sweet-smelling meats, when a servant of Princess Iput approached him. She bowed her head in reverence to him and he pushed away his hunger.

"High Priest Kagemni, Princess Iput has sent me. You are to go to the room west of the great hall and wait. The princess has a message for you." She bowed again and left before he could question her.

He sighed. All he wanted to do was show the king the collections he had recorded, eat and sleep, in that order. He entered the room and sat on the wooden bench under the wall decorated with scenes from one of King Unas's great hunting expeditions. A servant entered the room and gave him some *henqet*. He gulped it down, wiping his mouth with his hand. At least his thirst was quenched. He told the servant he wanted another one and was glad it was not his rotation for his priest duties. He was staring at the carvings of the hunting expedition on the wall when he was handed a second cup of *henqet*.

"You have been gone for over *senuj* full moons, and I have missed you."

He stood. Her voice was sweetness to his ears. "Anhai, it is good to see you. Thank you for the *henqet*, but you must leave—Princess Iput requested to speak with me."

"You need to shave."

Although he was the one drinking, Anhai was the one who looked relaxed. "I will, there's time before my next priest rotation. I have just returned from collecting the king's taxes."

"I know. It seems you have been gone for a lifetime. It is I who needs to talk to you."

He shook his head. "I can't. I told you, I am expecting the princess."

"No, my love, you do not understand, it is she who granted me this visit with you."

His face tensed, showing his wrinkled forehead. "I don't understand; I need to show the *nesu* his collections."

"In due time. This matter of which I need to speak to you is of great importance. Come sit with me."

He sat, and Anhai joined him on the bench. She placed her two fingers over his lips. He had longed for her touch and kissed her fingers.

"Please listen, I do not have much time." She cupped her hand and began stroking his face, taking in a deep breath. "I am with seed. You have been gone for the last *senuj* full moons. My belly has been full for that time plus a little longer. I did not know until after your farewell." She whispered in his ear, "The baby is yours, and Princess Iput knows this. She is willing to help us, as it helps her."

He leaned his head against the wall reliefs. He was too tired to know what to feel. He only knew he just wanted to eat, sleep and then think about what she had said. But he knew he had to say something. "I am married. It may be a loveless marriage from the gods, but you know I am married." He pressed his hand over his eyes to gather his thoughts. "Are you sure?"

"Sure I am with seed, or sure the baby is yours? Yes to both." Her voice was brusque. "I really do not have much time."

"Show me your breasts!"

She turned toward him. "I cannot. Someone may enter."

He didn't care. He needed to see the difference in them. "I said, show me your breasts."

She looked toward the archway, hoping no one was near. She slowly lowered her sheath and exposed herself to him. Kagemni swallowed hard. His eyes were fixated on them. They were almost double in size. There was a richer darkness of brown color around her much larger nipples. He moved closer and touched her breasts.

She bucked, pushing him away. "They are tender to your touch. *Sjsu* moons out, or a little longer, I will bear your child. Shh." She placed her finger over her lips. "Listen very carefully to what I have to say."

TWENTY-SIX

2350 B.C., ANCIENT EGYPT

Princess Iput pondered on her husband, the future King Teti. He was of small stature with a pudgy face and bulbous nose. He had dark hair and his appearance was of one who never lacked for a meal. His only outward assets were his deep voice and his *Sekhemti* crown, which ensured his commanding presence, due to the fact he was the future king and, because of King Unas's recent illness, the acting king.

Inside of this commanding presence, she knew he was full of insecurities, the lack of him producing a male heir being the biggest one. The need for more wives to produce this heir was not something she really wanted for him or herself. She thought he probably was really in love with her. She had brought out something in him his first wife could never do, and that was excitement. Every time they made love, she knew he felt powerful. She could always make him laugh, and because she was also a royal, she understood the trials of being the ruler behind the ruler of this vast Egyptian empire.

King Teti had just returned to the palace grounds with his cavalcade of horsemen behind him. He was returning from his hunt of the great crocodile. Certain times of the year the crocodile was prominent on the banks of the Nile, and during these times royals would hunt them, not to kill, but to bring them home for their children, wives, and to give as gifts to the priests for the temples. They would adorn the crocodiles with jewels, let them roam free in their homes and pray to them daily during this season so the Nile would provide good soil for a decent crop and be abundant with fish. The crocodile represented the god Sobek.

Sobek had a man's body with a head of a crocodile. He was an all-empowering god and the most frightening of deities. It was Sobek who first came out of the waters of chaos to create the world, making him a link to the sun god Ra. So when the future king came back to the palace with his crocodile, she knew the god would be pleased. Deeply pleased. One of his servants, or maybe a slave, would parade the crocodile around the palace. He would want to show her and his first wife, Khuit, along with his soon-to-be wife Weret-Imtes, his good fortune.

Princess Iput shook her head. Enough thinking of Teti's other wives. She was eager knowing her father, the great King Unas, had helped her by requesting Teti's presence. Her *abi* was going to tell him he had to summon his royal wife. Now. Before he entered any other room of the palace or spoke to any other person. He would wonder why his vizier had not told him this and should see the urgency of the situation. Thanks to Anhai, she knew before he left, his last conversation with Kagemni was telling him he was going to be replaced soon, by his son-in-law Mereruka.

As she tried to calm her nerves, a guard entered and made his announcement. "The almighty future King Teti is here to see you." He banged the wooden pole he held twice against the floor and left. As the future King Teti entered, Princess Iput bowed the way the servants and slaves do, all the way onto her knees, her head dropping to his sandals as she kissed his exposed feet.

When she got up, she found him staring at her, so she spoke. "Come, sit here. You must be tired and thirsty from your travels. I have a cup of *henqet* waiting for you, and after I hear of your great conquests, I have some news of importance for your ears." She smiled, handing him his cup of *henqet*.

He sat and spoke. "You are as beautiful as the stars and today you are as luscious to me as the Nile itself. I do not have much time to prepare for tonight's banquet. It is only out of respect for your *abi*, King Unas, that I stop here first. What did you want to tell me?" He threw back his *henqet*, and then seemed to drink her in with his eyes.

"I wanted you, no, I needed you to know before you become too busy at the banquet that... well, it has been *senuj* full moons since my last bleeding. My nipples are sore, and I am sick when I try to eat. I spoke with the women who study the herbs and they confirmed, I will bear your seed before the next *sefekhu* full moons rise in the sky." She bowed before him again.

"Get up." He went to her and picked her up off of the floor and laid her onto the bed. "Don't say false words before your future king."

"Never," she said.

He leaned in and kissed her lips with such force, his tongue going deep into her mouth. She knew he felt ever so powerful. As she spoke, her breasts were pressed against him, enticing him. "Are you pleased?"

"As ever, my princess, you are full of surprises." His smile turned into laughter.

"Will this help you with your decision tonight?" She smiled.

"Ah, I see. Well, you will never know." He sat up. "What I promise you, my dear, dear, wife, is that if you produce a son, you will be made queen. I will tell everyone tonight the reason for the banquet is to announce that you are with seed. Everyone had assumed I was going to proclaim who would be queen tonight, and I was, but no one really knew for sure, not even your *abi*. So tonight, since you have pleased me so, tonight is now your night. It has been nearly a generation since the palace has produced a baby, and for that I am truly in love with you." His grin was etched into his face and his boisterous laugh showed he indeed was very much pleased.

She got up and bowed again, keeping her head low as she spoke. She knew she had won her husband over to her side with her news and even perhaps her charm. "If I may request a favor from you, since I have pleased you?"

"Stand, I will not have you hunched over in your condition," he commanded. "What is the favor you ask?"

She stood. "In my condition, I am afraid to anger the gods. It took so long for my womb to fill with seed... I ask, no, I beg of you, that you do not make any changes. With my *abi* ill, please keep Kagemni as your vizier until after his death. He has honored my father and you, and if the gods become displeased with any move you may make, I may lose the future heir of Egypt." She wiped a tear, then looked up through her lashes to see if he was moved.

"Do not do anything to upset yourself. This is a small request, a mere delay. I grant you your request. Settle yourself. Now I must prepare for the banquet. Make sure you eat heartily tonight. My son needs his nourishment."

He stood and kissed her, stopping when they heard someone sneeze. It startled her. She had thought they were alone. Who could this be? Teti walked out into the courtyard, just beyond the bedchamber. A scribe was sitting cross-legged writing with his reed pen on papyrus. When he saw the future *nesu* he immediately bowed before him.

"What have you heard?" yelled King Teti.

The young scribe stayed bowed, his face at the king's feet. "Nothing, nothing, your majesty. Only that Princess Iput is with seed. But I know nothing." The scribe never looked up, he stayed bowed with his face touching the ground.

"Go! And if you speak of this to anyone, I will have your tongue cut out."

The scribe stood, scrambling to gather his reed pen, ink and papyrus. He ran through the bedchamber, out into the hallway.

Princess Iput was confident he wouldn't say anything. For she and everyone else knew the wrath of the future king. He really would have his tongue cut out.

TWENTY-SEVEN

2350 B.C., ANCIENT EGYPT

Kagemni and Anhai both stood when they heard someone enter. The stranger bowed. "King Teti sent me here to practice my writing. I am the new palace scribe Hezi, and I am here to record tonight's banquet."

The vizier gave a nod and pointed for him to go sit at the opposite end of the room. He turned back toward Anhai and leaned in closer, whispering, "Why did you not see the women with the herbs and ask them to give you acacia?"

"This is the first time my womb has been filled. When I was sick I thought it might have been due to something I ate; I did not even think I might be with seed until my breast changed and grew tender. Then my bleeding stopped. When I realized, I was scared. I prayed to the gods to help me. I had no one, for you were not here at the palace. I swear to you, I told no one, until Princess Iput found out."

"Out of all the people to tell…" He glanced at the scribe, who was busy with his writing. Placing his hands on Anhai's arms, he pulled her closer to him, whispering, "I swear by the god Ra, of all the people you could have sworn to secrecy, you chose the princess, someone who could ruin your position and send you into slavery?"

She spoke softly. "When I smelled the food for the banquet, I became ill in her chambers, and she asked me if I was with seed. I was scared and told her yes. She guessed. She knew the symptoms—seems she has been trying to bear seed for some time now. She has even been praying to the goddess Meskhenet."

Kagemni looked again at the scribe. His face was buried in his papyrus. He turned back to Anhai. She placed her hands into his, taking a deep breath before beginning. "Princess Iput is the one who created our plan. Listen to what I tell you, because what happens to us also benefits her. She is going to ask you to make arrangements for me to stay in the temple with the priestesses, where I will finally be able to fulfill my dream. While I wait to bear your seed, I will be taught the duties of a priestess. And the princess will swear them to secrecy. You as a priest know, when a royal swears you to secrecy, your life is dependent upon keeping the secret."

He nodded, so she continued. "They will never know of our plan. They will only know I am to stay here until I have the baby, because I am favorite handmaiden to the princess and do not wish to disgrace the royals, for the baby's father will not marry me. Which is true, so I am not risking angering the gods or lying to the priestesses. They will never know it is yours."

He sat back down, swigged his *henqet* then rubbed his hand over his mouth, never taking his eyes off her. She sat next to him. "Then the princess chooses a new servant girl, one who is young and stupid. She must be stupid. And as handmaiden, she takes over my duties. They will go into confinement until after our baby is born. The princess knows how she should look and feel when with seed."

She continued, never skipping a beat. "After she learns I have given birth, she sends a request for me to come back to the palace. Saying she wants me here, for she is in fear of her labor with this new servant girl, because she is so stupid. Before I arrive, she dismisses her, then I come during the night, bringing the baby with me, going into confinement with the princess. Remember, only the priestesses know I have given birth. Within the night, my baby dies, upsetting the princess so deeply, her labor begins. This is the story we tell the priestesses."

He swallowed the last of his drink. "This will never work," he said, putting his chin to his chest, sighing. "It is full of risks."

"It will work. And I am willing to take the risk, as this helps you, the princess and me. As for everyone else, after she dismisses the servant girl, the princess will ask the midwife to go to the medicine woman and bring back some herbs, for she is not feeling well. Everyone knows it takes a while for the medicine woman to cut and mix the herbs. Once she leaves the palace, and I arrive, she pretends to have her baby, which I say I helped to deliver, because no one knows of my baby. When the midwife returns, the princess is elated and shows her the baby. She is so grateful she elevates me from servant to caregiver of the future *nesu*'s baby. And I will privately be his wet nurse for my breasts bear milk."

Learning of all that had occurred while he had been away from the palace, Kagemni had forgotten the scribe was there. He turned, fearful that Hezi had overheard everything, but the scribe seemed buried in his papyrus. He whispered, "Where do you get a dead baby to show the priestesses? How do you come up with that inside the palace walls?"

"To ensure her plan will work, she will have a slave prepare a cosset for an offering. Then that night she and I will sacrifice the baby lamb to the goddess Meskhenet. When we are done, we will carefully bundle the dead lamb several times in royal cloth. The lamb's blood inside the princess's bedchamber will be proof that she has given birth. And the royal cloth ensures the priestesses will not unwrap it, for fear of wrath from the gods. And you alone will carry the bundle to show them."

She leaned in closer to Kagemni. "You will tell them Princess Iput has made arrangements for the burial on temple grounds. Then, after the priestesses pray to the gods for my baby's *ka*, you take the bundle and bury it yourself." Anhai's speech slowed. "I am now the main caregiver of the future *nesu*'s baby. I get to live in the palace and raise my own child and when it is my rotation, I am also a priestess. This is unheard of for someone from my low birth."

He pressed his fingers together. "But you or I can never claim the baby as our own." His mind was full of mixed emotions. He lowered his head.

Anhai brought his face to hers. Even after everything she was saying, he longed for her touch. "Don't you see? It is well worth the sacrifice!" Her voice went back to a whisper. "If this baby is a boy, we will see our bloodline become the future king of all of Egypt. The princess becomes queen and takes her rightful place. She is of royal blood, being a *nesu*'s daughter herself. And she knows…"

"Knows what?"

"She knows she owes you a favor. She is already acting upon it as we speak. She is telling King Teti out of respect for her and her *abi*, now that she carries the future king's seed, she is asking for you to remain the vizier until King Unas passes."

He raised his empty cup, but his voice was sarcastic. "Long live King Unas."

"Long live King Unas," she repeated, her voice sincere.

He was quick to face the reality of the situation. "This buys me time but is not a permanent solution. And the princess came up with this idea?"

"Yes! She does not want Khuit or Weret-Imtes to be made queen. She is the direct descendant to the throne." Her tone grew brazen. "Her father is King Unas and her grandmother was also a queen."

"What if the baby is a girl?" This seemed to be the only downfall in the plan.

"Then this baby gives everyone time. The future King Teti will say if the princess can bear one child she can have another. I am still caregiver and priestess. You are still vizier and advisor to the *nesu*, because the favor has already been granted. He also wouldn't want to do anything to upset her chances of bearing seed again. She then has more time to produce an heir. The plan remains the same."

They stood and she leaned closer to him. "Oh, one last thing," she said. "You are to attend tonight's banquet. After all, you are still the vizier." She looked too young to be so clever and ambitious.

He whispered in her ear, "I will go along with the princess's plan." Then he kissed her cheek.

"Now go get ready," said Anhai. "What I wouldn't give to see Mereruka's face when the future King Teti announces the princess's womb is filled and you are staying on as his vizier."

Kagemni bid Anhai goodbye, not noticing the scribe Hezi rapidly etching onto his papyrus. He worried about what the gods would do to him in the afterlife, and there was nothing he could do about it. Walking down the hallway of the palace, suddenly his doubt was replaced with calm.

If Anhai had a boy, the next future king of Upper and Lower Egypt would be of his bloodline. And he would have a resurgence in power, just like he had when Teti was a boy. The thought put a smile on his face. The future King Teti may have disgraced him, but the gods had just shown this vizier and priest justice.

TWENTY-EIGHT

2350 B.C., ANCIENT EGYPT

The smell of myrrh and lotus blossom scented the air as people arrived for the banquet. An archway along the far wall led to an outer courtyard, showcasing the sandstone colors of the buildings around the palace. The room was lined with pomegranate trees and slaves held palm branches, waving them in front of the guests to create a calming breeze. In the middle of the room was a fountain, not only filled with water, but also perfume to scent the heat of the night as the people arrived. The dais at the front of the room held two chairs—one was ebony, for the future King Teti, and the other was ivory, for whom he would declare as his queen. Both chairs were inlaid with semi-precious stones fit only for royalty. Multicolored tiles glazed the floor and paintings of past royals adorned the walls.

Around the fountain, musicians gathered, playing the harp, flute and double clarinet. Dancers rattled bone clappers in their hands while they danced and men beat rhythm sticks together, while women sang songs of the triumphs of Egypt. Roasted duck and goose scented with garlic and onions permeated from the kitchen, along with pomegranate paste and honeyed nut cakes. These were the scents and visuals engulfing Userkare as he entered the great banquet hall.

He was of great height, *jfedu* cubits, *senuj* palms and *senuj* fingers. His name signified, 'The Ka of Ra is Powerful,' meaning the soul of the sun god is strong. He was not only a member of the king's guard. He was the lead guard, head of the *Khenty She*. He traveled with his retinue, where he was ranked of the highest importance. He had medium brown hair and green eyes.

His mother had been from another land. She came to Egypt and became a sacred intimacy performer, one who gave men favors. Then she died when he was *medshu* plus *jfedu*. He never knew where she came from, but because of his complexion, he knew he was only half Egyptian. He did not know who his father was, and because of this he had no money or position and had to spend his entire life fighting for what he needed and wanted.

It was a member of King Unas's guard who had seen him in the marketplace stealing food. Because of his height, the guard thought he was much older and recruited him into the *Khenty She*. He demonstrated his fighting capabilities against any slave they literally threw at him. He excelled in battle and was an excellent bodyguard, but was also aloof, arising from his birthright. He did not feel comfortable around people. But tonight, the future King Teti had invited him, not as a guard, but as a guest, because of his past military achievements.

So here he stood against the wall, bare-chested in his loin skirt, which ended just above his sandals. A slave stood by him, waving a palm branch, casually thumping him in his face. If looks could kill, the slave would have been dead as Userkare moved away from the wall and closer to the fountain. Suddenly the trumpets made of silver and bronze sounded the signal for the arrival of the king and his wives.

"Bow for the honorable future King Teti, whose name means, 'He Who Pacifies the Two Lands.' Preordained by the gods and his title having been bestowed upon him by the great and powerful King Unas, who is represented here tonight by his daughter Princess Iput. Accompanied by Khuit, the honorable future King Teti's elder wife, and their daughter Seshseshet, and her husband Mereruka. Followed by Sesheshet, mother of King Teti, succeeded by Weret-Imtes, concubine of King Teti." He blew his trumpet again. When the sound stopped, everyone arose.

King Teti's *Sekhemti* crown made him appear taller than he actually was, and Userkare noticed how young Weret-Imtes looked, still a child. Beside her was the future king's mother, beholding a regal confidence he had never seen before in a woman. Next to her stood Mereruka. He was not a man in his eyes. Everything was handed to him because he was the king's son-in-law. His wife Seshseshet was rather plain in beauty. Good thing she was adorned in ornate jewelry. Next to her was Khuit, aged by her endless wait for who would be made queen. And then there was Princess Iput.

Her sandals dazzled with blue lapis jewels. Her movements were lithe. And she stood taller than the other women, looking noble standing next to her husband. Gold charms arrayed in a circle adorned her wig. Her eyes were blazoned with kohl and her eyelids dusted with flecks of gold. Her lips were red with ochre. She wore a necklace of aventurine and carnelian, which led enticingly to her hennaed breasts. He was having licentious thoughts and needed to adjust himself. He was used to women being merely for relief, not pleasure.

The future King Teti ascended the dais and sat in the ebony chair. People started to talk amongst themselves and the servants began dispensing the date wine. He felt somebody nudge him and turned to find Kagemni offering him some wine.

"I didn't expect to see you here," the priest said, handing him a cup.

"Tonight I am an invited guest." Userkare took the cup of wine.

"It is good wine." Kagemni smiled. "I have been invited by the *nesu*; however I do not know which *nesu* invited me."

"I see by the hair growing on your head that it is not your rotation for your priest duties?"

Kagemni shook his head. "No, I am here as vizier. I only returned to the palace a couple of hours ago."

"Is all well with the people of Egypt?" asked Userkare.

Kagemni took a sip from his cup. "Yes, the Egyptian people have once again paid their taxes. Is all well within these palace walls?"

Userkare's gaze strayed to Princess Iput. "Yes, and the view is stunning." He couldn't keep his eyes off the princess.

Just then a guard put a mouthpiece made of gold to his lips and the trumpet's sound resonated everyone to silence. The future King Teti began speaking. "I have some news of great importance." He breathed heavily through his small and portly frame. The dais he stood upon raised him above the people.

His crown and deep voice were what made him look sovereign and kingly. Without them, he would have looked ordinary.

He raised his arms in praise. "I am pleased to announce Princess Iput's womb is filled. Before the full moon rises *sefekhu* times, she will birth. And if it is a son, Princess Iput will be made queen of Upper and Lower Egypt. My kingdom, bow before the woman who may be carrying the future *nesu* of Egypt."

The people were obedient, although you could hear whispers. "Arise, for now we make a toast to Princess Iput." The people cheered. "She had only one request to be granted and it was not for herself. This is why she pleases the gods," he said. "I have granted her request to keep Kagemni as my vizier until the death of her father, King Unas." Everyone held up their cup. King Teti also held his cup upward, looking at the princess, then Kagemni, nodding.

The trumpet blared again. "We are also making a toast to Weret-Imtes, who before the next full moon will become my wife." The people cheered a second time. The musicians returned to playing their music, while the dancers rattled their bone clappers and danced around them.

Weret-Imtes took a sip of wine before speaking to Seshseshet, Teti's daughter. "I thought I was supposed to be his baby-maker? Why, then, is he marrying me? I have no hope of ever becoming queen."

Seshseshet spoke. "You are a noble friend, but what of my mother? She is my father's first wife and has paid her dues to him. He owes her."

"He owes her nothing." Mereruka said to his wife. "Your mother failed to produce an heir. He is fond of her, but she is not from royal blood like Princess Iput."

"You're telling me this decision does not bother you?" said Seshseshet. "I thought when he made you his vizier this secured my mother's position as queen."

"Well, we have no security, I am not vizier. Displaced before I even started. And your mother Khuit and good friend Weret-Imtes have no hope of becoming queen." Weret-Imtes began crying. "You are acting like a child. Stifle your tears," said Mereruka. "Both of you need to pray to the gods for Princess Iput to have a female child. Why do you think he is still going to marry you? It took the princess a long time for her womb to fill, and no one knows if she is capable of producing a boy."

"Yes, my *abi* is covering all possibilities," said Seshseshet. "There is nothing we can do but wait."

"And wait we must," said Mereruka. Weret-Imtes began crying again as the servants started to bring in the food. Roasted duck, boiled pig, goat, and heart of a plucked goose in onions and garlic were set upon the banquet tables.

Khuit sat next to King Teti's mother. "I should have seen this coming, since I am past my womb-filling years." She gulped her wine.

King Teti's mother, Seshseshet, spoke. "You are ungrateful. You have had many years with my son as his main wife and you have produced no heirs. Yet upon King Unas's death he will elevate your daughter through your son-in-law being made vizier. You are treated well and lack for nothing. What more could you want?"

"My son-in-law Mereruka was already the king's vizier and he has just had it torn from him," said Khuit.

"No, he is going to be the future king's vizier. King Unas still lives, and while he does Kagemni has always been his vizier. Your son-in-law's status was premature, just like him," said Sesheshet.

"Admit it, you want Princess Iput to be made queen. After all, she is of royal blood like you, and so you favor her," said Khuit.

"It is her destiny, as it was mine, to be queen."

"Well, please remember this—he has not yet made her his queen. Why do you think he still intends to marry Weret-Imtes? She is young and fertile," said Khuit.

"She is boring and acts like a child," said Sesheshet. "If the princess produces a son, he will tire of Weret-Imtes, and although she may be a wife, he will treat her like what she truly is—his concubine." King Teti's mother held her cup in the air and a servant came over, pouring more wine. Khuit drank quickly and had the servant also refill hers.

The food was all laid upon the banquet tables. Userkare noticed Kagemni was seated by the future *nesu*, and had been asked to sit there by Teti himself, probably as sort of a peace offering, or so he thought. He had also been surprised when the future king had told him to sit next to Princess Iput. However, where he sat, it was so close to the music, he wished it would stop so he could start a conversation with her. He wanted to order a *henqet*, but thought manners dictated wine tonight. When she noticed him, he got up and bowed from the waist. "A pleasure to meet you."

"Sit down. What does it take to get a servant to bring me some wine?"

He started to sit, but instead left the table, picked up a cup of wine from a servant's tray and brought it back to the princess. "For you." He bowed again.

"Quit doing that, but thank you. I don't need you to bow every time you see me, only when I enter the room. Besides, I know who you are, even if you have never met me. All the royals know which guards protect the kings."

"I see." Userkare couldn't think of anything to say. "You are very beautiful, even if you are with seed." His words had a certain temerity to them.

Her eyes locked onto his. "I could have you killed for saying that."

"I meant nothing by it. Please, I have no grace in my manners. It's just you are truly beautiful, if I may say so, only to your ear."

"Shh, don't let my husband hear you say that, but I am pleased to hear you say it. I am discouraged that I hold the future king's heir, and he still wishes to marry Weret-Imtes, in case I fail."

"You won't fail in providing an heir. I doubt you fail at anything," said Userkare.

"Well, you compliment me again with such boldness. But seeing you are the head of the *Khenty She*, I will keep what you have said to myself. Where are you from? Your hair is light and your eyes are as green as palm leaves."

"Oh, my princess, would your curiosity about me get you killed?" She smiled and Userkare knew she was interested. The king might be a royal, but he could fulfill her in every other way.

"No," she said. "I was born a royal. I can say what I like as long as my father, King Unas, lives."

"I do not know who my father is or was. I only know he was born a true Egyptian."

"And your mother?"

"She was not from Egypt. But what does it matter? She is dead, since I've been a boy. I have been with the palace guards since I was *medshu* plus *jfedu*. They mistook me for being older than my youth because of my height."

"And build," said the princess. They observed each other in silence.

He was again at a lack for words knowing she was frivoling with him. Suddenly the future King Teti got up and stood behind the princess, whispering something in her ear.

She finally spoke. "We have been discussing the flooding of the Nile. It has not been so well for Egypt's crops the past few years and we hope this year's flooding will help them thrive."

"Ah," said the future king. "I was just speaking to Vizier Kagemni about that. He says the people were unselfish in paying their taxes even though the past year has been lean." He looked directly at Userkare. "Fear not, my loyal guard, the gods are pleased with us—it has been a generation since a royal birth has taken place. The gods will be bountiful with the flooding this year."

*

Anhai was about to enter the banquet hall carrying a tray filled with cups of wine. Kagemni rushed to help her, taking the tray. "You can't carry something this heavy. Have you forgotten you are really the one with a full womb?"

"No," she spoke. "What would you have me do? The princess has told me after dinner is served I am free to go. She told me I could go to her room and rest. She assured me she would be staying in King Teti's bedchamber tonight."

"I would not count on that. In the past he has not slept with his concubines when their womb was filled. He never even touched Khuit each time her womb was filled."

She took the tray back. "No matter. If that happens she will need me to console her, so I will still be staying in the princess's chambers tonight." She paused. "I have to go now. I need to serve the guests."

Kagemni took several cups of wine off her tray so it would not be as heavy. He entered the banquet hall first, noticing the scribe Hezi sitting on the floor against the wall on the other side of the entrance. The scribe had his reed pen and papyrus in hand and was writing down the events of the night's festivities.

And while Anhai was serving the wine, King Teti addressed his guests. "Let us all say a prayer to the gods before this most charitable meal for their generosity toward Egypt today." The hall became quiet. A slave entered the room with a crocodile on a leash. It was the crocodile the future king had caught in his hunt.

As Kagemni placed a cup of wine before the future king, he heard him praying to the feared crocodile god Sobek. He placed a cup of wine by Teti's mother, Sesheshet, and Khuit, Teti's elder wife, and heard them praying to Hathor, the goddess of protection and daughter of Ra. After placing Princess Iput's cup of wine on the table, he heard her whispering Meskhenet's name, the goddess of childbirth, in her prayer. Next to her he gave Userkare, head of the *Khenty She*, another cup of wine. He was praying to Osiris, god of the underworld, who judged everyone's soul. When he was done, Kagemni said his prayer to the sun god Ra. The most powerful of them all.

TWENTY-NINE

A.D. 1988, CAIRO, EGYPT

All the Ph.D.s in the lab were engrossed in their research, or in Mark's case syntactically writing and analyzing the photos from the Pyramid Texts. He had each hieroglyph symbol blown up on the monitor and was examining them one pixel at a time. Those that hadn't found anything were recording the events of their excavation under the bright lights of the laboratory.

"I need everyone's undivided attention." Mark looked up along with everyone else to hear what Dr. Ramsey had to say. "I want to inform everyone what the samples have generated with the genetics lab. As you know, we were able to obtain some D.N.A. from both arm bones as well as from the baby's bracelet, however not from the pottery shard. This, however, is a new test, and it will take weeks to actually determine, but because of the same sequencing in the D.N.A. bands, there is a high probability the baby and the adult are related. The minister of Egyptian antiquities has given his approval to continue our research, because of the high probability." One by one the Ph.D.s began to clap.

Mark had veneration for Dr. Ramsey. Looking around the room he wanted others in his field to someday venerate whenever he spoke. It seemed everyone was enthusiastic and talking about this new field of D.N.A. testing. He was getting ready to join in when he saw Cassie. She too looked happy with this outcome and because she wasn't talking to anyone he thought he should say something. Approaching, he noticed her hand. "Dr. Seldon, what happened? Your hand is swollen."

"It's just a cut. I've been putting triple antibiotic ointment on it. Really, it's nothing."

"Let me see," said Edmund. He turned her hand over to take a look. "How did this happen?"

"I don't know, I noticed it when I was in the pyramid."

"Yeah," said Ian. "It happened right before she showed me the papyrus."

"No, when Dr. Richards noticed it, I was wrapping my hand with my bandana to stop the bleeding."

"This happened inside the pyramid?" Edmund looked alarmed.

"It's no big deal," she said. "I'm fine."

"You should have that looked at," said Ian. "Remember what happened to the people who discovered King Tut's tomb. They all died of infections."

"You really should get it looked at," agreed Edmund. "We wouldn't want to take any chances. Between your thumb and index finger is a fragile part of the hand."

She nodded. "But for now I'll go into the break room and get some ice for it."

Mark noticed Dr. Ramsey had begun looking at Cassie's notes. "These are rather elaborate about what is written on the papyrus." He moved closer to see if he could also get a glimpse of her notes. After a few minutes, Dr. Ramsey spoke. "There seems to be more theory here than fact." He looked like he was about to say something else, but then Dr. Seldon reappeared.

"See, the swelling is beginning to subside now that I have applied some ice."

"Dr. Seldon, I was just glancing at your theories on the papyrus." Edmund tapped his finger on her notepad. "Interesting—however, I need you to stay focused on the pottery shard. We must take our time to re-examine the picture, so as not to overlook anything. After all, it does show a king wearing the double crown."

Mark kept quiet on the subject of the double crown. He still wasn't finished examining his photographs of the hieroglyphs written in King Unas's tomb.

"Okay, but these are not theories," said Dr. Seldon. "This is what it actually says." She spoke adamantly. Mark wished she had just ended her sentence with okay. "You can ask Dr. McCormick, as he has been trying to piece the story together with me." He swallowed hard. *Unbelievable. Now I'm involved.*

"But I don't see any notes on the shard," said Dr. Ramsey. "Dr. McCormick has still been analyzing the photographs he took of the Pyramid Texts and trying to determine the findings of the Sed Festival and Ritual of Valor, and their meaning pertaining to the red crown." He noticed Dr. Ramsey frowning before he continued. "I suggest you leave the papyrus to Dr. Richards and you get back to the pottery shard. I will continue to examine the bones and Dr. Granite is trying to get more information about the baby's bracelet."

"But the story within the papyrus is of great importance."

"It is of great importance, but not to our timeline. Your tomb yielded results and since we are on limited time here, you are to stick to that."

"But the papyrus talks about Princess Iput. And it might mention some of the artifacts I found in her tomb."

"And if it does, Dr. Richards will find it."

"But what if he overlooks something?"

Mark really wished Cassie would just stop trying to get her own way and get back to examining the pottery shard. After all, Dr. Ramsey was in charge of this excavation.

"No disrespect, Dr. Richards," she said, "but the papyrus is telling not only of a banquet but also about two pregnancies. One is of Anhai, a servant who became pregnant by a priest, who was also the pharaoh's vizier. And the other pregnant person is Princess Iput, but her pregnancy may not be a pregnancy after all. It may have been fake, a ruse to help her become queen."

"A fake pregnancy, Dr. Seldon?" Edmund's voice had a tone of ennui.

"Excuse me," said Ian. "Dr. Seldon has been very helpful in the dissection of the writings."

Now Mark wished Ian would just keep quiet. Both of them should not be questioning Dr. Ramsey's decisions on what to examine. Cassie spoke again. "Well, if Dr. McCormick does not wish to explain… then I will."

Here we go again. Why does she keep on trying to pull me into what she shouldn't be doing?

"We already know Princess Iput did become queen." She spoke fast. "And the history archives show that she gave birth twice. The birth of two sons consecutively put an end to the rumors that the future Pharaoh Teti was incapable of producing a male heir, which was common in their time due to too much inbreeding."

"So you have all the answers now that you searched her tomb?" said Dr. Ramsey. "As for Anhai, a priest sleeping with a servant… well, that would have been beneath him."

"Dr. Ramsey, have you ever heard of falling in love?" she asked. "A forbidden love. It does happen, you know." She turned toward Mark. "What about you, Dr. McCormick, do you believe in love?"

This is it, he thought, *now I have to say something.*

"You have been very taciturn throughout this discussion," she said. "You've been following along with the story just as much as I have. Do you want to weigh in?"

"No," said Mark. *Why couldn't she have just let Ian take over the deciphering?* His stomach ached again. "Only royals wore jewelry in the Old Kingdom. This makes the baby's bracelet definitely from a royal baby. So the real question is does this bracelet, found in Queen Iput's tomb, have anything to do with the baby's bone, which was found in King Teti's tomb? And why was either bone not given a proper burial or mummification?"

"Especially when ancient Egyptians even mummified their cats," said Dr. Barrington.

Mark inhaled deeply. He felt he had appeased both sides. He had mentioned the baby in relation to the bracelet and bone, but not to the papyrus. Observing Cassie with Ian looking at the images of the fragmented papyrus, he also wanted to go over there and continue with the reading, but logic stopped him.

"Dr. Seldon!" said Dr. Ramsey. "Do I need to tell you

again? Let Dr. Richards do the research on the papyrus," he said peremptorily.

"It's just... I was... it's really fascinating. And to me, it is relevant to our findings. I'm sorry. I won't try to read the papyrus anymore," she acquiesced.

Mark went back to examining the photographs he had taken of the Pyramid Texts. *Finally*, he thought, *can everybody just get back to work?*

THIRTY

2350 B.C., ANCIENT EGYPT

Userkare was waiting for Princess Iput by the fountain in her courtyard. She had to dismiss all her handmaidens before he could enter into her bedchamber. Since he was the head of the *Khenty She*, and Egypt was not at war, he was in the palace with his men guarding the royal family. He always knew where the future King Teti was and so, it seemed, did she. Whenever the acting king was out hunting, or hearing the concerns of the people, she appeared. It started with the princess asking him to accompany her. She walked to ease her so-called condition.

Everyone thought the princess was with child and she played her part well. She arched her back when she walked and wore cloaks. Underneath she had roped her stomach in cloth to make it appear larger. As the months passed, he looked forward to accompanying her on her walks. It was the first time he'd really got to know a woman. She was the first woman he ever longed for emotionally as well as physically. Over time he fell in love with her, deeply in love. He knew he shouldn't, but her attentions gave him a new zest for life that matched no other, and he did not fear death. He trained every day for hours, which chiseled his chest. And he was strong, much stronger than the future *nesu*. With Princess Iput's attention on him, he attained a type of arrogance that was matched only by the future King Teti, and he only took orders from the kings.

On the first night they spent alone together, he told her of his childhood and how he had become a member of the *Khenty She*. And in one vulnerable, intimate moment, the princess confided in him about her and Anhai's plan. She was lonely and also depressed. And even though she appeared to carry the future heir of Egypt, Teti still wedded and bedded Weret-Imtes. Startled at first, Userkare soon understood the plight she and Kagemni were in, and even though Anhai was a woman, he understood her ambition, being that she was from low birth like him.

And now here he was, standing with his helmet tucked underneath his arm, trying not to sweat. He was anxious to see the princess. He noticed her shadow in the late-afternoon light. She was wearing a cloak with the front opened, exposing her translucent sheath and powdered skin. She herself was powdering her skin with crushed mother of pearl to appear paler. After all, to everyone else she was with seed. Upon seeing her, he felt strength beneath his loincloth. She noticed him and put her finger to her mouth to make sure he remained quiet, then motioned for him to come into her chambers.

As soon as he entered, he laid down his helmet and tore off her diaphanous sheath. Hearing her sigh made him eager. He embraced her, lowering his mouth onto hers, pressing his bulge against her warmth. She smelled of lotus and honeysuckle. Looking into her eyes, he ran his fingers through her hair, placing his lips onto hers once again, while his other hand fondled her breasts.

Then, gently lowering her onto the bed, he took off his loincloth and vest. He ran his hand up her leg, his fingers touching the part of her that was his. She moaned. Hearing her pleas, he inserted the touch of his fingers into her warmth, causing her to lift upwards. He ran his tongue across her stomach, and then, moving his hand upon himself, he guided his insertion into her warmth.

He looked directly into her beauty, and with each movement he made, she moaned again and again. With each thrust, he knew he was lucky to have her, and each time she arched her back, he wanted her more. Hearing her satisfied him. And he knew she wanted him as much as he needed her. He lifted his body once more, gave a final push, and now it was him who was moaning.

THIRTY-ONE

2350 B.C., ANCIENT EGYPT

Kagemni ran up the steps and into the temple with the servant boy who had summoned him. Anhai was in labor. Running past the raised wall reliefs with epithets to the gods on them, he slipped on the glazed tile floor, grabbing on to one of the pylons to prevent himself from falling. The skylight above showcased the stars and the terra cotta bowls lit the temple.

A priestess greeted him and told him it would be soon, for Anhai was already squatting on two large bricks. He wanted to see her and be by her side to comfort her, but he knew he couldn't. The priestesses did not know he was the soon-to-be *abi*. He ordered the servant boy to stand outside the door, and to come to him when the birth was confirmed. He had told the priestesses because Anhai was Princess Iput's favorite handmaiden, and also, him being the king's vizier and priest, he was here to make sure they kept this secret so the palace would not find out, causing the handmaiden disgrace, since she had bed a married man. He heard deafening screams resounding off the temple walls, and he knew what he had to do. He walked down the hallway, his sandals clicking on the slanting floor, and opened the cedar wood doors to the darkened room where the gods and goddesses resided. He knew he needed to make them an offering.

*

"You stupid, stupid girl." Princess Iput slapped the handmaiden across her face. The girl grabbed her cheek and bowed to the floor. "Go, you do me no good tonight and I grow weary of your mistakes. *Out!*" The servant girl arose and scampered out of the room.

She really was stupid. Princess Iput had chosen a girl who had a lack of mental means. It was all part of the plan. However, she had grown weary of the girl's inability to aid her in any way. After all, she was the future queen and she had been doing all of her own dressing. The girl was barely capable of bringing in a tray. But she reminded herself this was also part of the plan.

She knew the servant girl would not question Anhai's arrival, or her own dismissal, which she wished for soon. But before she could rest, the stupid girl was back again. She dropped to her knees. "Forgive me, Princess Iput. But a servant is here to deliver an important message from the vizier."

"Well, what is it?" The girl got up, motioned for the boy to enter the room and left.

He bowed. "Forgive me, but Vizier Kagemni said I could only bid his message in private, for your ears only."

"Then speak, I am the only one here."

He bowed again. "The vizier has sent me to tell you…" He paused. "To tell you…" He swallowed. "The stars have aligned, the gods are pleased, he will deliver your wet nurse tomorrow's eve." He looked at the floor, breaking eye contact. "You are to have a slave prepare an offering to the gods at that time." Before she could say or do anything, the boy turned and left as quietly as he had entered.

So it had happened. The stars had aligned. Anhai had given birth. The gods were pleased. Iput knew she had delivered a son. The wet nurse is arriving tomorrow's eve. Anhai was coming back to the palace. It had to take place at night. The slave would prepare the cosset, and then bring the lamb for her and Anhai to offer up to the gods for what they had done. And the blood from the lamb would prove the princess had given birth.

After the offering, they would wrap the cosset in royal cloth, and tell the slave the vizier would be burying the carcass since it was used in a royal offering. But Kagemni would really be taking it to the priestesses and saying Anhai's baby died at her bosom after living one day. And he was here to bury her baby on temple grounds himself, since she was now a priestess and did not want to be disgraced. They would not question the vizier because of the royal cloth.

He would then tell them Anhai was in deep sorrow, and Princess Iput was so upset over her favorite handmaiden's loss, her labor had begun. And they should start making offerings to the gods for the *ba* and *ka* of both babies. Again, they would never question him, not because he was the vizier, but because he was the priest known as 'The Pure One.' The plan was flawless.

She smiled. Tomorrow she would pretend to be feeling ill and in a foul mood, and she would fire the stupid servant girl. She had done it, and like her grandmother before her, she would become queen.

*

Iput was immersed in sentiment watching her favorite handmaiden Anhai sleeping on her bed. Her newborn son's true mother would be his caregiver until he reached his manhood. He would never know who she really was, but he would always be very fond of her. Royals were always affectionate and tender-hearted to the women who raised them.

Anhai was also now a priestess and she could see Kagemni more often. He did seem to love her and not his wife. And Anhai and Kagemni's bloodline would one day sit on the throne of Egypt. Just envisioning herself as queen made this sacrifice worth it. But just in case, earlier in her bedchambers, they had performed the sacrificial offering of the cosset to the statue of Meskhenet, goddess of childbirth, newborn babies and destiny.

And while Anhai slept to regain her strength, Kagemni was burying the cosset. She had just sent word to her husband, the future King Teti, telling him she had been feeling pains in her stomach and would be taking to her chambers. She wouldn't even waste her breath bothering to tell him she was distraught over Anhai's baby's death, as kings did not concern themselves over servants. This display was only for the priestesses and servants, the ones who must have a reason for her going into labor now. Soon she would order the midwife to go to the medicine woman and get the herbs to help her childbirth.

By daybreak this would all be over. Her fake labor and delivery would happen in the dead of night, before the predawn light. And she had the perfect excuse as to why only Anhai was there for the royal delivery, because the midwife had not yet returned with the herbs.

*

As all of Egypt waited for the royal birth, Hezi the scribe not only wrote everything he saw and heard, but also everything he presumed.

THIRTY-TWO

2350 B.C., ANCIENT EGYPT

Princess Iput was lying on her ebony bed when she heard her husband shouting from the hallways of the palace.

"My son. Where is my son? My wife has given me my heir. Where is he?" Teti entered her bedchamber. He was in full royal regalia, wearing his gold loin skirt. Its top edge extended up and over his left shoulder and ran along his back, ending just above his knees. His leather belt was emblazed with carnelian stones, as was the *wesekh* he wore around his neck.

His head was adorned by the formal *Sekhemti*, a combination of the red *Deshret* crown of Lower Egypt and the white *Hedjet* crown of Upper Egypt. On the front, entwined with a vulture, was a uraeus ready to strike, which made the future king look taller. "I heard I have an heir. Where is my son?" He grabbed one of the engraved bed columns as he spoke. "You have done me well. Where is my son?"

Iput smiled. "I sent for him when I heard you shouting from the halls. Forgive me if I do not get up to bow to you, my king."

He waved his hand to excuse her from bowing and leaned over to kiss her forehead, stopping when he heard his son cry. He turned. Anhai handed him the baby and bowed. He gently held his son, looking longingly at the new royal. "A boy, a healthy, screaming baby boy. I shall name him Tetiankhkm. Meaning Teti, ankh, the black, named after me, and the spirit of the gods. And black is for Egypt, because it is the color of the silt around the Nile. Someday, when he becomes *nesu*, he will ascend to the status of the gods." Tetiankhkm quit crying and gave a yawn. "Look, my son is sleepy."

He handed the baby back to Anhai. "I shall need to be informed daily of his health and I will see him every night before he sleeps." He sat on the edge of Iput's bed. "You look weak, but the gods have favored us, for you have survived the birth. You rest now, and I will see you after your purification is over and you have made your offering to the gods in the temple." He bent over and kissed her on her cheek. Then he left the room.

Anhai sat cradling the baby. Iput noticed she looked pale, so she got out of bed, looking for a servant to bring a cup of water. She did not see anyone. It was probably just as well. They would wonder why she, a princess, was asking for the water and not her handmaiden. She did, however, see a youthful man in the hallway and shouted to him. "You, what is your name?"

"Hezi. I am the palace scribe." He bowed to the princess of Egypt.

"Draw me a cup of water and bring it to my chambers." She pointed behind her. "It is for my wet nurse sitting in the reed chair."

"Yes, of course." He bowed again before leaving.

"Go quickly."

He soon returned, and Princess Iput snatched the cup, handing it to Anhai. "Here, take it, you looked like you needed water." She gulped it down. Princess Iput handed Hezi the cup. "Get her more water," she ordered. He left with the cup, re-entering the room soon after.

"Thank you," said Anhai as he handed her the cup. "I feel much better." She drank the water, then stood. "Tetiankhkm is done nursing; I must lay him down to sleep." She handed him back the cup.

"It was my pleasure," he said. "I hope we will meet again, as it is my position to record the events within these palace walls."

"*Shhh*," said Anhai. "You must go, Tetiankhkm is trying to sleep."

"You have a mother's love for this baby and—"

Princess Iput interrupted. "I remember you. And what the future King Teti told you." Staring at Hezi, she continued. "You need to bite your tongue, so as not to lose it." He turned and bowed to the princess, then left. Watching him walk down the hallway, Princess Iput hoped he did not know the true meaning of what he had just said.

THIRTY-THREE

2350 B.C., ANCIENT EGYPT

Princess Iput needed to see Userkare before her purification ended. They had met in secret during her confinement and even after Tetiankhkm's birth. But she had not seen him for several sunrises. She only had *khemet* sunrises left before she was to make her offering to the gods and goddesses in the name of her child. She had sent several servants to give him a message, but no one as of yet had found him. She hoped he was still guarding the palace and that her husband, the future King Teti, had not sent him off to another land. To her it was becoming a matter of life or death. She needed to explain everything to Userkare before she made her offering and saw Teti. In the meantime, she must tell Anhai, and had her summonsed to her chambers.

Anhai was always her favorite, but now, sharing a secret together and spending weeks in isolation with each other, they were close and had developed a friendship. Princess Iput had elevated her to be the caregiver of the future *nesu's* heir. And since she was also a priestess, a friendship with her was acceptable.

"You called for me, Princess?" She lowered her head and gave a small bow, pushing her black ringlets out of her eyes.

"Yes. Since Tetiankhkm is with the women who have knowledge of the herbs, and it is a pleasant day, I have drinks for us outside." She began walking to the courtyard outside of her bedchambers, passing the scribe Hezi, who was practicing his writing by the fountain. Her light linen sheath clung to her body as she sat on the bench along the far wall away from the scribe. Anhai followed her, the mist from the fountain spraying her as she passed. The princess sat next to a tray with an egg-shaped earthen jar plugged with grass. Beside it was two cups. There was also a gold plate, laden with figs, dates and bread with honey.

"Well, what a surprise. I must say, I am rather hungry," said Anhai. "The women who will be examining Tetiankhkm will make sure he is progressing well?"

"Yes," said the princess. "Sit and have a cup of milk with me. Do not worry. We both know Tetiankhkm is in good health. His cry is so loud, it's as if he wants the entire kingdom to hear." She smiled.

"Milk! This is special."

"I have something to tell you," said Princess Iput. "It is another secret we must share. Do I have your loyalty in this as well?"

Anhai popped a date into her mouth, nodded yes and pulled the grass out of the top of the egg-shaped earthenware jar. She poured the princess and herself a cup of milk, took a big gulp, and wiped her mouth with her hand.

"You know the head of the *Khenty She*, Userkare?"

"Yes, I have seen him around the palace now that we are not at war." She took a bite of the bread with honey and drank more milk to wash it down.

"Slow down—now that you live at the palace there will always be plenty of food."

She smiled. "I know, but Tetiankhkm suckles much and I am always hungry. Go on."

"Anyways, I have gotten to know Userkare much better since the banquet. I don't know how it happened. I was insulted the future king still married Weret-Imtes, even though he knew I was carrying his heir. I was lonely, and Userkare always seemed to be in the palace."

Anhai quit eating. "You've lain with him?"

"Don't look so shocked. You sleep with a married priest."

"But, my princess, sleeping with a married priest when I was only a servant would have caused me shame, but not death. I fear for you. Who else knows?"

"No one. Only you. And I know you will keep your mouth shout, for we share more than this secret." Princess Iput gave her a long stare.

"You make me nervous," said Anhai, "for I value your life and our friendship. If any of the other wives find out... or the future King Teti... not even your father, the *nesu*, can save you." She poured herself another cupful.

"I know, but I had become bored with my confinement. He gives me attention and I am well loved by him. I can feel it when we are together." She paused. "He shows it in ways I have never seen or felt before."

"I know the feeling," said Anhai. "It is how I am when I am with Kagemni. I feel sorry for you. You now have to go through what I do to see the man you love." She took another fig.

"I called for you so you would talk to Kagemni. It is urgent that he finds Userkare and ensures he comes to me." She inhaled. "Now you will also be the first to know this—last month I did not bleed. My breasts are bigger and my nipples are dark and tender. I feel sick when I eat, until dinner. Then I am starving. I know the signs because of you. I am carrying Userkare's seed."

Anhai's mouth dropped. "Oh, I knew what we did shamed the gods. See what happened? What do we do now?"

Princess Iput grabbed both of Anhai's hands and squeezed them tight. "We did not shame the gods. It was by their blessings that our plan has worked. We keep quiet, but I must sleep with my husband the night I get out of my purification." She let go of her hands. "Then, after I miss another bleeding, I will tell him and also my *abi* that my womb is once again filled. Teti's arrogance will make him believe he is the most fertile man in Egypt. With me bearing him another child before Weret-Imtes, he will believe the gods have only made him fertile with me."

"How can you be sure she will not bear his child?"

"The future king, has not produced his seed in many years. I am only a couple of years older than his daughter Seshseshet by Khuit. No, our plan would have never come into form if I had felt he could produce an heir to the throne of Egypt."

"You are certain to become the queen of Egypt," said Anhai. "His mother Sesheshet will be so proud of you, as well as King Unas. But what of Userkare? Should he tell one person it would mean death to you."

"He loves me too much. He will tell no one because his son's blood will be of royal lineage. But you can never tell Kagemni this. I need you to swear on the blood of your son, our son, I need you to swear your loyalty to me." Iput's eyes implored her.

"I swear, I swear."

"Nothing will change with our plan. You have my word. Your son is first in line to be *nesu*." She placed her hand on her belly. "Besides, this baby may be a girl." The princess took a sip of her milk then spoke. "Userkare was a street boy, his mother a sacred intimacy performer. And he does not know who his father is; he will be satisfied enough to know his child will be a royal. Besides, being the secondborn, if this child is a boy, he will be molded into a great warrior, ensuring Userkare's future at the palace. And he himself will be his teacher. Then he will be able to watch his son grow."

"It will not bother you that you were born of royal blood and your child will not sit on the throne of Egypt?"

"How was I to know I would fall in love and bear seed? And as I said before, this baby may not be a son. But if it is a boy, I picture him as a soldier riding beside his true father." Princess Iput already felt proud.

"And what about when you birth the baby early?"

Iput finished her date before speaking. "I have been asking for honey and fenugreek and will continue to do so. The women with the herbs have always said this loosens the womb. Besides, women whose wombs fill so soon after having a baby sometimes birth early. I will say this, and my love of fenugreek and honey, is why I have birthed early."

"Well, I see you have already started with the honey."

The princess laughed. "Here, I have something for you. She reached underneath the bench and handed her a small statue of a cosset. My *abi* gave this to me when I was a child. It has special meaning to me."

Anhai lowered her head before hugging Princess Iput. "You want me to have something King Unas gave you?"

"Yes, it is yours. Look on the belly of the lamb."

The statue fit into the palm of her hand. She turned it over. *Sefekhu Shenet* was written on the belly. "The number represents the length of time the shepherd kings ruled over Lower Egypt, before Upper and Lower Egypt unified," said the princess. "This unification was honored by sacrificing the shepherd kings' lambs to the gods, and now I give it to you because of the sacrifice you made for me."

"It is beautiful," she said. "Since you treasured it as a child, I will give it to Tetiankhkm. It will have special meaning to the three of us."

Princess Iput took off her bangle bracelet made of gold and held it out to Anhai. "I also want you to have this."

"No, I can't." She pushed the princess's hand back.

"But you must. Tetiankhkm also has a gold bracelet. I gave him the bracelet I wore as a child." She folded Anhai's hand around the piece of jewelry. "This symbolizes the bond the two of you shall share. It is the first of many good things coming to you, since you and I now share *senuj* secrets that have secured our future." She paused. "Come, we must make a blood offering to the goddess Meskhenet, for the seed within me and for our destinies."

"Where will we cut ourselves?"

"Across our finger, palm side. No one will see it." Iput stood.

"I fear the gods will not like our second secret, but I will do the blood offering with you because you have requested this from me."

"Then as soon as we have sacrificed, you need to tell Kagemni to bring Userkare to me. I need to tell him he has filled my womb and ask him for his promise of secrecy. Again I tell you, Kagemni must never know. I do fear his loyalty to the priests may prevent him from keeping this secret." They began walking through the courtyard.

"And you do not fear his loyalty to the future King Teti?"

The princess put her arm through Anhai's as they walked. "No, not after he displaced him for his daughter Seshseshet's husband, Mereruka, as vizier. Kagemni has much ambition. It does not benefit him to see my downfall." They both stopped walking. "But he won't, because you mustn't tell him." She stared at Anhai. "Do you understand? If you tell anyone, you will not be the caregiver of Tetiankhkm. I am grateful and fond of you, but this secret is to be kept. No matter what the cost."

They entered into the princess's bedchambers, standing before the shrine of Meskhenet. "And if the gods are displeased, cost us it will," said Anhai, bowing before the goddess, while Princess Iput found a knife.

THIRTY-FOUR

2350 B.C., ANCIENT EGYPT

Userkare took off his helmet when he entered the palace hallway leading to Princess Iput's chambers. He had just returned from inspecting the prisons—another one of the duties he did when the country was not at war. He stopped to acknowledge another member of the *Khenty She*, and then proceeded. A guard at the princess's door announced his arrival and then Userkare entered. No matter how many times he had been invited, the riches of each room still amazed him.

The suite he entered was larger than the house he had grown up in, and it had columns with carvings of birds, women dancing and lotus flowers. She had cushions on her chairs and a bed stuffed with feathers, making it appear plump until you laid on it, then it would flatten, but it always felt soft against his body. He placed his helmet next to one of the chairs, took his sword out of its sheath and laid it down beside his feet. He was making himself comfortable on one of the chairs when the princess entered, carrying two cups of *henqet*.

He bowed. "Why do you carry your cups?"

"I sent everyone away to service the wet nurse and Tetiankhkm, so you could enter my chambers. He grows stronger by the day. He already tries to hold up his head. Impressive for such a young age; he must know he's a royal."

"Your time of purification is nearing its end. Have you enjoyed your peace and privacy?"

She sat, before sipping her *henqet*. "You know I have, since I have spent many a peaceful and private night with you." Seeing her smile, he looked her up and down. "Do you find the chair to your comfort? The cushion has been newly refeathered. I want you feeling at ease, for I have news to tell you. News about us."

Userkare drank his *henqet*. He felt hot. "What news do you have about us that I do not know?"

"I missed my bleeding, so I had a servant bring me barley and wheat grains in pots of dirt." She showed him the pots. "I have been pouring my urine on the grains of barley and wheat, and look—they sprouted." Her face lit up when she showed him the pots. "Look again, the barley is taller than the wheat, for it sprouted earlier." She paused. "Do you know what this means?"

His face disclosed his ignorance. She started to laugh. "The sprouting means my womb is with seed. And the barley being taller than the wheat means our baby is a boy." She sighed. "I will bear him by the time the Nile starts to flood, around Egypt's fertile season."

He placed his cup on the table and got down on one knee. Then he took off her sandals and began rubbing her feet. "You must make yourself at ease. Please make sure you rest. And you must eat well." He loved her. He didn't want her to know what he was thinking, so he just continued to rub her feet. He knew he could never claim the baby as his. The future King Teti would be given that honor.

She leaned forward and cupped her hand under his chin. "When I look into your green eyes, I see not the face who fights for Egypt, but the face that fights for me."

He placed her feet back into her sandals and leaned in toward her ear, tenderly biting her left lobe before whispering, "I love you and I will love this baby."

"Shh." She looked to her left, then right. "To love me is to die."

"Not to love you is death." He put his head on her lap and she stroked his hair for a moment. Then he lifted his head, leaned in and kissed his princess, the future queen of Egypt. She smelled like lotus flowers. He ran his hand up and down her leg over her linen sheath. The softness of the linen against his rough hands made him desire her and he wanted to pleasure her now.

"I love you too." Her voice was trembling. "I am sorry to cause you this pain, but I need to be called into Teti's chambers. I must lay with him once so the baby can be claimed as his. I will say my love of fenugreek and honey has caused my early birth."

He knew she was right, but his heart was aching. He cleared his throat before speaking. "When your purification ends, you cannot just walk into his bedchamber without being summoned."

"I know. Last time I asked my *abi*, the great King Unas, to tell King Teti to summon me, but our *nesu* grows weaker by the day and I do not wish to ask him any more favors, only to tell him the good news."

"As head of the *Khenty She*, I can request that he sees you. I will have the scribe put you on his list to be seen the day after tomorrow. You will be his last subject for the day. After he lays his eyes on you and knows you are pure, he would be a fool not to take his evening meal with you and your persuasive charms. I know if you can be presented, you can ensure what comes after."

She leaned forward. "You know the second son of a king enters the military to help maintain our borders. You will see your son every day and train him to be a mighty warrior just like you."

She seemed to be able to read his thoughts, which gave him some comfort, knowing he could raise his true son to be more like him than the future king. She brushed her lips against his mouth. She could always put him into a trance-like state. The taste of her ignited such desire in him, he would have done whatever she had asked.

*

The future King Teti was sitting in his ebony chair on the dais of the great hall. "There is one more to be presented," said Userkare. The palace scribe Hezi looked over the list before nodding to his future *nesu*. "Princess Iput has waited all day to see the great and honorable King Teti. Her purification is over and she has made her sacrifices to the gods. May I ask her to enter?" Teti gestured to Userkare for her to come.

Userkare motioned to the guards to open the doors one last time. To him the princess looked luminous. As she brushed by him, he noticed her full figure and swelling bosom.

She was far enough along to look healthy but not with seed. The future *nesu* would assume the extra weight was from the birth of Tetiankhkm.

Userkare watched her walk and then bow at the foot of the dais. He saw the look of pride and lust on Teti's face and he knew first-hand what it meant. As he walked out, the door to the great hall closed, and the knot in his stomach tightened. He suddenly felt ill.

THIRTY-FIVE

2350 B.C., ANCIENT EGYPT

Vizier Kagemni sat in a chair on top of the dais, with a rug underneath. A cushion was placed in front of the chair for his feet to rest upon, and another one was behind his back. While kings held their crook and flail, viziers held their baton, which he had in his left hand. The receiver of the palace's treasury was on his left while the master of the palace was on his right. Hezi, the palace scribe, was also at his right on the floor in his cross-legged position, recording all the business of the day.

The people needing to see the vizier were lined up in an aisle, hoping to get their demands heard by him. First to be seen were the overseers of the people of Egypt—the governors, with their petitions, problems and requests for him. Next were the people who were in charge of life in the palace—from the cook to the baker, the servants of the chambers, to the servants of the livestock. All daily palace business was reported to him.

After them came the district officials with real estate cases, division of land boundaries, wills, etc. Then came the people who cut the timber, followed by the dispatchers of the water supply and then the overseers of any labor being done in Egypt. The tax collectors and inspectors lined up behind them, followed by the *Khenty She*, who were the palace guards, and after them were the guards of the Egyptian army. Last in line were criminals of all sorts. They would go to prison if they could not disprove the charges the messenger had against them. The vizier would determine their fate, after hearing from the messenger.

All these proceedings happened daily in the reception room, which exhibited massive carved columns and marble floors. And when everyone else's day was done, Kagemni then had to take what the scribe had written and recap the entire event for both kings. King Unas, who was ill, and his chosen heir, the future King Teti, next in line to the throne to become *nesu*. And although he welcomed his priest rotations, where he could put the government of Egypt out of his mind to focus on the *ba* and *ka* of his soul and the souls of all the royals throughout Egypt, he felt in his place as the vizier of the palace.

It angered him to think Teti really wanted him replaced with his son-in-law, Mereruka. After all they had been through together. He had taught Teti everything there was to know about politics. As a youth, Teti constantly hung around him, and he definitely was his advisor and friend growing up. You would think he would have his position for life, like the *nesus* have theirs, but after all this he was to be replaced when the great King Unas died. If it weren't for the secret he shared with Princess Iput about his child, he would have already been replaced. But even this only bought him some time.

He would pray to the gods for them to keep the great King Unas alive until his son, who the princess claimed as hers, grew to manhood. Tetiankhkm would never know, but if he kept his position as vizier, he could become close to the boy and actually have a say in how he would be raised, as he had with Teti in his youth. That was why it was highly important in Kagemni's eyes to keep his position. But with King Unas being so ill, he didn't think it likely. However, today, he felt the gods spoke to him. And as soon as the head of the *Khenty She* came to the front of the line, he would declare his need of thirst and rest. He would then take Userkare to the temple and tell him of the plan the gods and goddesses gave him.

*

Userkare and Kagemni proceeded up the temple steps and entered the opening between the giant obelisks, passing painted walls and colorful decorated pylons with raised wall reliefs showing epithets to the gods. Beneath their feet were mosaic tiles inlaid into the floors. The most powerful Egyptian gods and goddesses were here, all in gold, and a great sense of ambience filled the room. Kagemni was walking ahead of Userkare and waved his hand as if to have him hasten. Behind the vizier was a servant carrying a tray laden with dates, figs, bread and wine. He was cautiously hurrying, trying not to spill the wine. And behind him was the palace scribe Hezi.

Userkare's helmet was tucked underneath his arm as he walked by the open cedar wood doors, which housed the gods and goddesses, giving them a half bow as he quickly passed. It wasn't like Egypt was at war. The land had two kings and a son who would be heir. The soon-to-be queen was also with child again. All was good in the land and the people back at the great hall would wait, as they had traveled far to be heard. They weren't going anywhere, so he couldn't fathom why the rush. They made a right and finally entered Kagemni's inner post. This was where the vizier made all of his plans during his priest rotations.

"Sit," said Kagemni. "And both of *you*... close the temple doors on your way out." He waved his hand again, this time dismissing the servant and scribe.

They bowed and quickly scurried out of the vizier's sight. The servant ran down the hall. But the scribe Hezi sat on the floor, on the other side of the unbolted door.

Userkare placed his sword by his feet next to his helmet and sat down. "May I?" He then took a cup of wine from the tray and popped a date into his mouth before Kagemni could answer.

"I have asked you here as my friend and ally." Kagemni chugged his wine and poured himself another one. "What would you say if I offered you the chance to become co-regent of Egypt along with me until Tetiankhkm comes of age?"

Now it was Userkare chugging his wine. "What are you speaking of?" He poured himself another cup. "There already is one ill *nesu*, one waiting to rule and one in line as the future heir. Egypt does not need a regent or co-regent for that matter."

"I'm talking about the future king's demise. Not our beloved King Unas."

His eyes widened. He took a deep breath. The vizier was known throughout all of Egypt as being a man of good conscience and reason. He was also chief priest. Userkare couldn't believe what he was hearing.

"Before I tell you of my plan," said Kagemni, "I want you to know, that I know, you are the future king's bastard half-brother. I also know you were not born from Teti's mother, who is a royal. Because of this, you were robbed of any royal birth. Your mother was one of Sesheshet's husband's sacred intimacy performers." He picked up his wine and drank.

"What!" said Userkare. "I did not know this!" He suddenly felt as if he was going to be sick. "Who else knows?"

"Only King Unas and I. And, of course, Teti," said Kagemni.

"The future *nesu* knows I am his bastard half-brother?" He put his head between his legs. He was sick to his stomach.

"You think it was fate that the *Khenty She* just happened to find you in the marketplace? Because you and Teti shared the same father, Unas had his guards keep an eye on you from a distance. King Unas had heard about your mother's death, so he sent the palace guards to look for you. Many intimacy performers were dying of plague. But when you ended up at the marketplace in need of food, they brought you to King Unas, and when he saw your height, it was only natural that you would be trained for war."

He lifted his head. "What if my mother had not died? What if I had not grown tall? What then? What would have become of me?" He kept questioning, not waiting for answers.

"You would have been sent for when you became of age. And if your height and build had not offered you an advantage, you would have been made a gatekeeper, or maybe a dispatcher." Kagemni took a bite of fruit. "Nothing of great importance. You're lucky your build offered you a chance to be trained at a higher position."

"And what of Princess Iput?" Userkare gulped more wine. He went from feeling ill to becoming parched. "Does she know?"

"No, only a few of the *Khenty She*. The ones who found you, those who no longer walk among us, knew. The great King Unas wanted Teti and I to know, so when his time came to join the gods, there would always be a place for you at the palace. After all, you never will be a threat to the future King Teti, for you are not of royal birth. The father you share was a noble, but not a royal. Not even Sesheshet, King Teti's mother, knows, or I'm sure you would have been poisoned by now." Kagemni gave a guttural laugh.

Userkare swallowed hard. He knew he must speak his only thought. "I have slept with Princess Iput, my half-brother's wife. I could be put to death." Userkare saw Kagemni's eyes widen.

"My, my, this is interesting. You have slept with your sister-in-law and never knew. All the more reason to have the future king meet his demise, before he finds out and kills you."

Now Userkare not only wanted but also needed his wine. "You know this act would be regicide, not to mention the most powerful of sins against the gods? You are vizier, you know this. So why?" He drank some more.

"The future king sees himself as a god. The great King Unas will tell you a *nesu* is not godlike until his death. Teti's decisions are reaping havoc amongst the people of Egypt. He is not well liked among the royals, the guards and the Egyptian people. It's just a matter of time. If he doesn't destroy himself, the people will do it." Kagemni took a drink.

"Then let the people destroy him and we can wash our hands of any royal blood."

"I want to do this for the greater good of Egypt. The great King Unas is ill and will die soon or linger, but either way he cannot rule. I would then become regent of Egypt until Tetiankhkm comes of age. The gods will understand because they know I have a claim to the throne through Tetiankhkm. You do know I am his true father?" asked Kagemni. "After all, you said you have lain with the princess."

"Yes, I know he is yours and Anhai's, of which the princess claims as her own."

"And you know I am the highest of all priests. The gods command my destiny."

"Which gods command your destiny?" he asked.

"All of them. But this comes from the highest and almighty god—Ra himself."

Userkare knew Ra was the highest of all the gods. He was named after him. "If so, what have you done to please Ra?"

Kagemni's eyes gleamed. "I have guaranteed Ra that King Unas's religious beliefs will remain intact and be upheld for the people of Egypt."

"But even if Teti doesn't rule, one day Tetiankhkm will. And he may make the country worship a different god."

"I will mold the boy and we will continue to uphold the great King Unas's religious beliefs."

Userkare looked puzzled. "But you have known Teti since he was a boy and he still tried to replace you."

"But Tetiankhkm is of my blood," said Kagemni.

"Yes, but he will never know of this."

"But don't you see?" asked Kagemni. "Part of me is in him, and without his father he will need me to show him how to rule. We will be close, and he will not betray me, for he is of my blood."

"When are you planning to do this?"

"At the banquet when the princess is crowned. No one will suspect anything happening at the festivities." Kagemni poured himself more wine, started to eat then stopped. "She has to be crowned first or chaos may follow, as any person who has one drop of royal blood will be fighting for the throne. We cannot have the country divided like it was for our ancestors. As queen, she will put her son on the throne. Then as vizier, I now become regent until he becomes of age. And I will make you my co-regent."

Kagemni drank more wine. "I already attend to the affairs of the government. And you already rule over all of the guards. This way we can stop any revolt and we will have the *Khenty She* on our side. We will have the government, the guards and the priests all in our favor."

"Will you tell Princess Iput of your plan?" asked Userkare.

"No. No one knows except you and me. I need your help to divert the guards so I can poison him at the banquet. I need her to be distraught and surprised by his death. Then no suspicion can fall on her. The people of Egypt will feel sorry for her, as she has just become queen, and will not protest her putting her son on the throne with us as his co-regents."

"You mean your son." He drank more wine. "The future king has his tasters. How do you plan on poisoning him without poisoning the taster?"

"Ah yes," said Kagemni. "I have it all planned. After the ceremony, the taster will test the food and wine, and the feast will begin. When the pageantry of dancers, and you, divert his attention, I will slip the poison into his wine. It will be a mixture of opium, hemlock and *shedeh*. The pomegranate drink has the same color as wine and its sweetness covers the taste of the poison." He watched on as Kagemni took another sip of wine before continuing.

"I just have to request Anhai makes sure the wine is rich in aroma to be certain the poison will not be discovered. Teti always eats and drinks much at these feasts, and if he is washing his wine down with food he should not notice." Kagemni raised his glass. "A toast to the betterment of Egypt."

Userkare thought about raising his glass. He knew the future king was cunning by nature, not the most intelligent of *nesus*, and definitely more devious than the respected King Unas. If anyone knew the *nesu* well, it was Kagemni. Like Princess Iput had told him, the future king had much insecurity, stemming from his lack of being fertile. It was known throughout the land that his wives had trouble bearing children for him. And the future king did bully his people. It was rumored he tortured those who crossed him. But didn't all kings do this?

Little did Kagemni know if Teti did not become *nesu*, it put Userkare's future child one step closer to the throne. And the prospect of Princess Iput needing him to console her on her loss caused him to raise his glass and repeat, "For the betterment of Egypt."

THIRTY-SIX

A.D. 1988, CAIRO, EGYPT

Cassie saw the hotel lounge on her way to the elevator. A nightcap after she showered and changed seemed perfect; she needed to unwind after Edmund's reprimands. She didn't know which bothered her more—his scolding of her for spending too much time viewing the story within the papyrus or treating her like a child about her cut. Regardless, she felt his treatment of her was juvenile.

After running a quick shower, she dried herself and chose to wear the purple satin cami again, but this time she chose the black panties. She was glad she had gone shopping at the airport, seeing how her lingerie was limited when she traveled. Looking at herself in the mirror she felt sexy, until she noticed her hand was oozing pus. She applied some antibiotic ointment and rebandaged the wound. She then pulled out a syringe from her toiletry bag, found her vial and tipped it upside down, filling the syringe before injecting herself in her left arm.

She recapped the syringe and gently began putting on her stocking with the seam in the back, past her knee and upward.

She hooked it to her garter then sat back on the edge of the bed and daintily embraced her left ankle as she smoothed the entire length of her stocking. She repeated the process with her right leg. Standing, she critiqued her entire body in the full-length mirror hanging on the outside of the bathroom door. The purple satin cami with the empire waist helped accentuate the natural curvature of her full bosom. A far cry from when she had been pregnant in high school and the size of her growing breasts clinging to her clothing had had the boys goggling, the girls sneering and everyone whispering.

She felt the soft material. Her luminous smile radiated how she felt within her body. Grabbing a hand mirror from her toiletry bag, she turned and held it up to the mirror to study her backside. Not bad. She was proud of her body's accomplishments.

Her hourglass figure was firm and the stockings accentuated her legs. Too bad no one else was going to see her in this. She examined the front and side once more, before putting on a black skirt and blazer. She was grateful her outfit wasn't wrinkled. If she had been in her own closet, this outfit and the lingerie would have been hung on satin hangers.

Lingerie was her confidence-booster. And her confidence needed boosting after Edmund had made her feel like a child. What was it that made her feel so unworthy? Was it the scars from her teen pregnancy? Or her unfit mother? Probably both, and the death of her baby followed by the suicide of her boyfriend Chad, Cassandra's father, didn't help. She knew this had all been too much to take while she was still in high school, but since going to college and becoming an Egyptologist, she had thought this was all in her past.

Maybe since her childhood had been taken from her, a part of her still needed to feel like a child. Was this her internal struggle, that she didn't feel like an adult? And Mark hadn't helped much today, keeping his mouth shut about the papyrus. He was just as interested as she was in the story it was beginning to reveal, but yet said nothing when Dr. Ramsey spoke to her. It was like he was trying to undermine her at every turn. And at other times he acted like he was trying to help her, but then he would end up questioning her reasoning. She couldn't see how he was helping the excavation.

And his silence today was pushing her to her limit. She breathed deeply. She felt her stomach flutter. She would have a talk with him; he would either have to come on board with her findings once she established the earlier timeline theory, or she would suggest he head back to the States. After all, the timeline was leaning in her favor according to Dr. Granite, and he was an expert geologist.

She shivered, as if this would take her mind off him. Grabbing her purple peep toe shoes with the three-inch heels, she sat on the edge of the bed, crossed her left leg over her right, and shoved her foot into the shoe. She did the same for the right foot. Looking one last time at her image in the mirror, she regained her confidence. Yes, lingerie always made her feel like an adult. She grabbed the keycard and her purse, shut the door of her hotel room and sashayed her way to the elevator.

THIRTY-SEVEN

Mark sat at the bar of the hotel and ordered a Manhattan on the rocks. Today was one long day. He was tired but too tense to settle. Once the alcohol kicked in, he would be able to relax. He tried to get comfortable in his seat but ended up adjusting his backside, trying to conform into the barstool. It didn't have a back and it was shaped like a cup made from some reddish see-through plastic. It looked very space-age, along with the red running lights on the black transparent bar and the neon blue lighting above. *Disco Egypt*, he thought.

A huge white alabaster pillar stood on the right side of the bar, and to the left in the distance was a mesmerizing view of the pyramids at dusk. The lights at the end of the hotel property seemed to illuminate them, and the lotus-shaped palm trees gave it an essence of wonderment. On the left side of the glass wall was an exquisite white spiral staircase, which brought you down from the lobby to the lounge, where wafting sounds of instrumental music permeated through the air. He took a drink from his glass. It tasted pure, but he smelled nutmeg and cardamom. Seeing a waiter, he realized the smell was coming from the kitchen. Between his drink, the soothing scents and the view of the pyramids, his tensions of the day were beginning to mellow.

And then he saw a stunning pair of legs descending the spiral staircase, diverting his attention from the pyramids. He was smiling at the thought of what the woman attached to those legs might look like. Slowly but surely, the legs began to wind along the spiral of the stairs wearing purple heels. He took another swig of his drink waiting… and then began to cough, violently.

Cassie? No, not Cassie, anyone but her—out of all the women staying at this hotel. What if she's meeting someone from the group? "Awkward," he mumbled.

She was on the bottom step when she noticed him, stopping in her tracks. It was too late to escape, so he flashed a quick wave and she sort of smiled, hesitating before approaching. "I guess we both had the same idea."

He gulped his drink. It gave him what he needed to get back in control. "Just trying to unwind. I have a headache from staring at all the photographs. Are you meeting someone from our group?"

She looked back at him and shook her head. "No, it's just me. I thought I'd have a drink, maybe check out the pool."

He could let her go on her way. He was used to drinking alone. Or he could invite her to join him. It couldn't hurt. They'd gotten off to a really bad start. He gestured to the empty seat next to him. "Would you care to join me? I could order you… a glass of wine?"

"Alright, sure, but I'd rather have a cocktail." Just then the bartender appeared to take her drink order. "I'll have an amaretto on the rocks. Thank you."

Mark held up his glass for a refill. "This hotel is stunning," she said. "I really like the red neon lighting on the bar. And the blue lighting on the ceiling is so… I guess… modern, for being among ancient ruins."

He nodded, trying to think of something to say. Silence encompassed them, and when the bartender returned with the drinks, he was first to quench his thirst. "Look, to the view on your left."

She turned. "*Wow*, it's breathtaking." Placing her glass on the bar, she walked over to the window. He followed her, and when she turned, her heel sank right into his foot. She was so close to his face their lips could have brushed. Except he was in pain.

"Ouch."

"I'm so sorry!" she said, backing away. "I-I didn't know you were behind me." She reached for his arm. "Can I help you back to the bar?"

He laughed. It wasn't that bad. "I'm fine." He looked down at her shoes. "How do you women walk in those things? Don't get me wrong, they make your legs look gorgeous, but they must be uncomfortable." The second the words left his mouth, he realized what he'd said. He'd just told Cassie her legs were gorgeous. He hadn't meant to say it out loud. He headed back to the bar, sat down and threw back his drink. He held up his glass for another Manhattan.

She sat next to him. "Tell me, Mark, which of our encounters has been more awkward—the first one on the plane? Maybe today, when you didn't speak up at the lab, when you were also looking at the papyrus? Or tonight?" She took a sip of her drink, sounding far more confident than he'd heard her before.

He cleared his throat. "Well, since we don't seem to agree on the timeline theory, and I didn't feel the need to have to speak up and subject myself to the same criticism you were receiving at the lab today... tonight is the most awkward for me. Because, well, you look rather attractive in your attire." The bartender returned with his drink. He felt the alcohol kicking in, and it made him feel more confident.

"I like your purple shoes; they match your ensemble. Am I allowed to say that, or will it induce another awkward moment?" He drank some more. "But, after all, you wore it," he mumbled.

"Thank you, I think." She downed her drink. "Bartender, I'll have another, please." She repositioned herself on the barstool. "You don't look so bad yourself in your... jeans."

"I only brought one suit and I'm saving it for the dinner party on our last night. I don't want to chance spilling something on it." He looked down at his clothing and then he drank some more to drown his inadequacies.

Her drink arrived, and she sipped this one, looking at the view. "The pyramids have always enchanted me. The mystery within them is spellbinding." She took a deep breath.

"Well, what you found in Queen Iput's tomb is indeed a mystery. You hit the pyramid jackpot in artifacts. A pottery shard and a baby's bracelet."

"And don't forget the papyrus."

"I didn't, but it seems to be a sore subject with you tonight." He grinned, feeling slightly more relaxed.

"Well, your pyramid also yielded results."

"Somewhat. I'm rather pleased at the translation of spell 220."

"And let's not forget spell 221," she said.

"My, my, you really were listening to what I was saying regarding the Sed Festival, and the wearing of only one crown by the king for the Ritual of Valor ceremony."

"I listen to everything anyone says regarding the theory of the timeline. But what I want to know is, why are you so opposed to the unification of Egypt starting earlier than Dynasty One?" There was a nuance to her tone.

"I'm not. But I have proof from the pyramid spells that the king was wearing the *Deshret*, or red crown of Egypt, and it represented the Ritual of Valor. There was no indication in the hieroglyphs of it representing Lower Egypt. I know it did come to represent Lower Egypt, and the *Hedjet*, or white crown, represented Upper Egypt. But not at the predynastic time of Narmer and the Sed Festival. This proves to me the existing timeline, starting with the unification of Upper and Lower Egypt in Dynasty One, 3050 B.C., is correct." He chugged once again.

"But what if I told you I have deciphered the word etched on the back of the pottery shard?" She sipped her drink.

"And?"

"And it says Narmer," she whispered.

"So?"

"*So!* Do you remember the picture on the shard? It had an image of two tiny men looking at each other holding lotus stalks entwined with papyrus. And next to it was a *serekh* enclosed with one word—NARMER. And next to the *serekh* was a tiny etching of a man wearing a *Pschent* crown. This represented the two crowns worn together, symbolizing the unification of Egypt." She took a breath. "So if Egypt was unified in Narmer's time, and the current timeline starts with King Menes as the first king of a unified Egypt in Dynasty One, well, then we need to add Narmer. And there is no place to put him unless you make him the pharaoh of Dynasty Zero, starting at 3150 B.C." She paused. "It's a hell of a lot easier to add him to a Dynasty Zero and push the timeline back, rather than putting him in Dynasty One and redoing all the reigns of every king for the next thirty-one dynasties."

He noticed her breathing deeply trying to keep her emotions in check. "Don't look at me as if I don't get this. I do. But I still don't buy that Narmer was the king of a unified Egypt. I need more proof."

"Well, do you at least believe that Menes and Narmer are not the same person?" she asked. "Some in our field think they are. And do you think Narmer was the Scorpion King?"

He shrugged. "I do not believe Menes and Narmer were the same person. There is evidence Menes came after Narmer when Egypt was unified. And yes, I do think Narmer was the Scorpion King." He noticed Cassie rolling her eyes at him.

"And a lot of other people in our circle think this as well."

"Scorpion came before Narmer." She hesitated. "You'll see—Dr. Granite is working on what he perceives as the date of the pottery shard."

"Yeah, along with the bracelet and the age of the bones found in Pharaoh Teti's tomb. And the date of when the pyramids were possibly built, because of the two different types of erosions. The fact is, Dr. Granite has too much to do and too little time to do it, since he is the only geologist on this excavation." He held up his glass. "Another round, please." The bartender was quick to please as the tab added up.

"Are our drinks included with our hotel?" asked Cassie.

"I don't know." He noticed she had pushed her empty glass to the end of the bar. "I'm running a tab."

"Can I ask why you are sort of afraid of Dr. Ramsey?"

"I'm not, but you should be. He's got his eye on you and your cut." He pointed to her bandage.

She sighed. "It's no big deal, and neither was his reprimand. He chose me to go on this excavation. So he must value my opinion."

The bartender brought their drinks and he raised his glass. "To your opinion."

She raised hers in return. "He's just a little fastidious," she said. "But he also seems to be a little pensive. He has many layers. But then, don't we all?"

"Well, since we're using big words tonight, do you think he sort of has an avuncular charm? After all, he was very concerned about your cut."

"I don't know," she said. "I just think he has an old-world sophistication about him, and after all, he is in charge."

"Well, I can manage to get along with Dr. Ramsey." He looked at his watch. "Oh, it's late, we'd better get going. We have another long day in the lab."

She downed her drink. "Whew." He grabbed her elbow to steady her. "I think I drank too fast."

"Not too much, just too fast?"

"Not too much if I would have eaten."

"Here, let me help you up the stairs. The spiraling can make a person dizzy on any day, much less tonight," he said.

"I would appreciate that. But only if you don't mind. And can you find my keycard? It's in my purse. Have you seen my purse?" She started to bend down, but Mark grabbed her and helped her back onto the barstool. He didn't want her to fall. He saw her purse on the floor, picked it up and then put his arm around her waist, helping her to stand. He placed her arm around his neck and led her to the spiral staircase. Someone was yelling behind him.

"You need to pay." It was the bartender.

He turned back. "Bill the charges to Dr. Edmund Ramsey, and include a twenty-five per cent tip for yourself."

The bartender was grinning from ear to ear. "No problem. Dr. Ramsey's tab. Thank you, sir."

He looked at Cassie. "It seems everyone really does know Dr. Ramsey." He didn't want to think about the lecture he was going to get when Edmund received the bill.

THIRTY-EIGHT

Cassie's held on to Mark, her arms draped around his neck. Her thoughts were muddled. How many drinks had she had? He laid her onto the bed and took off her shoes. She opened her eyes and touched her forehead. "Ouch." He came over and adjusted her pillows. She shut her eyes again.

"I'll bring you some water." She opened one eye to see where he went, but she only saw the ceiling. Shutting her eyes again, she didn't know if seconds, minutes or hours went by before she heard him say, "Here, drink this." She felt him propping her up. She opened her eyes again and he handed her a glass of water. She sipped. Then he took it from her and placed it on the nightstand.

"Cassie, can I help you get comfortable underneath the covers?" She nodded, so he moved her slightly forward and pulled off one sleeve of her blazer, then the other. She saw him placing it on the chair by the television. Without her saying anything, he unwrapped the bandage from her hand and threw it out. She heard him in the bathroom. When he came back, she saw he had triple antibiotic ointment and some fresh bandages. She watched in silence as he put some ointment on her wound and then rebandaged her hand, giving her a smile.

She knew she was tipsy and, seeing that he was a good guy, she took a chance on speaking, hoping she wouldn't slur her words. "Would you help me take off my skirt?" Nodding, he rolled her on her side. "Wait a minute," she said as she unzipped it. Then, laying on her back, she arched upwards and he helped her wiggle the skirt down her hips, past her knees, throwing it on the chair by her blazer. She was going to say thanks, but he spoke first.

"Whoa, I didn't realize... I was just trying to get you into the bed. Eh... um... wow!" She opened her eyes again to see him grabbing a blanket out of the closet. "Here." He draped the blanket over her body. "This will cover you up and it's easier than trying to have you stand to get underneath the covers." He cleared his throat and continued.

"Cassie, your skirt is on the chair and there is water on the nightstand. You really should drink the entire glass. It will help. When I get to my room, I'll place a wake-up call for you. I guess we should have eaten while we talked. I feel like I owe you a dinner. I'm going now."

"Wait." She couldn't lift her head. "Can you turn off the lamp?" He did; she sensed darkness and opened her eyes. There was only a slit of light coming from the bathroom. "Thank you. I guess liquor here is a higher proof than in the States." She heard him laugh. "Really, thank you—nobody has ever tucked me into bed before." She tried to focus to slow the spinning.

"Sleep tight," he said, and then he looked back. "Nobody has ever tucked you into bed before? Not even when you were a little girl? Before you wore garters?"

She laughed, and it made her head hurt. "No, Susan sort of had some emotional problems. I kind of raised her."

"Who was she?" he asked.

She propped up on her elbows. Her head was throbbing. "My mother."

"You call your mother by her first name?"

"Yeah, ever since my daughter was born. I had to become the adult in the family, so that's when I started to call her by her first name." She laid her head back onto the pillow.

"I'll get you a warm washcloth for your head." She held one eye open with her finger on her brow and saw him running the water through the mirror's reflection on the open bathroom door. "I sort of had that type of a mother too. She was the adult, but she favored my brother. So I kind of raised myself." He walked over and placed the compress on her forehead. She lay back down. "Who's watching your daughter now? Hopefully not Susan."

She closed her eyes. "God. He's watching over her now. She died of S.U.D.C., Sudden Unexplained Death of a Child. It's similar to S.I.D.S., which is Sudden Infant Death Syndrome, except they call it S.U.D.C. when the child is over twelve months old. She was sixteen months when God took over as her guardian. I guess I wasn't a good enough mother either."

He sat on the bed next to her and touched her shoulder. "Hey, don't say that. Sometimes we aren't to question his reason, but when you see your daughter again, you'll get your answers."

She took the compress off her forehead. "I have my answer. I believe for every baby or child God takes, there is a mother who had to leave her children on earth before her time. In my heart I know these mothers who had to leave earth too early care for the children that left this world too soon." She leaned up toward the darkness. "Anyways, that's what I tell myself. It keeps me going, or rather, it keeps me from going crazy."

"Don't forget about the fathers. There are fathers up in heaven too."

She propped her pillows against the headboard, raising her upper body slightly, then reapplied the washcloth to her forehead. "I know. Cassandra is with her father. He died a few months after she did." She felt for the water and took a sip.

He turned the lamp back on. "Geez, Cassie, I'm sorry. I had no idea. I thought you were this carefree single professional."

She squinted her eyes. "No, but that must be what you are, because you come across as uptight and full of responsibilities."

"Well, I only have to worry about me, if that's what you mean."

"No girlfriend or significant other?"

He nodded no. "I guess I'm just a loner by nature. Probably is an archaeologist trait, since we spend all our time in desolate ruins. People drain me when I don't get some down time. And my parents always seemed to love being around people. They have the same personality as my older brother." He pushed up his glasses.

The spinning stopped and she noticed how green his eyes were. He was quite handsome when he looked relaxed. "I don't have any siblings."

"You're lucky. No pressure to compete or be compared to," said Mark.

"But nevertheless lonely. I don't have any aunts or uncles either and my grandmother is deceased. My grandfather and my mother have been estranged since she became an unwed mother with me. I don't even know if he's alive and I have never met my father." She tried to smile, but her head hurt.

He must have sensed her pain. "Finish your water and I'll fill it up and rewet your washcloth." She drank, and then repositioned her pillows so she was sitting up against the headboard. He handed her the washcloth and set the glass down.

"Thank you, I feel like I could eat something."

"You need bread to sop up all the alcohol." He paused. "Hey, I know where we can get a pizza around here."

"Delivered?"

"Yep, at the bar. I'll go get us some pizza and soda, and uh, maybe while I'm gone, you could change into sweats or something?"

"Sweats? In this heat?" She lifted the blanket and saw her purple cami, panties and garter belt. She had a long run in her left stocking. "Oh, I owe you another thank you. Thanks for not judging what I'm wearing."

"Well," said Mark, "I couldn't help but look. That's why I covered you with the blanket." His cheeks were flushed.

She tried to smile again. "It hurts to smile. Thanks, I do owe you one—the pizza's on me." She started to get up to find her purse, but he stopped her.

"You can pay me later." Then he walked out. He was a true gentleman behind his nervous demure. Her head was still throbbing. "I know better than to drink like this," she whined. "I really know better."

*

She actually enjoyed Mark's company. Over pizza they were able to relax and get to know one another. They seemed to have a lot in common with their feelings of inadequacies within their families and feeling left out while growing up. She told him all about her mother's mental illness and her boyfriend, Chad Westin. And how she had her baby at sixteen and shortly after Chad turned eighteen, causing her mother to call him a molester, but the truth was he was just a scared teen. She told him how his father was a Methodist minister and when she was with Chad's parents, she finally felt like part of a family.

And even when Chad had to tell his parents about her pregnancy, they were upset, but told them both this was a family problem and everyone would work together to find the best solution. She unburdened herself telling him how after Chad and Cassandra died, the death of her baby was also the death of her. The death of who she was and where she came from, and when her baby rebirthed in heaven, she told him she also had a rebirth—the rebirth of herself.

She explained why she bought and wore lingerie. Because it was private, and a part of her life where she had total control. If no one knew you bought or wore lingerie, no one could criticize how you spent your money or how you looked in it. And that other than him, no one in a very long time had really seen her in lingerie. She found herself laughing when she remembered how he nearly choked on his pizza when she said that.

And then, feeling so relaxed and without much thought, she told him about the lamb statue. And now that she was getting sober by the minute, she wondered if she should have. *What would he do with this bit of information? Would he tell Dr.*

Ramsey? Or did he have enough alcohol in him to have forgotten about it when he woke up? She decided she would call to tell him she would return it tomorrow. This way neither she nor he would have done anything wrong and he wouldn't have to torment himself about doing the right thing.

She looked at the clock on the nightstand. They had to be back at the lab in a few hours. She thought a moment and decided she would tell him after she returned it.

THIRTY-NINE

Edmund sat on the edge of the bed, his hands sifting through his graying hair. He felt every bit of his sixty-plus years, and he was tired. These past few months had been a roller coaster of emotions for him. He missed his wife. She had recently died from breast cancer. He gazed upwards and remembered her final words to him: *Get in touch with your child.* He was not a good father to the only child he ever had, and his wife wanted him to make it right.

Whenever he thought of his wife, emotions and feelings ruminated through his mind. Always moving, never ending until his heart ached. God, he missed her. She was such a good woman. She'd also been his friend. That's the part he missed the most—that he could talk to her about anything. He still couldn't believe her final words: *Get in touch with your child.* His child was not hers, but yet she still wanted him to *get in touch,* even on her deathbed.

He had promised her he would. But he couldn't bring himself to do it now. He wanted to finish this expedition, and then he would begin a new chapter in his life. He knew this was his last. He had ridden on his reputation for some time, but there were those who wanted him out. And truth be told, he was ready, but not until after Dynasty Zero was settled.

He was not admitting to anyone that he wasn't exactly sure which timeline was correct. Upon doing his research on the topic, he had inadvertently started a debate. Now everyone of importance in the museum world expected him to settle it. Those who worked in the field of studying ancient civilizations could have the debate go on for infinity. But the museums dealt with the public at large, and if they settled it now, it would promote interest in visiting museums again.

He also wanted to go out on top and in the limelight. He hadn't had a quest for quite some time and he was ready. So what evidence did he really have? A baby's bracelet, however old, not old enough. A pottery shard, with an etched picture and writing, found in situ in Queen Iput's tomb. Possible. A long shot, but possible. And an adult woman's bone and a baby's bone. Although fascinating, they probably wouldn't prove if Egypt was united before Dynasty One. And, of course, the papyrus, the one thing everybody wanted to decipher.

He looked up at the ceiling. After this, what next? Eventually people would focus on the next thing. Then what would become of him? His wife had been right. *Get in touch with your child.* Or spend the rest of your retired life wondering: *What if?* Since they never had any children together, they had a career-driven, sophisticated life, and except for this one affair, they really had a wonderful marriage.

Looking back, he wondered how he could have done such a thing. It's just his wife was also so busy in her career, and loneliness had gotten to him. His relationships with people were all tied up in his career, and ironically this had been what led him to the affair in the first place.

She was young, but weren't they all? She was slender, but wasn't that a given? She had blondish hair, but didn't all men at some point in time fantasize about a blond? She knew him from a professional standing, which made it convenient. And wasn't convenience how all affairs got started? It had to be easy, at least in the beginning.

And it had the classic ending. It got harder and harder to conceal and she expected more and more. And when she couldn't get enough of his time, she became pregnant, in the hopes it would bring him to her, or at least to their baby. But it didn't. He told his wife only about the affair. He promised it would never, ever happen again. And out of sheer respect for their years together, she forgave him. Not one of the highlights in his life.

He saw his child a few times in the early years, but never told his wife. He was taking this one to his grave. But as life has a habit of turning on you, his wife went to her grave first. He watched as the cancer ate at her breast, bones, liver and life. And on her deathbed she whispered in a barely audible tone, "*Get in touch with your child.*" Her final words.

He never found out how she knew, or when she knew, or worse yet, how long she lived knowing. But she had known and her last words were about his life. She was the only person who recognized the darkness he kept in his soul, and she didn't want him to be lonely, even if the person she had in mind had caused her a lot of pain. He missed her so much. He closed his eyes and said a quick prayer, which gave him a measure of peace.

He yawned, finally feeling tired enough to sleep. Tomorrow was a new day. His career would not be the only thing in his life. As soon as this debate was over, he would try to get back into his child's life. He would enjoy all the hoopla, the interviews and the lecture circuit. But in between he would reach out, get in touch, and afterwards he would make building a relationship the main priority of his life. If for nothing else than to get his wife's voice out of his head and into his heart.

FORTY

Cassie flipped on the lights. It was chilly inside. Places in Egypt either had no air conditioning or an arctic chill. The lab was no exception. She put on her lab coat and a pair of cotton gloves, and then pulled out the tray where the artifacts she had found while in Iput's tomb were stored. Opening her purse, she took out the plastic bag containing the lamb statue. Then, taking off the plastic covering on the microscope, she put the lamb under the magnifier, glided its belly with her miniature brush and looked closely at the writing. "*Sefekhu Shenet*," she said aloud.

She knew this was the written form of seven hundred. She turned the lamb every which way and looked at it from all angles under the scope. She heard the lab door open; it was Ian.

"Hiya. How are you this morning?"

"Alright. A little tired." More like hungover. But she wouldn't admit this.

"What are you looking at?" he asked.

She shrugged. "Nothing new." As soon as he turned his back, she bagged the lamb and put it in the pocket of her lab coat. Picking up the pottery shard, she placed it under the scope. She heard the lab door open again but didn't bother to look.

"Boo," said Mark. The hair stood on the back of her neck. "Did I startle you?" Her heart was thumping so loudly, she thought everyone in the room might hear. He spoke again before she could answer. "How are you feeling this morning?"

He was standing so close she felt nervous. "Sluggish and tired, but I'm alright. How bout yourself?" He looked good for someone who had also had too much to drink.

"Same. I have a headache."

"Did the two of you go out last night?" asked Ian.

"Well, sort of," said Cassie.

"I was at the hotel bar," said Mark, "and Dr. Seldon came in. We conversed while having a few drinks, that's all."

She smiled. "I would kill for a cup of coffee." She rubbed her temples, as if that somehow showed her desperation for caffeine. Anything to change the subject, but Ian was oblivious and just kept on.

"I wish I would have known. I would have joined you two. My evening consisted of ordering food to my hotel room."

Dr. Ramsey entered, his voice booming. "Is everyone ready to share their research today?" He then disappeared into the smaller room.

"Where's the statue of the lamb?" Mark whispered.

She felt his breath on her cheek. She swallowed hard. Her back was against the table and he stood so close to her, his arms might as well have been extended, gripping the table on either side of her. "Why?" she managed to whisper.

"Because you need to tell Dr. Ramsey."

"I will, it's just… I'm not done looking at it under the scope."

"Well, you can do that after you tell him."

"Yes, I could, but I'm not."

"Cassie, this is theft. Antiquity theft." His voice was just above a whisper. "Any theft in the museum world carries a minimum twenty-six-month prison sentence. But we're not in the States. Under Egyptian law, you could get life. You can't do this."

"Shh. I'm not a thief. I just need a little more time."

"Time for what? To decide if you're going to keep it or not?" Mark turned, "Dr. Ramsey!" His voice was insistent. "Dr. Seldon has something to tell—or rather, show—you."

Edmund walked out of the smaller room. "You do?" His eyes lit up. "What is it?"

She quickly pulled the statue out of the baggie from her pocket and pretended she took it out of from under the microscope and set it on the table. Edmund put on his cotton gloves before examining the ancient artifact. "Amazing. Why didn't you mention this before?"

"I'd forgotten to mention it with all the other findings the tomb yielded." Her palms were sweaty. "I was just getting ready to catalogue it with the others."

Mark interrupted. "She had given it to me to look at, and I have concluded that the lamb is three inches in width and two inches in height. It has *Sefekhu Shenet* written on its belly."

She knew he was trying to help, but right now it didn't feel like that. Edmund was still engrossed in looking at the lamb and took it with him into the smaller room where he kept his notes. Ignoring Mark, she sat by Ian in front of his monitor. She needed to think if Mark had helped or hurt her by telling Edmund about the lamb statue. She took a deep breath. She knew she shouldn't, but she wanted to know more about the story within the papyrus. So she began to read aloud. "It says here Queen Iput laid on her bed with the statue of the cosset and began to cry for the loss of her servant, priestess and friend."

Mark walked over standing behind her. "That means Anhai died. Go on, Dr. Seldon. Dr. Ramsey's out of earshot."

She was silent for a moment, realizing this was probably the statue she had in her pocket only moments ago. Her anger at him jolted her back to her senses. "Really! It's okay for us to read the papyrus after we were told not to, but it's not okay for me to keep the lamb statue for a few more minutes." Her face reddened.

"Dr. Seldon, you're not making much sense. It's just, I didn't want you to go to jail." His voice was elevated. "Especially in a foreign country."

"Well, thank you for your concern, Dr. McCormick. I don't want to go to jail either, or, for that matter, to get into any more trouble with Dr. Ramsey. So here, you sit next to Dr. Richards and I'll stand behind you. That way, if Dr. Ramsey comes out, I can walk away and this time you'll have to own up to reading the papyrus." She felt hot.

"Dr. Seldon and Dr. McCormick!" Dr. Richards seemed agitated. "I'm the one who's in charge of the papyrus. So if both of you insist on doing what you're not supposed to be doing, you can both stand behind me."

Mark looked disheartened and that made her feel better, seeing how he was getting into everybody's business today.

"Alright now, where were we?" said Dr. Richards.

She moved in closer. She wasn't going to let anyone ostracize her from the fascinating story held within the papyrus. Now it involved one of her findings—the cosset.

FORTY-ONE

2349 B.C., ANCIENT EGYPT

Hezi was given a chair to sit on and a chest made of cedar wood, which he could and did use as a desk. This was uncomfortable for him. He was used to sitting cross-legged on the floor, his writing tablet on his lap. But the great King Unas sent his chief servant with the chair and chest, and told him to make sure he recorded the deaths and the story behind them.

Because King Unas was ill, Hezi was a scribe for both him and the acting King Teti. He had just had his sidelock shaven and was entering his manhood when he was asked to be the palace scribe. His youth ensured he would be the official written recorder of the palace for a long time to come. He knew if he recorded the events favorably, he would become the 'Royal Chamberlain.' Then he would be nobler than any other scribe—and he would also be the youngest inspector of the scribes.

Officials would come to him for the history of past events, for the record of present government affairs and for the recording of any future happenings within Egypt. He would be in charge of the history of Egypt during King Teti's reign.

But it was King Unas who was wise, and he knew to record every detail of the deaths and what led up to them would take a great amount of time. He wanted him to be comfortable so he could write for longer periods of time, so he provided him with furniture.

With his sharpened reed tip, he wrote his name and accomplishments on the papyrus, then ran his hand along the top of the chest. The cedar wood was smooth and smelled of spice. He tilted his head back and adjusted his rope necklace, which was entwined with amber-colored glass, straightened his back and ran his hand once again along the chest.

It had a beautiful bronze hue, same as the chair, and its legs had been carved to look like gazelle legs, right down to the carving of the toes. The etchings on the side of the chest were of a winged sun, with a uraeus, in the middle, wearing the *Sekhemti* crown of Egypt. He ran his hand over it and adjusted his seat. The wooden chair was inlaid with ivory and had a string mesh seat, and as he sat it molded to his body. He could fall asleep in this chair. No wonder royals were lazy. Furniture could do this to you.

He brushed his dark hair out of his eye, staring at the red clay reliefs on the walls. They were flecked with colors of blue, green and brown. There were pictures of cattle, gazelles, farmers and the gods. Sobek, the crocodile god of strength; Ra, the hawk god wearing a headdress of a solar disc showing power; and Osiris, the all-encompassing god of death, holding his crook and flail. He let out a big puff of air and then dipped his reed into the well of black ink. He wrote the date, making hieratic signs joined together. If he didn't have spaces in between each symbol, he wouldn't use as much papyrus in this administrative task. He used his black well over his red one, because this was official writing. Putting his reed tip against the papyrus, he began the task of recording the events for King Unas:

Princess Iput's purification had just ended since giving birth to her younger son, whom she named Pepi, meaning, 'to add another son.' His birth was celebrated by King Teti, who gave every man, no matter what his stature, a cup of henqet when they came to the temple to make an offering in honor of Pepi. The women were allowed to take as many lotus flowers out of the fountains as they could carry. And many of them brought baskets to hold the flowers, for the smell of the lotus was thought to bring enlightenment. All of Egypt, and especially King Teti, was joyous at the birth of another son, securing the entwining lines of King Unas and himself. No one would dare object to him becoming the acting nesu due to King Unas's advancing illness now that he was the abi of King Unas's grandchildren.

He started fiddling with the reed. He couldn't write that King Teti was high-handed, having no regard for the feelings of others, only himself. He couldn't write that the acting *nesu* was short, chubby and full of insecurities. Or that he would do anything to validate his existence, for many of the Egyptian people did not see him as a direct line to the throne. Most of them considered King Unas to be one of the greatest kings of

Egypt. No, he wouldn't dare write that. He dipped his reed back into the black ink well and continued writing:

Princess Iput had lived up to her part of the bargain and had given King Teti another son. She was to be made queen at the feast held on the next full moon, before all of Egypt. After a long drought of lack of heirs, the gods seemed pleased with their union because Princess Iput was from full royal blood. She not only gave him sons, but when she did, she was quick about it, bearing seed as soon as her purification was over from birthing Tetiankhkm. It was not the custom, but the princess enjoyed holding her newborn baby.

Her favorite handmaiden Anhai cared for her elder son, Tetiankhkm, who was only a full moon shy of celebrating his name day, following him as he crawled along the mosaic tiles. In spite of King Unas being ill and bedridden, the princess was finally happy and unafraid. Her sons gave her the security she needed within the palace walls.

His well was dry. The drama of recording the royals took a lot of ink. He must remember to tell the servants to crush more plants and mix them with water to make more ink. He took out another well from the chest drawer. Dipping the reed into the new black well, he wrote:

But before the queen was to be ordained, King Teti was told by King Unas to secure his people in their places within the government. King Unas wanted to make sure his daughter and son-in-law's reign would be secure before his death. Upon this request by the nesu, the acting king wasn't exhausting any more time on the matter of his son-in-law becoming the new vizier. He had earlier ordered Kagemni to step down and just retain his priest duties, but Kagemni must have gone begging to Princess Iput. So King Teti kept Kagemni for the sake of the princess's condition. He would not make the same mistake again.

No one knows what royals talk about behind hidden walls, thought Hezi, but for the record he would write:

King Teti had met with his son-in-law Mereruka, a man of slender build and average height. There was nothing special about his looks, but in the linen garment he would wear as vizier, he could command a royal presence. So he was promised the vizier position if he would implement his father-in-law's plan. It was political. King Teti wanted a stable dynasty. Any instability was a sign of weakness. And to maintain a strong dynasty, he needed high government officials to be family.

Mereruka was to take Kagemni to Saqqara and tell him King Unas wanted to turn his mastaba into a pyramid. It was already located north of King Teti's pyramid, and turning his mastaba into a pyramid, would show Kagemni had achieved the stature he had hoped to attain. Once inside, Mereruka would view the inscriptions and drawings on the walls and suggest how they might be revised and polished once the pyramid *was completed. He would then ask Kagemni to pray to the gods with him, and while in deep prayer, Mereruka would quietly leave and soldiers would be ready and waiting at the entrance to seal the tomb, ensuring death. The deed would be done while the banquet for the newly crowned queen was taking place.*

He dipped his reed into the well and continued:

Iput was officially the principal wife of King Teti. She would be given many titularies, as least as many as King Teti's mother, Sesheshet was given. She was to walk into the banquet hall wearing the insignia worn only by queens: The vulture headdress.

This cap, formed from the body of a vulture, has two wings spread along the sides of the wearer's head. The vulture's head juts forward from the queen's forehead. She also was given the uraeus headdress. The royal cobra could be substituted for the vulture headdress, but the princess chose the more elaborate one, for this was a formal occasion. And it showed her elegant neck. Originally worn by the vulture goddess, Nekhbet, Protectress of Upper Egypt.

Iput was as beautiful as a goddess and as regal as a royal could be. She was presented with the proclaimed document bearing King Teti's signature and seal of his signet ring pressed onto wax. It was rolled and had King Unas's seal pressed against it for closure, making sure when she opened it, the queen herself would be breaking her father's seal, but not her husband's.

This would be the one and only time King Teti would bow to her—when he presented her with the legal document, showing everyone she was to become his principal wife and queen.

"All bow for Princess Iput," shouted the guards. When everyone arose, she broke the seal, her brown eyes fixating on the document. She read it aloud, and when she was done, the guards yelled again, "All bow for Queen Iput."

After this the musicians and dancers arrived. Servants carrying wine on trays appeared and she was presented with the royal rock crystal cup. The trumpets sounded, and the king and queen drank first. Then the acting king raised his glass. "What has been done cannot be undone. Let us hope it pleases the gods." Everyone cheered and began drinking. The musicians played their instruments while dancers clasped their cymbals, starting the festivities.

That's how one guesses it was to have happened. Hezi stood, arching his back, when a servant entered the room bringing a tray laden with figs, nuts, some duck meat and wine. He smiled then waved his hand for her to leave. She gave a nod and returned his smile before leaving. He gulped his wine and took a few bites of food, trying to collect his thoughts on what to write next.

He wrote:

Kagemni didn't question why the great King Unas wanted him to leave after the ceremony, before the banquet began, because Mereruka informed him of the nesu's plan to discuss turning his mastaba into a pyramid. Mereruka would be the overseer of the project now that Kagemni had kept his position as vizier. It was thought Mereruka probably had enough of Queen Iput's party, seeing his wife was the daughter of King Teti's first wife, Khuit, the one who provided King Teti with daughters instead of sons.

The caregiver to Queen Iput's children followed her lover to his tomb, assisting him as a priestess. She brought a basket filled with wine, bread and other foods, covered with a blanket, to offer to the gods, telling Mereruka the queen had told her to accompany them. He didn't question this but stared into Anhai's big dark eyes for a moment, aware of what this meant for her, for her life as a servant was all relative. The king will have done what he wants done.

He put his reed down and opened the chest drawer, taking out a red ink well and another pointed reed. Then he brought out a new papyrus, spreading it on top of the desk and running his hands along the edges to smooth it down. He would write not in hieratic but in formal hieroglyphs, then he would hide it, for this record was going to contain the entire truth. He would make sure it would not be found until after King Teti's death or his own. He dipped his reed into the well and again wrote down his name and accomplishments on the papyrus before he began to record.

He knew why Tetiankhkm was with Anhai and Kagemni on the evening of Iput's crowning. He remembered all too well the discussion Anhai and the then Princess Iput had had before another banquet. Where Anhai told the princess she was with child. He knew this was Anhai and Kagemni's baby, for he had been writing by the fountain outside of the princess's chambers. He recollected what he had overheard that night, and in red ink on the papyrus that would hold the truth, he began writing.

When he was done recording Tetiankhkm's true story of how he arrived into this world, he went back to eating his duck meat and drinking his wine. He reminded himself he must pray to the goddess Maat for helping him become a palace scribe. Living here, he would always have a full belly and a place to sleep. He popped a fig into his mouth and dipped his reed into the red ink well again. His hieroglyph writing had to be sharp and fine to show the horror of it all.

He continued:

Anhai arranged part of the blanket in the basket then placed Tetiankhkm inside, covering him with the rest of it and closing the lid. She wanted her baby to be with her. For one rare moment, they could be together as a family.

*

The room was growing dark. He didn't notice the servant girl until she spoke. "I have the fire to light the room." He quickly placed the papyrus on the floor and switched back to the papyrus with the hieratic symbols, the one for the official record. Then he waved for her to enter and waited while she lit the torches, giving him the dim brightness he needed to go on writing. Once he was alone again, he wrote with his black-tipped reed:

The smell of lotus blossoms and pomegranate from the trees that lined the banquet hall filled the air. The slaves' rapid waving of palm branches staved off the heat for the guests. The fountain was not filled with water, nor perfume, but with wine. Guests helped themselves; everyone was happy. King Teti had just sat down on his throne made of ebony. The queen's throne was made of ivory. Both were inlaid with semi-precious stones.

The newly crowned queen was about to ascend the dais, when she grabbed her stomach and went to her knees. The king's servants rushed to help her. She smiled and told her husband not to worry. A sudden sickening feeling had come over her and she did not know why. The king took over, helping Queen Iput to her throne. He did not want servants on the dais.

As soon as she sat, a female servant burst into the hall, screaming, "The baby! Tetiankhkm is gone!" She bowed before continuing. "The baby is not in his chambers and his nursemaid Anhai cannot be found."

King Teti turned when he heard his newly crowned queen screaming in agony. She placed both hands over her mouth. Silencing herself, she bowed to her husband and calmly left the banquet. As soon as she was out of the room, she ran down the hallway to her son's bedchambers.

The king ordered all entrances to the palace be closed. He sent his guards to secure the city's gates. He ordered

Userkare to question anyone who was seen with a baby. Then the trumpeter blew his horn and the banquet hall became quiet. He announced the arrival of Mereruka, the king's son-in-law. He bowed and approached the dais. King Teti gave a look of relief. The deed with Kagemni must be done. He could now use his help with finding his kidnapped son, his heir.

He dipped his black-tipped reed into the well and continued:

Mereruka whispered to the king he had had the guards seal Kagemni's tomb. He spoke of the priestess, Anhai, telling him she had insisted on going to the mastaba with them. It could not be helped. But the gods should find favor with them because she had brought a basket of food and wine, so they had some nourishment to offer the gods in the afterlife. He then told his father-in-law he had lit the torches and quietly left the two of them praying, as their fate was sealed.

Hezi then picked up the papyrus he would later hide and dipped the other reed into the red ink well to show the true bloodshed of it all:

Mereruka and King Teti had no idea the future nesu's fate was sealed forever. They didn't know Anhai had Tetiankhkm inside the basket. There was no food or wine. They did not realize they had killed the future heir to the throne of Egypt. But Queen Iput did.

The queen let out a blood-curdling scream when a guard told her of the death of Kagemni and Anhai.

She mumbled. "No, no, not my little cosset… it cannot be, death of the cosset." She knew her handmaiden had taken the baby. For she wanted the planning of her baby's father's pyramid to be a family affair. Even if only Anhai, Kagemni and the newly crowned queen knew.

And now she would have to tell King Teti. She would have to be the bearer of bad news and possibly his wrath. And King Unas, as sick as he was, would have to know.

He recorded as he remembered:

The queen pulled out flowers from a clay vase and vomited into it.

He needed to write down the queen's thoughts, so he switched back to the papyrus on which he was ordered to record the events for King Unas and returned to using his black-tipped reed:

Queen Iput knew Anhai was Kagemni's mistress. She wanted to feel pity for Kagemni's wife, but she couldn't. Like most highbred Egyptian people, theirs was a loveless marriage. His wife would recover, but she never would— she had lost her best friend.

He switched again to the red ink well, dipped his reed, then began writing in detail on the papyrus that would hold the truth:

As the hours passed, the guards would whisper to each other how distressed and pale the queen looked. The queen returned to the banquet hall, bowed down and grabbed the king's ankles. Everyone in the room knew something was wrong. Her sobbing was uncontrollable. In a voice just above a whisper she would say, "Forgive me, my dear great king, but the gods…" She was gasping for breath in between sobs. "We must have offended the gods, they have…" Ever so slightly she rose, grabbing her sheath to wipe her nose.

King Teti bent down, lifting her up to him, whispering, "We have not offended the gods." He wrapped his arm around her waist and held her close so he could hear what she needed to say. Queen Iput's body was shaking as she moaned, "He's dead. Tetiankhkm is dead. I knew he was with Kagemni and his caregiver Anhai. I already spoke with Mereruka."

She fell to the floor, sucking in a big breath of air, sobbing and hiccupping. She lifted her head and chest off of the floor, trying to breathe. "Mereruka wants to speak with you too." She returned her face to the floor.

He bent down and whispered in her ear. "Tetiankhkm did not leave with them." It was then that Mereruka returned to talk to the king. He had a look of desperation upon his face. King Teti left the queen crying face down on the floor and led him out of the room.

He changed reeds, dipping it into the black ink well, and went back to the official papyrus:

King Teti was inside the temple and had no knowledge of how many sunrises had passed. In agony he tore his sheath at the shoulder and down the front, put his fist into the air and cursed all the gods. He fell to his knees and the priest heard him saying, "Why my son and heir? I would have willingly offered my slaves as a sacrifice to you."

The king tried to stand but stumbled, falling again to his knees. He was seen covering his face with his hands, crying. No one dared try to remove him from the temple. Several sunrises passed before the queen got out of her bed. She then only did so because she had another son she needed to hold. And they left it to the priests to tell the bedridden King Unas what had happened to Kagemni and Tetiankhkm.

He was to record the findings of the bodies and so he continued, using his black reed:

The baby Tetiankhkm, heir to the throne, was recorded missing during the banquet, after the crowning of Queen Iput. The nesu and acting nesu's vizier and priest, Kagemni, was also recorded missing soon after the religious ceremony of Queen Iput. Anhai was not noted as missing until after the queen was told her son was gone, since Anhai was her chief handmaiden and her son's caregiver.

He switched back to the papyrus, which would contain the truth, picked up his red reed and began:

Mereruka was able to seal Kagemni and Anhai in the mastaba and return to the festivities without anyone realizing he was gone. But he didn't leave quietly while they were praying, as recorded for the record.

He killed them with his sword, and left them for dead, only fulfilling the orders of his father-in-law, the king. Truth. He never knew Tetiankhkm was sleeping inside the basket. Mereruka's killings were quick and quiet. He never knew Tetiankhkm was Kagemni and Anhai's son, because Queen Iput claimed him as her own. It wasn't until after he returned to the palace and heard Tetiankhkm was missing, that the queen spoke with him. And then he was the one who had to tell King Teti the truth about his son and heir.

Seeing the future nesu unable to leave the temple, Mereruka went back into the mastaba, alone, in the middle of the night, with only a torch, and broke the seal on the tomb. He went inside and opened the basket. He saw Tetiankhkm. Lack of air had turned him azure in color and he looked so small. Mereruka started to weep but stopped. He wiped his face with his hand, realizing he had only done the future nesu's bidding. To do otherwise would have meant death.

Hezi quit writing, staring at the ceiling. If Kagemni had only stepped down when King Teti had asked him to, his mistress Anhai, and the future heir, would still be alive. He took a gulp of wine contemplating this. Iput had begged her husband to allow Kagemni to stay until after the great King Unas's death. And the acting king honored her request, even though he couldn't have that. Even he knew queens could never be the power behind the throne. King Teti had to make a statement that he was ruling Egypt. King Unas was too ill to rule and was *nesu* in name only.

He dipped his red-tipped reed into the well and then continued:

> *King Teti knew he had to give his elder wife, Khuit, something. So he made the husband of Seshseshet, the daughter they had together, the new vizier to carry out the law of the land. Mereruka knew he would need proof, so he cut off Kagemni's feet and the arm of Anhai and the baby. He took them to the acting nesu. Then, in his anger, he sent his slaves to retrieve the rest of the bodies and bury them in the desert, as if they were common Egyptians.*
>
> *Every Egyptian knows that if you mistreat a body after death it could rise up against you in the afterlife. But Mereruka wasn't worried because only the nesu himself could bestow an afterlife. King Unas was too ill to bestow any pleas to the gods. And Mereruka doubted King Teti would have bestowed them any privileges; he wouldn't want them coming after him. So he had slaves bury them in the desert, where they would be naturally preserved and where nobody would ever find them. Far away from Saqqara.*

He returned to the papyrus he was using to record the official events and dipped his black-tipped reed into a new ink well before beginning:

It will be recorded: King Teti was given proof of the deaths. He proclaimed the feet were Kagemni's, and the arm was Anhai's. He ordered Userkare to return the feet to Kagemni's mastaba and the arm of Anhai was to be kept inside his pyramid. He needed to relieve Mereruka from this task and turned it over to the Khenty She. The feet and arm were wrapped in a shear linen sheath and returned. Then Userkare sealed King Teti's pyramid, and he also resealed Kagemni's mastaba.

He went back to the papyrus holding the truth and picked up his red reed. He began writing:

King Teti also wanted Tetiankhkm's arm to be wrapped in a shear linen sheath and buried in his pyramid, hoping this would absolve some of his pain—keeping his son with him forever, spending eternity together. He buried Anhai's arm in his pyramid, to show the gods he was innocent in both of their deaths. He honestly did not know. But before Userkare returned the body parts to their final resting places, he showed them to Queen Iput. He knew by doing this she would never forgive the king and her heart would be his forever.

And Mereruka, in his anger, buried the rest of Tetiankhkm's body with the others in the desert. King Teti couldn't even give his heir a royal burial. The shear linen sheaths each body part was wrapped in would eventually rot away. But in everyone's haste, they lacked the time for a proper mummification.

And the acting nesu couldn't have all the attention that would come because of this. He had to be free from the Egyptian people finding out. So he told the people that Tetiankhkm was not missing. The medicine woman, who had knowledge of the herbs, had taken him because he was ill. He died from childhood fever and Pepi was now the future heir of Egypt. This would absolve Mereruka from Anhai and Tetiankhkm's death, since they were done in the innocence of the order he had given.

The lights from the torches were growing dim. Hezi got up, gulped the last of his wine and added more oil to the base of the torches. He needed to finish before dawn. He didn't want the sun god Ra seeing he had the official record and another papyrus containing the truth. He went back to the official record of events, dipped his reed into the black ink well and wrote:

This is what the people of Egypt were told: "The high priest Vizier Kagemni and the priestess Anhai died while overseeing the reconstruction of Kagemni's mastaba into a pyramid. Also, with great sorrow, King Teti and Queen Iput's son, Tetiankhkm, died of childhood fever. He was not missing. The medicine woman had taken him because he was ill. Pepi is now the future heir of Upper and Lower Egypt.

He put down his black-tipped reed and sighed. He looked up from his writing. The people of Egypt would believe this, for these were common deaths. He was done with the official recording of events for King Unas. He picked up his other

232

reed and dipped it into the red ink well and continued writing on the papyrus he would hide:

Userkare picked up the golden bracelet from the floor of the mastaba. He recognized it immediately. He knew Queen Iput had given this bracelet to her son. Only royals wore jewelry, and even sons of royals wore bracelets to show power. He would give this to the queen. Maybe it would help.

Queen Iput's rooms were filled with blue lotus flowers. This was to provide a relaxing, euphoric state of being, and only the blue lotus acted as a sedative in which to induce sleep. She spent many days lying on her bed crying, holding the cosset statue and praying to the gods for the soul of little Tetiankhkm. She then cried for the loss of her servant, priestess and friend, the person who saved her life and the stability of her throne.

Upon Userkare's arrival, she stopped her tears long enough to accept the bracelet and placed it around the small statue of the cosset. Since Anhai and Tetiankhkm's death, she always had the statue within her reach. She properly thanked him, whispered something and then dismissed him. There were servants around filling a stone basin full of water for her to bathe. It would be the first time since their deaths the queen was going to bathe, henna her toes, powder her skin and place kohl around her eyes. He bowed, thanking her for the pleasure it gave him for her to accept his gift. She nodded, and as soon as he left the room, she dropped her sheath to enter her bath.

He again dipped his reed into the red ink well and wrote:

Userkare feared for his life. As head of the Khenty She, he knew well King Teti had ordered Kagemni's death. He also knew Anhai and Tetiankhkm were not supposed to be with him. But what did that matter now? Kagemni was dead, and if the king could order the death of a high priest, he could also order the death of one of the Khenty She. Possibly even the death of his queen.

Hezi was aware Userkare and King Teti knew they were half-brothers, having the same father. He had overheard Kagemni telling Userkare in the temple. He wondered what would happen if Teti ever found out Pepi was not his blood son. He probably would have Userkare and the queen killed. He also knew if Teti ever found out Kagemni had planned to kill him with poisoned *shedeh* at Iput's crowning, it would have justified everything. Hezi knew Userkare would not give Teti that reassurance. Telling the acting *nesu* could place suspicion on him. He knew Userkare would never talk. To know of a plan to kill a royal and not say anything, also meant death.

So he wrote:

On the other hand, it put Userkare's son, Pepi, next in line to the throne after King Teti. To some gods Pepi meant, 'to add another son,' and that is what Queen Iput told everyone. But to other gods, the name meant, 'established and good,' and that is how Userkare thought of his son. No matter what, Pepi

*was from the royal lineage of King Unas and his
daughter Queen Iput. Whereas Tetiankhkm was not,
and had he lived to become of age, a fake royal would
have ruled Egypt. And everybody involved would
have let it happen, just so King Teti could appear
to be fertile. Userkare would have let it happen too,
because he knew it saved the love of his life. So the
gods had intervened to put a real royal on the throne.
A half royal was better than a fake royal.*

He put his reed down and arched his back. It hurt. How
royals endured furniture he would never understand.
However, now that he had recorded the official events of
what happened for King Unas, and another papyrus holding
the truth, dawn had arrived, and he was glad to have finished.
He said a prayer to the goddess Maat for helping him with
his writings. He would pull out the hidden papyrus as time
went on and continue to record the truth of events. And,
of course, he would always record the events for the official
royal record.

He took off his rope necklace entwined with amber-
colored glass and placed it inside the chest drawer. He was
again admiring the winged sun, with the uraeus, in the middle,
wearing the double crown of Egypt on the side of the chest
when he heard voices. He stood up and looked down the hall;
he saw servants working and whispering to themselves.

Everyone was busy cleaning Mereruka and his wife
Seshseshet's rooms. It seemed the honorable King Teti had
asked his daughter and her husband, his new vizier, to move
out of the palace. The king had requested only to see Mereruka

at official functions, on official policies and he would only see his daughter in the presence of other people. Khuit, Seshseshet's mother, King Teti's elder wife, was whispered to be heard crying all the way down the hall as she entered the empty rooms.

FORTY-TWO

A.D. 1988, CAIRO, EGYPT

Everyone in the lab was quietly working as the desert sun cast its slanting shadow over the building. It was too quiet for Mark, so he began reading aloud from the scanned papyrus. "From what I can decipher, it says here Hezi had a modest tomb located in the Teti cemetery of Saqqara. The inscriptions in his tomb proclaim he was at the front of the scribes." He pushed up his glasses. "His inscriptions also declare he was more distinguished than any other scribe, 'For his majesty knew his name.' Probably because he was the scribe for both pharaohs."

"Boy, he knew how to blow his own trumpet, didn't he?" asked Ian.

"King Pepi even made him the royal chamberlain. It seems all three pharaohs really needed his services," he said.

"This means he was probably one of King Pepi's personal confidantes." Cassie spoke as she walked over to the others. "I would say he was very well trusted. So help me put this all together. Do you think the papyrus we have been deciphering was not official knowledge and that's why it was placed in Queen Iput's tomb?"

"Seeing that you found it in her tomb probably means it was hidden," said Ian.

"If the contents of this papyrus had ever become the official record, everyone would have known Mereruka killed the future king's heir," said Mark. "And then Userkare taking Kagemni's feet and Anhai's and the baby's arm to show Queen Iput…" He stopped, nodding his head. "They would not have wanted that for the official record either."

"I think you're right," said Cassie. "Userkare knew his son was next in line to the throne after Teti, due to this twist of fate. He must have felt he needed to show her proof, knowing she would never forgive Teti and in his mind ensuring her love for him."

Ian interjected, "And Mereruka must have been furious, because he was close to his father-in-law. So, in his anger, he had his men bury the bodies deep in the desert. Hey, maybe that's where the mob got the idea, from the ancient Egyptians." Everyone grinned.

"It's as if Mereruka knew this would change things with the king forever," said Cassie. "And it did—Teti never saw him or his daughter privately again, only in public and with others around him."

Dr. Barrington added to the conversation. "King Teti had Kagemni's feet mummified and placed in Kagemni's mastaba, where they were found when they originally excavated. That is why I didn't find anything relevant when I was in Kagemni's tomb. His mastaba has been excavated several times prior. Same thing with Pepi's tomb. Too many excavators and nothing relevant."

"Well, getting back to the papyrus," said Cassie. "They

had the perfect alibi for the Egyptian people. They could say they both died while working on turning Kagemni's mastaba into a tomb. Which would explain why he took Anhai. She was a priestess and he a priest. They would both bless the reconstruction."

Mark spoke up. "Don't forget about the basket. It supposedly had food and drink for them."

"That's right," she said. "Speaking of Tetiankhkm, the papyrus says Iput gave Anhai the cosset, and in return Anhai gave the lamb to Tetiankhkm. Whereupon hearing about their deaths, Iput then kept the baby's bracelet Userkare had brought her from Tetiankhkm's arm, and hung it around the lamb, keeping the items close to her. So close she even had these items put in her tomb when she died, so they would be with her forever." She took a deep breath.

"This confirms that the rooms I found the artifacts in had never been excavated before." She paused. "Probably because the entrance looked like a wall and was only eighteen inches wide. The papyrus explains the baby's bracelet and the lamb statue I found in Queen Iput's tomb. It also explains why she would have the papyrus in her tomb. The only artifact we still don't know about is the pottery shard."

They all turned when they heard the door open. Dr. Ramsey entered. "I have the findings from Egypt's Antiquities Minister." Mark was grateful to have this conversation interrupted before Dr. Ramsey found out they were discussing the papyrus.

"It has been confirmed—well, the final D.N.A. report will still take weeks, but he has stated the probability at ninety-nine per cent…" Everyone stood still.

"Continue, Dr. Ramsey," said Dr. Granite.

"Like I was explaining, there is a ninety-nine per cent probability that the baby's bone was that of King Teti's firstborn son, Tetiankhkm, due to the fact that the D.N.A. on the baby's bone matched the D.N.A. found on the bracelet. And we know it was a bracelet for a royal. Also, the D.N.A. on the bone of the woman proved she was the baby's biological mother, who was not Queen Iput."

Mark was pleased. "These test results are running parallel to what Dr. Richards has been deciphering." But before he could explain, he saw the anticipation from Dr. Ramsey's face disappear.

"Are you trying to say the explanation of the bones is in the papyrus?" Edmund's voice had a solemn tone.

"Yes," said everyone almost at the same time.

"See, Dr. Ramsey," said Cassie. "This does make the deciphering of the papyrus relevant to our findings."

"No." Edmund's voice was stern. "It makes it interesting, not relevant. We are here to try to end the debate on the timeline. The future of Dynasty Zero is relevant, not the story within the papyrus. The bones are relevant, but not to us. Seems they are from Dynasty Five. This does nothing to prove or disprove Dynasty Zero."

Mark looked at the faces of his colleagues. Everyone seemed disillusioned. Cassie's smile had vanished, Ian's head was down and Tom? Well, he was the first one to speak.

"If the cosset you speak about in the papyrus is the one I have been researching and examining, well, the papyrus may be relevant to our quest in proving or disproving Dynasty Zero. The belly of the lamb says *Sefekhu Shenet*, which means seven hundred. We have to find out the significance of this date." Dr. Granite looked directly at Cassie. "I heard you say, Dr. Seldon, that the story in the papyrus has Queen Iput giving this to Anhai, her friend, handmaiden and caregiver of... should I say their child? You also said the papyrus states Queen Iput said her father gave her this statue when she was a girl, and it represented when they took control over Lower Egypt from the shepherd kings?"

"Yes, Dr. Granite. May I explain?" Mark leaned in. He really wanted to hear Cassie's explanation, since she supported the earlier timeline theory.

She began, "History tells us after the shepherd kings, Upper and Lower Egypt became unified, with one king. And we already know lambs were the representation of shepherd kings, but later in Egypt were not thought of too highly, probably because shepherds did not signify Egypt's unity. So *Sefekhu Shenet*, or seven hundred, may represent how long the shepherd kings controlled Lower Egypt before they were defeated in the war that unified them with Upper Egypt. The end of this war may have been the cusp, or start, of Dynasty Zero."

Mark turned when he heard the other Ph.D.s gasp. "Now I'm not buying this story so quickly. We need more proof. We need to find out what year the war ended." He shook his head. This wasn't happening. He'd been the one who insisted Cassie hand over the statue of the lamb to be researched. He knew she wanted to keep it for whatever reason she had. And yet, by being honest and doing what he felt was the right thing for his fellow coworker, this might just be the one object that ruined his side of the debate which he had fought so proudly for.

He heard a bang. From the corner of his eye he saw Cassie's arm hit the table as she began to fall. He grabbed her as she collapsed in slow motion, stopping her fall short from becoming a sudden crash. Her weight had dragged them both down to the floor, but on these tiles, she could have really hurt herself.

"I'm okay, I just feel lightheaded." She stood, but only with his help. "Too much talk about mutilation and death, especially about the baby."

"She needs to lie down and rest," Dr. Ramsey intervened. "Will someone please take Dr. Seldon back to the hotel?"

"I will," said Dr. Barrington. "I'll see she gets back to her room."

"I'll help you," said Mark.

"Don't be silly, I'm feeling better already." He noticed she looked pale. "I'm just feeling a little weak. I'll have the bus take me back to my room. I just need to lay down and rest."

"That would be for the best," said Edmund. "Dr. Barrington will accompany you on the bus and make sure you make it to your room."

Dr. Barrington agreed. "Yes, we wouldn't want you fainting or falling again." He put his hand on her back and escorted her out of the lab.

Ian whispered to Mark, "What do you think happened?"

"I really shouldn't say, but I think all this talk about the baby and death really bothered her. You know, she lost a baby around the same age as Tetiankhkm."

"Really?" said Ian.

He shook his head and whispered, "Yeah, she had a rough upbringing."

"Does anyone here know?" whispered Ian.

"I don't know." Mark shrugged his shoulders. "I only know because the night she and I were having cocktails we started talking about our past, and, well, that's when she told me she lost a baby girl to S.U.D.C."

"What's that?"

"It's similar to S.I.D.S.—you know, Sudden Infant Death Syndrome, except S.U.D.C., is Sudden Unexplained Death of a Child. It's called that when the baby is over twelve months old." He paused. "Cassandra, that was her baby's name, was sixteen months when she died."

"She named the baby after herself?"

"Apparently so. People do it all the time with baby boys. You know, juniors."

"Yeah, I know. Who's the father?" Ian whispered again.

"It doesn't matter, he's dead too. He died shortly after the baby."

"Jesus!" said Ian.

Dr. Ramsey gave them a disapproving look.

"I don't know anything else," said Mark.

"Well, if I was in her situation, today would have bothered me," said Ian. "You're probably right, that's probably why she felt weak."

"Alright everyone, enough. Dr. Seldon's in good hands. The rest of us need to get back to our research," said Dr. Ramsey, once again, giving them a disapproving look.

FORTY-THREE

Cassie walked to the bathroom and unwrapped the bandage from her left hand. Yellow pus was oozing from her cut and it hurt. Her hand was red and swollen, so she ran cold water on it for several minutes. Then she let it air dry as she went through her toiletry bag looking for antibiotic cream. She didn't want any more bacteria from using a towel. She pulled out the cream, a couple of ibuprofen, a new bandage and an Ace wrap. She figured if she Ace-wrapped it, no one would ask to see her wound.

She changed into a plain pink nylon teddy and opened one of those small single-serving bottles of wine from the room's refrigerator. Once in the bathroom, she sat down on the toilet lid, swallowing her ibuprofen and drinking the wine from the miniature bottle. She rummaged through her bag until she found her syringe and vial. She injected herself and went to bed. She knew she shouldn't be mixing wine and drugs, but she wanted to calm down after what had happened in the lab and she needed to sort through the day's findings.

She propped her pillows against the headboard. Then she turned off the light and closed her eyes. She already felt better. What evidence today had brought. The lamb statue might very well help her prove Dynasty Zero by the number *Sefekhu Shenet* written on its belly. Imagine that—a child's toy helping her theory.

Cosset, that's what she kept reading in the papyrus. The cosset lamb was the same gift she had given her baby Cassandra, as it had once been given to her. It was stuffed, but nevertheless. *Thousands of years later and we still give our children toy animals.*

And the baby's bracelet was for a royal baby, since only royals wore jewelry in the Old Kingdom. The ninety-nine per cent probability confirmed the baby's bone was related to the larger arm bone, probably his biological mother. Even if they couldn't prove one hundred per cent, these were Anhai's and Tetiankhkm's. *Who else could it be after what the papyrus unfolded?*

Feeling relaxed, she slid down under the covers and began to drift. She was a little girl in a smock dress. She was holding a man's hand and skipping. In her dream she was five years old, with long blond hair and bangs. The man kneeled down to her level, giving her something. A gift? No, a toy—no, a small stuffed animal, a lamb. She hugged the stuffed lamb, and then hugged the man, who was still kneeling at her level. "Thank you, Daddy."

She opened her eyes, staring into the darkness. She felt her heart beating inside her chest as if she had been frightened, because she had a memory of being with her father. It made sense now why she subconsciously loved that lamb so much and why she had given it to her own daughter. Maybe this would trigger more memories she possibly had cached in her mind. And it had taken a statue of a cosset and a story within a papyrus of another woman and her baby to trigger her own childhood memory. She rolled onto her side, hoping sleep might surface more subconscious memories, but instead, everything began to make sense—sudden clarity. She was beginning to make the connection between the ancient queen and herself.

Queen Iput had lost her son Tetiankhkm. Even though it was really Anhai's baby, this son she claimed as hers had saved her life, giving her security in ensuring her to be made queen. It was an ancient version of her life. Although she had lost her daughter, her baby had also saved her life, forcing her to grow up and giving her life a purpose. Cassandra's death was also the death of who she was and where she came from. She had been trying to make peace with her past, to help her overcome her present, to ensure her own future. And becoming an Egyptologist was also about bringing the past into the present to ensure the future.

And just like Queen Iput losing her closest confidant and friend Anhai, she had also lost hers—the father of her baby, Chad. Anhai's death was unforeseen to Iput. It was an indirect death. They wanted Kagemni, but it was just like Chad's death—an indirect accident.

He had pressure from her mother for being a teen father with no job. Susan never worried about paying her bills—she relied on the government to do that—yet she never let Chad forget he was an unemployed father. And he had tension from his father. Being a minister, he wanted his son to do the right thing and marry her. But her mother fought this; she thought marriage would seal her daughter's fate.

Then add the stress of her mother's constant aggrandized harassment of calling him a molester to anyone and everyone who would listen. Escalated by the police coming to investigate, and the shame of possibly ruining his father's ministry. Susan didn't seal Cassie's fate. She sealed Chad's, by driving him to kill himself.

And as with Anhai and Tetiankhkm's death, the sorrow should have been for Iput, but no, she had to stay in the shadows with her sorrow; all sympathy was with the king, for he had lost his heir. The same with her; the chasm she felt in her life over the death of her baby and her boyfriend had been overshadowed by her mother's mercurial being. This breakthrough and the day had her finally feeling sleepy. Yawning, she adjusted her pillows and blanket; her breathing became heavy and she felt herself slumbering into a deep repose.

*

Cassie's breathing was fast and shallow. The walk to the pyramid seemed endless. The closer she got, the farther away it seemed. The desert wind had picked up, so she grabbed the strings of her cowboy hat and lowered her head. Finally she made it through the sandstorm and arrived at Queen Iput's pyramid. She touched the side and a chunk of sand fell on her shoe.

She leaned her back against the pyramid and lifted her foot. While wiping the sand off her shoe, she heard a rumble, then felt vibrations. The sound grew louder. She felt the sand shifting beneath her feet. She ran a while, then stopped and turned, just in time to see Iput's tomb collapse into a huge pile of rubble. The dust permeated her lungs; she could barely breathe. Her stomach started to spasm from all the coughing. Her eyes were watering. She tried to catch her breath. She screamed.

Cassie awakened, startled. She kicked off the covers, her body veiled in sweat. She was on her back, looking at the ceiling, tears running down her face. She felt the wetness on her pillow. Her memories were vivid. She sat up, once again propping her pillows against the headboard. Her life seemed to be running parallel to Queen Iput's.

She needed to get back to the lab and finish deciphering the papyrus. She took this as a sign that she was running out of time and she needed to find out how the queen's situation ended. She knew it would sound crazy if she said it aloud, but it might give her some insight on how her own grief would turn out. She turned on the lamp and looked at the bedside clock. It was a little after three in the morning. If she got dressed now she could be back at the lab before daybreak to finish reading the papyrus before anyone else arrived. And then she would make her conclusions on Dynasty Zero. If anything, this vision unmasked what she needed to do, before it was too late.

FORTY-FOUR

Mark stood, beer in hand, on the patio off of his room, overlooking the city with the lit pyramids in the background. He leaned on the railing and took a swig.

Seeing the darkness of the night made him feel solitary, isolated. For once, being right wasn't enough. Nor was being an archaeologist. He respected Dr. Ramsey and chose him to be his mentor, but he often wondered what Edmund did in his free time. Did he have anyone to go out with, to dinner or a movie? He didn't want to end up that way.

He knew his quiet demeanor sometimes hindered any possibilities his looks might have to offer. He gulped his beer and felt himself mellowing. This trip had made him realize although he was a loner, he did need people, and he smiled thinking about having pizza and beer with Ian the other night. But the evening with Cassie at the hotel's lounge, it sure had been different than their encounter on the plane. Was he ready to admit he liked her?

He belted down his beer. He was ready to admit it. He liked her. Seeing her half drunk and in her lingerie might have sped his emotions along, but he really did like her. She challenged him. She was independent, career-minded and liked to travel. She also liked the same type of music as him.

They seemed to have much in common. In fact, after their time together at the hotel, the only thing he could think of that they didn't have in common was the timeline. Whether they were in agreement or not, he wished she would refocus. If he hadn't mentioned the lamb statue to Edmund, he knew she would not have turned it in. It wasn't that she was trying to steal an artifact. She just couldn't part with it.

It had something to do with what she had told him when he had helped her into bed. About the child—well, baby—she had lost. This murder of Queen Iput's baby seemed to hypnotize Cassie. He likewise was interested in the papyrus but was not so obvious to Dr. Ramsey. But then again, he hadn't lost a child. He made up his mind. He would help her get her answers held within the story the papyrus was unfolding. He also knew Ian would help them too.

With the last of his beer gone, his decision seemed clear. He was tired of being overly cautious and lonely. He was drawn to Cassie. He didn't have a choice. It was as if the feeling chose him. No matter what the outcome of the timeline, either at the airport or on the plane, he was going to ask her out. Not just a chance happening for drinks like before. It would be a real date. Dinner and all. He just hoped she would be wearing her lingerie underneath. He threw his beer bottle into the trash, adjusted himself and went to bed.

FORTY-FIVE

Cassie opened the door to the lab, switching on the lights before she even fully entered the room. The place looked sterile and downright depressing. She hung her blazer on the hook and put on a lab coat, which covered the jeans and T-shirt she had thrown on. She hadn't even bothered to put on any makeup. Not that it mattered; this was her, take it or leave it.

She brought up the scanned papyrus, scrolling down to where she'd left off before she fainted. She needed to know how Queen Iput's story ended. It was fragmented and difficult to read. She squinted but couldn't make anything out. She continued scrolling and at last found a section that was legible. She enlarged the area and was finally able to decipher some of the hieroglyphs.

She read. 'Egypt had just ended their seventy days of mourning over the death of King Unas. The year was 2345 B.C.' So Queen Iput lost her father when her second and true son, Pepi, was four years old. She felt herself twinge. Another thing she and the queen had in common. No father. Whether by death or desertion, grief was still grief. The poor Pharaoh Unas's illness did have him lingering, bedridden for a few years. She scrolled the papyrus, trying to find if it said how he died, but it only mentioned the seventy days of mourning.

She made a few notes on what she had deciphered, then scrolled up to before the papyrus became fragmented, before King Unas's death. She read. 'Kagemni was supposed to have the future King Teti's wine mixed with poisoned *shedeh* at the banquet, which was to take place directly after Princess Iput was made queen. But instead it was Kagemni who was murdered, along with Anhai and the king's firstborn child, Tetiankhkm.'

She looked up, as if this would make the words sink in. What a horrific end to such a beautiful day. Then, scrolling down past the fragmentation, she was back to the part of the story after the death of King Unas. She finally came upon a large portion of the papyrus intact. She enlarged the hieroglyphs and read, 'King Teti was squiffed.'

She read it again. *Okay, the pharaoh was drunk. We've all been there.* 'He was squiffed beyond belief, till he fell dead.' Wait, what did that mean? Dead drunk or dead? She continued reading at an expeditious pace, not sure what she was looking for.

FORTY-SIX

2333 B.C., ANCIENT EGYPT

Queen Iput sat in her reed chair with the carved gazelles on the ebony legs. Her ladies of the bedchamber were on either side of her trying to adjust her wig. They each tugged the sides of her head until she waved her hand. "Enough." Stopping, they began to apply the beads onto the wig. Next was the queen's jewelry. The ladies of the court fastened the aventurine, lapis and carnelian choker around Iput's long sleek neck. It lay just above her golden amulet of the Eye of Wadjet. Another lady handed her the polished copper with the handle of a naked girl holding a bird to show her reflection.

She was satisfied with the image looking back at her. Waving her hand again, she dismissed them. Many ladies in waiting had replaced her servants once she became queen. There were several to groom her, apply her makeup, and help with her wigs, beads and jewelry. The more ladies in waiting she had, the more she missed Anhai.

It had been *medshu* plus *sjsu* years since her friend, favorite handmaiden and confidant in secrets had died, and she missed her. She especially thought of her at any occasion involving her son, Pepi. King Teti had taken him crocodile-hunting today, and then they were going to honor him, the future king, at the feast tonight. He had had his circumcision and was declared healed and cleansed by the high priest. He was considered a man today.

Pepi would enter the banquet hall wearing his sidelock and present his kill to the priest. The high priest would then cut off the sidelock, because he was no longer a boy. He was now a man. Then the priest would shave his head, representing purity, for he was now circumcised. How she wished she could share this with Anhai. But then, if Anhai were alive, it would not be Pepi being honored at the feast, it would have been Tetiankhkm, her son in name, but Anhai's true son.

She walked through her bedchambers and into the courtyard. It was dusk, and a small breeze was blowing in from the desert, rippling through her linen sheath. She adjusted her rope belt, then sat on the bench next to the fountain, looking at the floating lotus flowers. This was where she found her peace, or rather where she eased her guilt. Anhai's indirect sacrifice had made her son Pepi become the future *nesu*. And in the last few years there wasn't a day that went by without her praying to the goddess Wadjet, the ancient goddess of protection. She wore her amulet every day and prayed daily for Wadjet to protect Anhai, Tetiankhkm and Kagemni as they journeyed through the afterlife.

As she flicked her hand back and forth in the fountain, the water quivered. She watched a single lotus flower float by. Her sadness deep from within surfaced. Without realizing it, she found herself caressing the amulet she wore for the goddess Wadjet, which was also called the Eye of Horus, for the sky god Horus—one of the gods her father, the great King Unas, had prayed to as well. It was the Eye of Wadjet, when praying to the goddess and the Eye of Horus, when praying to the god. She wore it daily because the amulet represented everyone in her life whom she had lost to the underworld.

It was her comfort. She no longer had the cosset her father had given her. She had given it to Anhai, who gave it to Tetiankhkm. Then it was passed down to Pepi, who had since outgrown it. Nor did she have the pottery shard also given to her when she was a child. After her *abi* died, when her seventy days of mourning were done, she took the pottery shard and cosset and placed them with him in his tomb.

When she knew the great King Unas's *akhu* was with the gods, she then asked Horus to protect him and lead his *ba* and *ka* on their noble journey, praying, "*May all of Unas's affairs be of good fortune and his heart be lighter than air.*" She kept his *Sekhemti* crown and his *wesekh* beaded collar made of electrum and faience with the carnelian stones, because it always made him look royal to her when she was young. She was saving it for the day when Pepi would be crowned king.

It seemed so long ago. Almost like it had happened in another lifetime. "I will always love you as my great and powerful *nesu* and *abi*," she said aloud. Standing, she glanced into her bedchamber. Her ladies had returned, watching her wipe her wet hand from the fountain onto her *kalasiris* woven with gold thread.

"No, no," said the lady of the court, frowning as she hurried, bowing before speaking. She straightened her *kalasiris*. "It is time. King Teti and the future *nesu* Pepi have entered the palace. You must be in the banquet hall before they arrive for their entrance. The priests and guests are all waiting for you."

Her son was a man now. Tonight would be a grand event. Her husband's mother Sesheshet's *akhu* was also with the gods, crossing over not long after her *abi*. But his other wives would be present. However, that did not matter anymore. Once she was secure as queen, they became lesser royals and moved to where Sesheshet used to dwell.

Userkare, the head of the *Khenty She*, would be there, and that always put a smile on her face. She dismissed her ladies in waiting. She knew her part and played it well. Holding her head high and with the grace only a royal could attain, her lithe figure started walking, taking in the sweet aroma of meats and figs. She stopped at the doors of the great hall, waiting while the guards announced her arrival. Inside, the scribe Hezi sat... writing it all down.

FORTY-SEVEN

A.D. 1988, CAIRO, EGYPT

Cassie had trouble comprehending what she had just read. She'd have to get back to King Teti's drunkenness. Right now, she had found a new part of the story about the death of King Unas. She looked for a notepad. She realized what she had just read, about Queen Iput putting the cosset and pottery shard into her father's tomb, was making the pieces of the story slowly start to come together. This bit of information about Pharaoh Unas's burial was relevant to her theory on Dynasty Zero. What was unfolding tied all of her findings from Queen Iput's tomb together. She grabbed her pen and wrote down word for word what the papyrus revealed.

The scribe had taken meticulous notes about the event. She translated, "His majesty the great *Nesu* Unas, King of Upper and Lower Egypt, will live forever on his journey with the god Horus. He will take on his journey his entire royal clothing, festival perfume, oil, prime linen, food and gold. Also in his tomb are his majesty's magic oars to ferry himself through the waters of the underworld. Hundreds of spells adorn his pyramid walls, which will help his soul's voyage into the next world."

She couldn't believe the next bit she deciphered. "…the wine jug, with the carving of *senuj* men, looking at each other holding lotus stalks tied with papyrus, with King Narmer wearing the *Sekhemti* crown unifying them, was made for the ceremony named Receiving the South and North. It was taken from the tomb of Queen Neithhotep at Naqada." She knew through her research that Queen Neithhotep was King Narmer's wife. She shut her eyes to concentrate for a minute. She had to sort out her findings.

The pottery shard she had excavated was from a wine jug. It had an etching of two humans looking at each other holding lotus stalks entwined with papyrus. She knew *senuj* meant two in ancient Egyptian numbers. The shard she had discovered represented a ceremony called Receiving the South and North. The papyrus indicated King Narmer was the figure on the wine jug wearing the double crown, the *Sekhemti* crown, or as we call it today, the *Pschent* crown. It also denoted the representation of the tying of papyrus around lotus stalks, symbolizing the entwining of Upper Egypt and Lower Egypt as one.

The wine jug was especially made for the ceremony Receiving the South and North, meaning the unification of Upper and Lower Egypt, making the timeline of Egypt's unification at 3150 B.C.—one hundred years earlier than the accepted theory. She pulled out a stool and sat down, wiping her sweaty palms on her lab jacket. She had to let this digest. And this wine jar was taken from Queen Neithhotep's tomb, King Narmer's wife. She wished she had found the entire jug intact.

It showed the unification of Egypt in two ways. First, with King Narmer wearing the double crown, and second, with the lotus stalks entwined with papyrus. Plus, its final resting place—well, at least for a while—had been with the queen. Leave it to a woman to notice the significance of it all. Otherwise it would have been in King Narmer's tomb. He probably considered the battle a conquest, since he was from Upper Egypt, while she regarded it as the finalization of unifying the country, since her family was originally from Lower Egypt.

Cassie continued to decipher. "It was given to King Sekhemkhet, a *nesu* from Dynasty Three, for he had great interest in building up Egypt's military." It didn't say how he acquired it, probably from the raiding of Neithhotep's tomb. She knew royals themselves, trying to increase their own wealth, authorized many of the tomb robberies. And it was known by Egyptologists specializing in the Old Kingdom period, that Pharaoh Sekhemkhet respected King Narmer's conquests of Egypt and wanted to be a great military pharaoh himself. She deciphered more.

"He died in battle six years into his reign as king..." She remembered in her previous research that all Dynasty Three pharaohs had a strong interest in Egypt's military. She continued reading, "...where it was buried with him in his tomb, protected by the god Horus and the Eye of Wadjet, until such time as King Unas's men unsealed King Sekhemkhet tomb."

She recalled from her studies of the Old Kingdom that Pharaoh Unas did have an interest in King Sekhemkhet's tomb. He was the last pharaoh of Dynasty Three to be buried at Saqqara. And word had been passed from generation to generation of the wealth in his tomb. She read, "King Unas's men took with them much gold, statues and the wine jug, for it signified the ceremony Receiving of the South and North. The wine jug was dropped and broken, along with some statues, by a slave or servant."

She looked up. Surely this slave or servant met an untimely demise because of this misfortune. She continued reading, "Now that it was broken, King Unas gave a piece of the pottery shard to his favorite daughter Iput, who laid it to rest in King Unas's pyramid when he died. Later her son Pepi unsealed the *nesu* Unas's tomb and took the pottery shard and the cosset, and put them in Queen Iput's pyramid, which he had built for her during her lifetime, for they had great meaning to her."

Well, there was the proof. The four-by-four-inch pottery shard had a paper trail, or rather a papyrus trail. The pottery shard showed a picture of a man, whom we now know was King Narmer, because a *serekh* was enclosed around his name. He was wearing what we now call a *Pschent*, the two crowns representing Upper and Lower Egypt. It had two tiny men looking at each other holding lotus stalks tied with papyrus. This symbolized the entwining of Upper and Lower Egypt as one. And the wine jug was made for the ceremony called Receiving of the South and North.

She wanted to jump up and scream, but instead she got up and drank a cup of water from the cooler. She looked to her left, then her right, even though she knew she was alone. She wrote down where she had deciphered this from the scan's sequencing. She would have to tell Dr. Ramsey the papyrus helped prove her theory. She wondered how he would react, especially since he'd thought the papyrus was not relevant to their findings on this debate.

And she couldn't wait to tell the others, especially Mark, that she had discovered a new dynasty. Dynasty Zero. And how this would affect the entire museum world. She wanted to go out and celebrate at the hotel's lounge with the entire team. This information would not only help her career but would gain her respect. It would give her the validation she sought and fought so hard for in her field. She took a deep breath, suddenly realizing this same information would disassemble Mark's theory. He would still be a respected archaeologist, but would he be able to handle being on the wrong side of this debate?

She didn't know, but she wanted Mark to understand and be happy for her. She wanted to scream for joy. So she did. Jumping up and down, she yelled, "I did it! I did it!" And then she went back to deciphering the papyrus, looking for any additional information to support her theory. All before dawn.

FORTY-EIGHT

2333 B.C., ANCIENT EGYPT

The musicians were playing, the dancers were dancing and the ladies with the clappers were clapping. The way the light reflected off the lit torches in the banquet hall illuminated an intellectual and spiritual presence, and all the people present looked illustrious in their regalia. The aroma of food wafted through the air. Platters of fish and foul with dates and figs were aplenty and the wine and *henqet* flowed freely. Queen Iput smiled, realizing Pepi was allowed to drink. Now that his sidelock was shaven, he was a man.

"You look nice, Queen Mother," said Pepi.

"Thank you, my son." She lightly touched the vulture headdress. "I chose this crown, for today is a formal gathering."

"Come, Queen Mother, sit beside me on the dais."

"I see you have on your *schenti* made of leather, for the proclaiming of your manhood."

Everyone had gathered waiting for King Teti's announcement. A few minutes later, the king stepped up onto the dais. "Tonight we proclaim my son, Pepi, the future king of Egypt." Everyone clapped. "But before the festivities begin,

I want to present him with his *Sekhemti* crown, once worn by the beloved King Unas."

Pepi stood. The king then placed the *Sekhemti* crown upon his son's head and secured what also used to be King Unas's *wesekh* beaded broad collar, made of electrum and faience with carnelian stones around his neck. A tear came to her eyes thinking about her *abi*. He continued. "Here is your future *nesu*. You will all proclaim your loyalty to the future King Pepi and to Egypt."

All the people in the banquet hall bowed to her son. No matter his or her age, size or health. Her heart swelled with joy. This was all for him. He looked at his *abi*, grabbed his hand and held it entwined with his, high in the air for all to see. Then suddenly she felt the energy from the room. She saw Pepi experience power. She knew he felt the power. And she knew he *wanted* the power.

All together the people chanted, "Long live King Teti and King Pepi." The *nesu* held up his vessel of wine and the party began. The queen knew her son's taste for *henqet* and wine was not yet acquired, so she saw him watch more than indulge. It was good he was keeping his head about him, for all the royals and heads of government wanted to talk to him. They wanted to know where he stood on matters of importance to Egypt.

Truth be told, her son just wanted to talk to the girls with the exposed henna breasts—a practice women did when preparing for an event where they wanted to impress the men. Applying henna made their breasts darker, causing them to stand out from their linen sheath, a form of flirtation. She wanted to make sure she made a match for Pepi with a pretty girl. Nothing less would be tolerated now that he was someday going to be king.

The room was loud with all the musicians, clappers and people, but she heard her husband's voice rise above the noise. He had had much to drink, and whenever he was like this, he spoke loudly and freely. "I am so squiffed from all the pleasures of the day that I don't even care how much wine everyone drinks." Then the *nesu* took a big swig from his jug. He had eaten and drunk much today, but it wasn't unusual for royals to eat, then purge and eat some more, so when she saw him fall off the dais, she laughed.

Everyone laughed, even the dwarfs, which were brought in from Nubia to entertain. Then she heard someone say, "What's wrong with the king?" A scream silenced the hall. There on the floor was her husband. It was not spilt wine encircling his head. It was blood and foam from his mouth. The people were still, somewhat stupefied. And so was she.

Still bewildered, Queen Iput saw her son act like a man. He jumped onto the dais and picked up the vessel of wine. Holding it in front of him, he shouted, "Who brought my *abi* his wine? Where is the servant who brought this jug? Where is the king's taster?" He turned to the guards and shouted, "Shut the doors to the palace. No one leaves until we find out who poisoned the king."

Commotion broke loose. No one knew what to do. In a daze, she just stood there as people revolved around her. The slaves and servants who had served the food and drink were brought into the banquet hall. Userkare bolted the doors. Not only could no one leave the palace, no one could enter.

FORTY-NINE

A.D. 1988, CAIRO, EGYPT

Cassie stopped reading to process it all. Pepi was sixteen when the pharaoh he knew as his father died, and in one instance he couldn't just act like a man, he had to become a man. It had been the same for her. She'd become pregnant at sixteen, and in one instant her childhood was gone and she had to become the adult in her family. Thousands of years have passed and people still dealt with the same issues.

She went back to the papyrus, scrolling down to where she could decipher the fragmentation. "The people prayed to Ra, the most powerful of all gods, and Sobek, the feared but beloved god of King Teti." She scrolled down. "There are certain men in Egypt who practice the art of mummification. It is their business.

"They used a crooked piece of iron and took out the brain of King Teti through his nostrils. Then they cleared his skull by rinsing it with drugs." Cassie looked for what type of drug had been used but couldn't find anything. She continued reading. "Next they took a sharp stone and cut the left side of his chest down to the abdomen, washing it out with palm wine. His lungs, heart, liver, stomach and intestines were placed into canopic jars.

"His cavity was then filled with myrrh, cassia, frankincense and other spices, before sealing the opening. The king's body was then placed in natron and wrapped. After *jfedu medshu* sun risings, his body was unwrapped and filled with linens and sand to give it shape, then rewrapped. After the expiration of time, which was not exceeded by even a sunset, after *sefekhu medshu* sunrises the linens were removed, his body was washed and wrapped again from head to foot with the finest of linens smeared with gum."

Cassie looked up from the screen. *Jfedu* was the Egyptian number representing four and the word *medshu*, often depicted as a picture of a yoke, represented ten. This meant the body was in natron for forty days. Then it was filled with sand and linens for *sefekhu medshu*. She knew *sefekhu* represented seven. So seven *medshu* was seventy. The body was wrapped for seventy days.

She knew the gum used in ancient times wasn't the gum we chew today. It was a substance that had the consistency of glue. This was how the linens stayed wrapped around a decomposing corpse for centuries. What she read next surprised her. So she read it aloud. "After, Userkare performed the Opening of the Mouth Ceremony."

Cassie knew of the symbolic ceremony. It was done with a *peseshkaf*, a spooned blade, used to symbolize the opening of the mouth on a statue of a mummy, representing the deceased. So the person could breathe, speak, eat and drink in the afterlife. And the dead person's *ba*, their personality, and *ka*, their spirit, would be released. Of course it would be done to the pharaoh. What she couldn't believe she was reading was who did it. Userkare. Usually the person who was next in line to the throne, or the one who claimed his stake to it, did it. It was an unspoken message to the Egyptian people. Even before King Teti was buried, the people in the palace with power knew Userkare was going to be the next ruler of Egypt.

She continued reading, trying to process what she was deciphering. "After the ceremony, the honorable King Teti's body was then placed into a wooden coffin etched with carvings of the crocodile god, Sobek, and the god Ra." Cassie tried to remember what Ra was depicted as, and then it came to her—a falcon head adorning a golden obelisk, the sun. She continued. "The sides of the coffin were decorated with many paintings of the king's *akhu*, the immortal souls of his ancestors and himself. The coffin was then placed into another coffin, which was shaped like the body of the *nesu*, and the lid was carved to look like the king's face. This coffin was placed into the stone sarcophagus of the *nesu*.

"Then the cavalcade, made of royal and noble men, wearing a diadem of gold braided material, which bore a square gold charm at the center of the forehead, continued to the great honorable King Teti's tomb in Saqqara. They laid him to rest in the sepulchral chamber. The walls were overlaid in gold and inlaid into the gold was blue faience. The ground around the sarcophagus had many funerary emblems. And the oars the *nesu* would need to cross the waters of the underworld were painted with magic symbols." She looked up, trying to piece this all together.

The sequencing finished with the securing of King Teti's tomb with his seal, and the cavalcade proceeding back to the palace, with Userkare and the young King Pepi at its head. The rest was too fragmented. So she scrolled up, trying to find a prior set of sequencing. She needed to find answers on the demise of Pharaoh Teti, for this definitely was a case of murder and mayhem.

FIFTY

2333 B.C., ANCIENT EGYPT

It was the middle of the night when Userkare entered the bedchambers of Queen Iput. Only caliginous torches lit the room. They would finally be alone. His helmet was tucked upside down under his arm next to his sheath, which held his sword. They had to meet in secret. She could not be seen with him in public since she and Egypt were in mourning for her husband, the late King Teti. He would have to wait before she greeted him, just in case anyone heard him enter. As he bolted the door, he saw her pick up the polished copper with the handle of a naked girl holding a bird to look at her reflection and check her makeup. She then opened the jar of green powder and applied more malachite to her eyelids, then rubbed a pellet of incense under each arm. This would prevent sweating.

She walked over to him before speaking. "I have also been in mourning over missing you."

He let out a hearty laugh. "Well, this pleases me, since I have brought you a gift." He pulled out a small box that was tucked inside his helmet and handed it to her.

She opened it and took out a necklace made of lapis lazuli. Hanging from it was a charm of Apep, the snake god of darkness. Before she could say anything, he spoke. "The azure blue complements your eyes."

She grinned. "You make me feel like a girl who still has her youth before her. Thank you." Putting on the necklace, she turned her back to him. He knew she needed help tying it around her neck.

"Wearing this makes you look like a royal." He secured the necklace.

"But I am a royal." They both smiled.

"Which is why I knew it would be perfect for you." He took her to the ebony reed chair. Everyone else in the palace was asleep except the guards on duty, and they wouldn't say anything because Userkare was head of the *Khenty She*. It had seemed like an eternity, but King Teti was to be laid to rest in his tomb tomorrow after the Opening of the Mouth Ceremony. The queen was to meet with the vizier at sunrise to discuss who would become co-regent of Egypt, along with her son Pepi. By Egyptian law, he could not rule Egypt alone until his *medshu* plus *sefekhu* name day.

"Iput, I need to talk to you as my lover and not as my queen. The news I tell you must stay within these walls."

"What news could you possibly have?"

"You need to hear of the plot against the king."

"What are you saying? What plot? Against my Pepi? He's not even yet been crowned."

"Yes, we must prevent any instability against Pepi, but I'm talking about the plot against King Teti."

She patted her heart. "I must sit. I have felt instability in this land ever since my *abi*, the great King Unas, went to live in the afterlife with the gods. So you say he was murdered?"

"Yes." He bent down, placing his hands into hers.

She sniffled. "But why? And who?" She released his hands. "I feel sick."

He stood. "Teti was poisoned by the taster. He tasted the wine right before he gave it to the king. And he is still alive. So the taster was the one who put the poison into the wine the king drank."

"No," she cried. "Someone else has to be behind this. He has no wealth or power. He could not have done this alone." She shook her head as if confused. "Where would he have gotten the poison?"

"From the royal physician, who will be arrested at sunrise. He made the poison out of opium and hemlock and then mixed it with *shedeh*. It would make anyone ill with one sip. This mixture was added to his wine." He paused. "And the way Teti was drinking the wine, right out of the jug. He had enough in him to kill him. Only the taster would have known that the king had chosen to share his jug with no one."

"It still doesn't make sense. A taster would not have wanted the king dead. Who else wanted him dead?"

"I did." Userkare's voice was stern.

"Why?" She stood. "Did he find out about us?" Silence infused the air. "Look at me! Did he know about us?"

He grabbed her shoulders. "Sit down." He spoke firmly, lowering her back into the chair. He then sat on the edge of the bed. "The plot was planned many years ago by Kagemni.

He never forgave Teti for wanting him replaced as vizier before his time. Since it was he who nurtured and guided him as a boy and also taught him the ways of governing and ruling like a *nesu*." Userkare gathered his words carefully.

"If your father King Unas were alive, he would tell you Kagemni was the best vizier for Egypt and its people, because he knew Teti was not as strong a ruler as himself. Without Kagemni's help, your father never would have made him his heir. Or, for that matter, without you to secure the lineage as royal, he would have never been proclaimed as the next king of Egypt. Still, your husband owed Kagemni. And when things were grand for King Teti, he wanted to have his vizier replaced, and by, of all people, Mereruka, his daughter's incompetent husband." He shook his head no.

"Kagemni couldn't bear the thought that he would not be near his son. The son you claimed as your own, Tetiankhkm, to help raise and guide him as he did with Teti. It was his idea to have him killed at your crowning, when everyone would be full of drink and making merry. But before Kagemni could kill Teti…" He stood and began pacing the room. "Teti had Kagemni killed. At one time they were so close, I am not surprised they both had the same plan. But for King Teti, death was the only way out of the promise he made to you, because he also made the same promise as to whom would be vizier to his elder wife, Khuit, regarding their son-in-law, Mereruka. He felt he owed her something since he was making you his queen." He paused.

"Go on," she said.

He took a deep breath. "So with all of them dead there was no need for the plan, but then I realized, I felt the same way about my son as Kagemni did with his son. If the king who had everything handed to him throughout his entire life was gone, my son would rule Egypt." She stood shivering, so he drew her near to him. Then they both sat on the edge of the bed. The bed that brought them so much pleasure was now going to be her source of pain.

"I don't know what to think," she said.

"There's one more thing."

"There's one more thing! Speak!" she demanded.

"I also felt it was just a matter of time until the *nesu* would kill me."

"You speak like a fool. You're the head of all the guards."

"How do you think I became the head of the *Khenty She*? I am fit and good in battle, but so are all the other men in the king's guard. Your *abi*, King Unas, chose me to keep me close, for I am Teti's half-brother." He looked into her face. "Why do you not look surprised?"

"It is not that unusual for royals to have misbegotten children."

"Well, I never knew." He wanted to yell. "I had to find out from Kagemni."

"Who told you to ensure distrust in your king and trust in him." She stood. "And it worked. Look what you did." Userkare was filled with remorse and relief at the same time. In quietude he waited for her to process it all.

"If this was your plan, why did you wait until now to kill Teti?" She sat back on the edge of the bed.

"For the stability of Egypt. If the new *nesu* had died directly after King Unas, instability would have arisen. Being the head of the guards, I know about military ways. You would have had many killings for the throne, or worse, a civil war within the country."

"I suppose you're right about a civil war," she said.

"I was going to wait until Pepi could claim the throne for himself outright, but he needs training and guidance. As long as King Teti was alive, there would be no sense of urgency, but now with him dead… with your permission, I have *medshu* plus *senuj* full moons to mold him into a great warrior and king."

"I see," she said. "And with only *wa* year until his birthright, if anybody wanted to take the throne from Pepi, it would take them at least that long to form alliances or an army, and by the time they would be ready, Pepi would be king."

"You are as smart as you are beautiful." He hesitated before continuing. "I went to the same physician Kagemni was going to use. I told him the king had the vizier killed. This angered him. He had been close to Kagemni since boyhood. So he made me the poison to mix into the *shedeh*. You know the pomegranate drink is the same color as wine and its sweetness covers the taste of the poison."

She put up her hand. "Wait… wait a minute. The taster did not question this?"

"No, he is feeble-minded."

"Go on," she said.

"So I took the poisoned *shedeh* from the physician and gave it to Weni. He is one of my trusted men within the *Khenty She*. He in turn gave it to the taster and told him to add the *shedeh* to the *nesu*'s jug after he tasted the wine. For the king likes his wine sweeter than you or I." He took a breath. "Like I said, he is feeble-minded and would not question the *Khenty She*."

"It is bad enough the gods know about this, but what will become of us if Mereruka ever finds out?" She got down on her knees. "Oh, almighty Ra, forgive him." She buried her face in her hands.

Userkare bent down, helping her to stand. "The taster will be brought to trial by your son-in-law Mereruka, since he is the king's vizier. Although he was my pawn, he is dim-witted, and his loss of life will mean nothing to us; it will mean nothing to him."

"And the physician? He certainly isn't stupid."

"Anyone who agrees to help kill his *nesu* is committing treason. Weni understands this and will kill the physician before he is brought to trial." He paused. "If he hasn't already done so.

"And what do you tell Mereruka?" she asked.

"Weni will say the physician asked him to kill him, as a sacrifice to the gods, to save his soul in the underworld. Mereruka will not question this because the priests and priestesses will agree with the *Khenty She*, as this is an honorable death for the guilty, to sacrifice their souls for the gods."

"And you are alright with committing treason?"

"It is for the betterment of Egypt. Members of the *Khenty She* are trained that anything is acceptable for the betterment of Egypt."

"And what if Weni turns on you, for the betterment of himself?"

"He won't. He is a trusted guard and I am rewarding him by making him the head of the *Khenty She*. This benefits him greatly."

"But you are the head of the *Khenty She*. What will you do now?" She was confused.

"With you being of full royal blood and queen of Egypt, I want you to make me co-regent until our son, Pepi, can rule."

She began laughing. "Mereruka will never agree to this."

"With your persuasions," his voice projected an austere manner, "yes, he will. When you present it to him, you tell him being the head of the *Khenty She*, I am able to protect Egypt against any possible instability or threats to the throne. You let him know it is only until Pepi's next name day, then he can be crowned *nesu*. And in the meantime, you start searching for a wife suitable for your son. And after he takes the throne and is married, you and I can do as we please. But you must tell him tomorrow, before the ceremony."

"And what pleases us?"

"I want to marry you. I want you for the betterment of me. Think of it. We would have no responsibility in running the country, but we would have all of its privileges. Including palace life."

She stared at him, or rather through him. Watching Iput contemplating his offer made him nervous. Had he overstepped his bounds? After all, she was a royal. He could no longer hold her gaze. He looked downward, trying to hide his doubt. Then, out of nowhere, she cupped her hand underneath his chin, bringing his eyes up to hers. "I will agree to this plan before I will see Mereruka govern Egypt."

*

The silver disc was fading. And in the twilight hours when the golden orb was below the horizon, in the queen's bedchamber, Iput placed her hands on Userkare's upper arms. She felt the brawny muscles beneath his flesh. His physique was equal to the god Osiris.

And just when she was thinking, he wasn't *actually* the one who killed her husband... he pulled her body closer to his. The kiss he gave her took her breath. Her mind drifted. Tightened in his arms, her body tingled and then went numb—numb to anything or anyone that would prevent them from being together.

When he was this close to her, she lost all fears and inhibitions. She also lost her senses. Her love for this man crossed any and all barriers of morality. And she knew it could cost her everything she had—security, power and her offspring.

The queen also knew when kings died they became equal to the gods, and she wondered for one brief moment what Teti might do to her in the afterlife. But then Userkare's tongue thrust past her lips. His hand ran upward under her linen sheath, strolling to her spot. It was then she threw her life into the dust of the desert. She couldn't stop herself.

FIFTY-ONE

2333 B.C., ANCIENT EGYPT

Hezi stopped walking. He thought he heard a noise. He contemplated if he should try to see which room it came from. But he was not allowed in most rooms of the palace. Then the noise became a voice from behind.

"You who is walking, turn around, for I am Pepi, the soon-to-be-crowned king of Egypt."

He bowed all the way down until his face touched the mosaic tiles on the palace floor. "Forgive me if I awoke you. I am the scribe Hezi, and with the king's death, I have had much to record. I work better when it is quiet within these palace walls. I was just looking for a drink to quench my thirst."

"And I had been awoken by a night terror."

"I am sorry to hear that, my *nesu.*"

"They have only recently returned from my youth since my *abi*'s death."

"May I stand?"

"You may."

"So that is why you stopped writing? To quench your thirst?" asked Pepi. "I too cannot sleep and I am also seeking something to drink. Come, follow me; we will find someone to serve us. *Henqet* will help."

"Thank you, my king. May I call you that now?" His family would have been honored if they could have seen him talking to the young king.

"Not until my next name day, but it will soon be official. As for now, when the sun awakes, it will be time for the Opening of the Mouth Ceremony. Then my *abi*'s body will be placed in his tomb to begin his journey into the afterlife, with the help of Osiris."

Hezi nodded. "At sunrise, I will once again have much to record."

"Will you describe me as a virile man, one of greatness?"

"Yes, I think I will. Whatever you want me to write, I will."

"Good." Pepi stopped walking. "You see this wall?" He pointed. "It has no scene, no picture, no writing. It is the portion of the palace wall waiting to show my great feats and adventures. And will you write whatever I say for the wall?"

Hezi slightly bowed again. "Yes, for you are soon to be my king." He knew this was not a formal request, but the new king had just given him another job to do in the royal palace. He couldn't wait to tell his family he would have more money coming in. This would greatly help them.

Pepi patted him on the back. "Good, you have proven your faithfulness to me, as well as to King Unas and King Teti. You are older and somewhat wise, and I think I have found a friend in you. I do not have very many within these walls."

Pepi had just referred to him as a friend. This would greatly elevate his position. And it would be nice to have someone to talk to. "I feel I have found a friend in you as well."

"In time, I will want you to record how my father, the great King Teti, whose reign was short, was murdered. Murdered by someone he knew. Someone close."

He swallowed hard. "You know this to be true?"

"I will unfold this plot of revenge against my *abi*. And when I do, I want you to record every word, so it will be known forever. This too will be engraved within the palace walls."

"Do you know who murdered King Teti?"

"I think it was a cabal against my father, perhaps the *Khenty She*. They have nefarious ways and are always in close range to the *nesu*."

"And what will you do with these people who committed treason against our king?"

"You know from the king down to the lowest slave, everyone has at least a small statue made of themselves. Something to hold in the palm of their hand, so their soul will ascend into the afterlife. I will take that person's effigy and have their name chiseled off their statue and anything else representing them. Then I will burn it for all of Egypt to see what becomes of someone who betrays their king. This will damn their soul to the gods."

Pepi's voice became louder. "Everyone knows if there is no statue of a person when they die, no one can feed their spirit. It will be as if they never existed. Their *ka* and *ba* will be destroyed and they will never exist in the afterlife. They will be a non-being for all eternity."

They started walking, then stopped. "Did you hear that?" asked Hezi.

Queen Iput was hurrying down the corridor. "Pepi, who is with you?"

"My new friend, the palace scribe. We are getting some *henqet*."

"Please don't be long, the ceremony will soon take place." Hezi noticed she was rubbing her hand along her gold chains. The charm of Apep, the snake god of darkness, was jingling against the Eye of Wadjet, the amulet of protection. They dangled between her breasts and he found it odd she wore both. He wondered if she was trying to protect herself from darkness. How much more darkness could happen now?

Then Userkare came up from behind Queen Iput and Pepi started shouting. "Why are you still here? Shouldn't you be guarding outside these palace walls?"

"He is making sure the inside of the palace is secure; there are others guarding outside these walls," said the queen.

The future king put his arm around Hezi's shoulder. His face was turning red. "Come, my new friend, we must hurry, for I am parched and I must relieve my nostrils from this miasmic stench which has entered the air."

But Hezi knew there was more to it than that. Something had just happened between the future king and his mother. And he knew it had something to do with the death of King Teti.

FIFTY-TWO

A.D. 1988, CAIRO, EGYPT

Edmund turned when Cassie entered the lab, coffee in hand. So did everyone else. With clenched teeth and papers under his arm, he greeted her. "Follow me, please." He opened the door to the smaller room, the one where the C.T. scan was done on the bones, and entered.

"I see everyone's here. I can't wait to show you my findings," she said. Edmund noticed she smiled at Mark before entering the smaller room. "I've been here most of the night. I just ran out to get some coffee."

"Yes, I know," he said. "I saw your notes when I came in." He paused, inhaling deeply. "Sit down." He shut the door and extended his hand but remained standing. She sat, putting her coffee on the counter, but stayed perched on the edge of the stool. "How have you been feeling lately?" he asked.

"Fine. Other than my hand has been throbbing."

"I'm wondering if you have had temporary amnesia as to your job description while on this excavation, or are you now a papyrologist?" His voice was stern.

"I have no explanation that you want to hear," she said. "Look, Dr. Ramsey, I'm sorry, but I couldn't sleep so I came in long before daylight and on my own time."

"When you're on a paid excavation, there *is* no time that is your own."

"Yes sir," she said, "but I found answers to the mystery of the bones and more important is the time—"

He interrupted. "Yes, there probably are answers to the baby's mystery. However, that is not why you are here. It was not your job to decipher the papyrus. Your job was to excavate any artifacts from the tomb, sequence them and determine their time frame."

"But if you were reading my notes, then you know I have solved the timeline theo—"

He didn't let her finish. "Dr. Seldon, this isn't going to bring your baby back and although I feel for you, this isn't a personal trip. It's a professional one." He saw she was confused.

"Dr. Ramsey... how did you know I had a baby? I never told you." She stood, her hands flying freely as she spoke. "Hardly anyone knows. It was a long time ago. Dr. McCormick! He told you, didn't he?"

"What does it matter? I need to complete my excavation and if I allow you to continue not following the rules, no one else on the team will either. There's already starting to be discordance, now everyone wants to be deciphering the papyrus, and I can't have that, not on my expedition. Your contraventions of the rules have left me no choice. It pains me to do this. Dr. Seldon, you're fired!" He watched as she turned the doorknob to let herself out. "Wait!" He fumbled through some papers. "Here, I have a return plane ticket. You leave later today."

As the door opened, Edmund observed everyone wearing a stoic expression. He knew his voice had conveyed itself outside of the small room. No one spoke as she left and then the door closed. He phoned the attendant in the lobby, asking to collect Dr. Seldon's badge, keycard and to escort her off the premises. He felt so disappointed. This excavation was supposed to be the team's finest hour, not its darkest.

FIFTY-THREE

Mark replayed the events of the last few minutes in his mind. He couldn't believe what had just happened, so he kept on rehashing it. First he entered the laboratory, the lights were already on and he saw Dr. Ramsey reading notes from a pad by the last monitor. He greeted him and then everyone else started to arrive. He then noticed Dr. Ramsey began shuffling and reshuffling the papers he had with him. It was like he needed something to do, to look busy, but not actually be busy. Then it all made sense. He was waiting for Dr. Seldon.

She entered with her coffee. And upon seeing her, Dr. Ramsey appeared stressed and anxious. He then asked her to join him in the adjacent room. Mark had never seen him this way before and glanced at Dr. Richards, whose face conveyed he was thinking the same thing. Today was not going to be a usual lab day.

So he walked over to read what was on the monitor. As he continued to scroll up the sequencing, he thought about why he had been chosen to go on this excavation. Mark knew he was talented and good—no, wait, he knew he was great at his job. He took pride in his work and made sacrifices to get where he was at—not career sacrifices, but personal ones. He didn't have a wife, girlfriend or children. Not even a pet. Hell, he didn't even really have much of a social life. He buried all of his time and emotions into his work.

Yes. He knew why he had been chosen. And he accepted this because he knew the payoff would be big. Debunking Dynasty Zero would put him into Dr. Ramsey's league. And this was what he wanted, so the last thing he expected to find was that the timeline theory of Dynasty Zero was correct.

He reread the part of the papyrus telling the story of the wine jar, with King Narmer being depicted wearing the *Pschent* crown of Egypt, originally found in Narmer's wife, Queen Neithhotep's, tomb. He was trying to comprehend what he was reading. That was, until the door to the smaller room started to open. He heard Dr. Ramsey say something and then Cassie came out. He recalled looking around the lab; all eyes were on Dr. Seldon and hers on them, and without anyone saying a word, she opened the lab door and left.

Dr. Ramsey could not have seen the part of the papyrus he was now viewing. If he had, she would have never been fired. Cassandra Seldon, who would have gone to the ends of the earth for her theory. This was her baby. Her baby! It suddenly all made sense to him. It explained why she had to find out what happened to the baby whose arm bone was found in Pharaoh Teti's tomb.

She needed closure on this ancient baby, because she really didn't have closure on the death of her own baby. Cassie had told him her baby had died from S.U.D.C., Sudden Unexplained Death of a Child. She knew why her baby had died, but that doesn't give you closure when the explanation has the word unexplained in it. She had appeared to be a little sidetracked, but everyone in the lab was somewhat invested in the papyrus.

Mark had a newfound esteem for Cassie. She might have been the rule-breaker of the team, but she had been willing to go all the way for her beliefs. And it cost her her job. While he gave up certain principles and his personal life for this job, Cassie had lost her job for her principles and personal life. Would he ever be able to do the same?

Or in time, would for the good of the company, force him into early retirement? If the job didn't kill him first, literally. He knew people who had died on their jobs from heart attacks. No... he would probably be laid off if enough funding weren't approved. He took a deep breath. Dr. Ramsey must know about this discovery, even if it meant he would lose his job too.

And Dr. Seldon must be given the credit. Having her as a lifelong ally and hopefully friend would be worth it. The proof was on the screen and he knew he could clear this up. Turn this mishap into a misunderstanding. His decision was made.

Coming out of his reverie, he stood rather regally, and the ground beneath his feet was steady. Mark felt calm. He seemed to breathe easier as he walked. He opened the door to the smaller room and entered. "Dr. Ramsey, in light of what has just happened, I need to talk to you." Then he closed the door behind him. "Now!"

FIFTY-FOUR

Cassie slammed the door to her room, dropped her purse and kicked off her shoes before falling face down on the bed, crying. "How could he have fired me?" she screamed into her pillow. Everyone on the team had been caught up in the papyrus. "Why me?" She punched her pillow.

Could it be he was harder on her than the others because he did not believe in Dynasty Zero? She sat up, rubbing her eyes. That was probably it. He was on Mark's side of the timeline and this was a threat to him. That had to be it. She wiped her tears, got up and went into the bathroom, grabbing some tissues, and she began to convulse, spilling all the contents of her toiletry bag onto the floor.

Her body was shaking and her vision started to blur, but not before she spotted the syringe and vial by the toilet. Grabbing it, she pulled her blouse up above her midriff and injected herself. She felt nauseated, so she curled up into the fetal position on the tile floor and began taking deep breaths. The room began spinning, so she shut her eyes. Her vision might have been fuzzy, but her memories were clear and in focus.

She remembered the day she had told her mother she was pregnant. She had hidden her pregnancy for nearly five months, wearing baggy clothes and rarely eating. First it was because she was so sick and then because she was so scared. And there wasn't much food in the house, so it wasn't all that difficult. Her memory was sharp now as she recalled her mother yelling at her.

She was supposed to be finishing high school. Not having a baby. She knew her mother did not want her to have the same fate as she did, since she had dropped out of college and had always regretted her choice. So it was agreed upon that she would finish the last of her high school credits during summer school.

But even if Cassandra hadn't died, she had still planned on going to college. Chad was not like her father. He was going to be there, to help. And it took a lot of courage for her to continue her education after Cassandra and Chad's deaths. But what made her go was realizing that any life would be better than the life she had.

Feeling a little better, she used her hands to pick herself up, but the pain permeated deep into her left hand, as if her cut had widened. So she undressed it. Besides being red and swollen, she could also tell the infection was worse. She ran her hand under water and took some ibuprofen for the pain and swelling. She walked to the mini fridge, looked inside, and grabbed the expensive candy bar and water bottle.

Thinking about death made Queen Iput come to mind. She'd lost a father, husband, best friend and a child she claimed as her own. Cassie mourned for the father she never had, she mourned for Chad, the husband and best friend she would never have, and she mourned for her own baby's death, the baby who would never become a child. She sat on the edge of the bed, taking a big gulp of water, and then bit into her candy bar. *Ooh, chocolate.* Feeling hot, she undressed, leaving on her satin and lace panties, then pulled back the covers and hid underneath them.

Now that she'd disgraced her museum on this excavation, she felt like a failure. She didn't want to become like her mother—on the edge, barely having a grip on reality. And even though she had a doctorate degree, her mother could still make her feel inadequate in the conversations they had together. This was probably—somehow, in Susan's eyes—a way to keep her close, since her mother had let all of her goals die with Cassie's birth.

The guilt she carried because of her mother pricked under her skin. How long would she have to repent, not only for her own choices, but also for her mother's? She was career-driven and had no illusions of a family that wasn't, unlike her mother, who had kept memories and made plans for a fantasy family. At least she'd made a life for herself. She was a self-reliant, strong-willed woman.

When everyone was back in the States, she would contact Dr. Ramsey and tell him how she'd proved the Dynasty Zero theory. But for now, she was going to finish her candy bar and call her mother. She had to tell her she was coming home. As the phone rang, she took a sip of water.

"Hello." *Okay*, she thought. *She seems coherent enough.*

"Mom, it's me. I need to let you know—"

"Cassie," her mother interrupted, "where are you? You know you should be home by now, it's getting dark outside."

"Mother, I'm in Egypt, remember?"

"Oh, yes, of course."

"I'm coming home, Mom. I have an evening flight. It seems Dr. Ramsey fired me today."

"Why does a pretty girl like you want to hang out in musty, mold-infested tombs anyways? Come to the church and we can all talk about what happened."

"Church? Mom, I'll come get you at the house." *Oh God, she's really lost it now.*

"No, dear, meet me at the church."

"Mom, I'm not even at the airport yet. I'll meet you at the house. Tomorrow."

"That's alright, dear, the church will be unlocked tomorrow, I'll wait for you there."

"Mom, are you listening? Let me get settled at home first, and then I'll come over to your place. I'll take you out to dinner and tell you everything."

"That's not necessary, dear. Like I said, you can meet me at the church, I'll wait there. Cassie, you need to have your hearing checked."

"Mom, again with this—what are you talking about? I don't understand."

"See you tomorrow. I need to take a bath and get ready."

"Wait, Mother! What church?" Silence. "What church?" Cassie knew Susan was having one of her episodic flights of fancy. Her illusions were her reality. The only church they ever went to was the one where Reverend Westin used to be the minister. The United Methodist Church on Race Street. It was three miles from the Kreativ Museum.

FIFTY-FIVE

The blandness of the lab's décor was in qua with how Mark felt as he left the smaller adjacent room. Whether or not he had a job was out of his hands. It was all up to Dr. Ramsey. So he tried to lighten the mood of the circumstances surrounding him. "Well, now that I may be on the verge of getting fired, let's get back to the papyrus and try to decipher its ending, before Dr. Ramsey comes out and makes me a part of history." To his amazement, everyone joined him.

"If we're all doing it," said Dr. Barrington, "he can't fire all of us. The entire team? He would just admonish our behavior. That's all."

"You obviously don't know Dr. Ramsey very well, do you?" Dr. Granite arched his brow.

"Well," said Dr. Barrington, "what's done is done. Read on, Dr. McCormick, let's get to the end while we all still have our jobs." Mark scrolled a few sequences and began deciphering a larger portion of the papyrus. He read aloud to everyone the part where Userkare admitted to Queen Iput that he killed King Teti. He scrolled down a bit and continued. "There had been no other event to match this one. The royal makeup and wardrobe had been laid out for the crowning of King Pepi, *nesu* of Upper and Lower Egypt."

FIFTY-SIX

2332 B.C., ANCIENT EGYPT

Queen Iput looked on as Pepi's servants rubbed him with pellets of incense under his arms and date palm oil across his chest. A handmaiden had been brought in to line his eyes with kohl. They draped the purple robe over him. leaving his leather kilt exposed. Looking through the arch opening from his room's balcony, they could see people gathering outside the palace—crowds and crowds of Egyptians trying to catch a glimpse of the soon-to-be-newly crowned king of Upper and Lower Egypt.

She knew Pepi's first order of business after his crowning was going to be reinstating the gods, Sobek, Ra and Horus. When Userkare was co-regent with her, he replaced them and made the Egyptian people worship the god Osiris. Instead of moving forward toward a new Egypt, the man she loved had the people return to very old ways. She knew this, and everything else Userkare had instated, would end after today.

Mother and son walked down the palace corridor to the great hall where the banquet would be held for the ceremony of her son becoming *nesu*. His *medshu* plus *sefekhu* name day had passed and he could now be crowned king. It would begin with the placing of the *Sekhemti* crown of Egypt upon his head. She prayed to the gods for his reign to be long and prosperous. She knew Pepi would reinstate his half-sister's husband, Mereruka, as his vizier, even though she detested him. He would honor King Teti's decision, unlike Userkare, who didn't use Mereruka or anyone as his vizier. She found herself smiling because her lover had used her, a woman, as his co-regent for guidance. Thank the gods that the people had not complained, probably because they only had to endure this until Pepi became of age.

The guards opened the double doors and announced their arrival. Upon entering, she saw Userkare standing on the dais. The *Sekhemti* crown of Egypt was not on his head but in his hands. She took a deep breath; she could not be nervous. He son was going to be crowned.

Pepi looked left toward his teacher Meri and his wife Bebty. Queen Iput knew he would promote them. He would put them in charge of education for the entire royal family and soon-to-be royal children. His teachers would be able to live at the palace and enjoy a good, prosperous life. But first, he had told her, he must re-establish the gods and then find a wife. Another royal to be his queen.

She looked lovingly at her son. He looked back at her. This was a proud moment for her. She sensed he was nervous. She eyed the room one last time and saw her son's friend and ally, Hezi, recording it all and she knew this moment was meant to be. The gods preordained her son's destiny and he would soon become like them.

FIFTY-SEVEN

2332 B.C., ANCIENT EGYPT

The following sunrise Queen Iput was in the great hall with the vizier Mereruka, planning which pretty young girl or princess would be suitable to marry the newly crowned King Pepi. "Have we considered any of the Nubian princesses?"

Pepi burst through the door before Mereruka could answer. "No, we have not. I have my eyes set on the Mayor of Abydos Khui's daughters."

Mereruka bowed then looked up. "What? He has *senuj*."

"I am *nesu*, I do not need, nor wish, to choose. I have my eyes on both."

Mereruka laughed. "Well, this will be interesting since Khui gave them both the same name."

"Shall we call them Ankhnesmerire *wa* and Ankhnesmerire *senuj*?" Queen Iput had a sardonic grin on her face.

"We shall not call them anything today. For today is not about my marriage, Mother, it is about yours."

"What do you mean?" she asked.

"Now that I am king, my first request is to grant you permission to marry Userkare. After all, it is only a fortunate few of us royals who can marry for love. And when I marry, you will be queen mother; my wife will be queen. So this campaign we go on against the Sand Dwellers to expand Egypt's borders will be his last. It is time for you and him to do what you wish for your remaining days. Userkare has more than shown his loyalty to me by crowning me as king."

"Mereruka, may we have a few moments?" Queen Iput extended her hand toward the door.

He bowed before his king. "If you do not need me, I will grant the queen's request."

"Yes," said Pepi. "We are done plotting my marriage for today."

"Come, my son, please join me on the dais. I need to talk to you."

She was glad the thrones were positioned so she would not be looking at her son when she spoke. "It pleases me that you have found favor with Userkare. For now that you are ruler of Upper and Lower Egypt, I want you to be a strong ruler, stronger than the late King Teti."

"Stronger than my *abi*?"

"You have the knowledge and physical height of your grandfather, the late, great King Unas, and the military prowess and physical strength of your father, Userkare."

Pepi laughed. "Just because I granted you permission to marry him does not make him my *abi*."

She got up and kneeled before her son, the *nesu*, kissing his feet. "Forgive me."

He stepped off of his throne. "Mother, what do you

mean?" He lifted her by her arms and flung her into the queen's chair. Then, standing in front of her, he said, "Watch what your tongue tells me. It is treason for the wife of the *nesu* to lie with another."

"You need to understand," she pleaded. "King Teti's elder wife, Khuit, only bore him daughters, years before, and then nothing. He married me to secure the throne. King Unas, having no male heirs, made Teti his heir. I was supposed to be made queen—"

"And you were!"

"Yes, but not right away. Time passed and nothing, so he made plans to marry Weret-Imtes, a young, stupid girl. I am of royal birth!" She poked her chest. "I was not going to be made a fool or bow down to a non-royal queen. That was not going to happen. I knew I would only be made queen if I produced an heir." She paused.

"At the same time the goddess Meskhenet had blessed my favorite handmaiden and friend, Anhai. She was with child by Kagemni. Back then he was the vizier and head priest, and also married." She sighed. "So we hatched an elaborate plot as to when Anhai gave birth it would become my child. If the baby was a girl, it bought me time, because it proved the king and I were fertile. If she bore a son, then I would become queen."

"So Tetiankhkm was not my brother?" He gave her a quizzical look.

"I ate a lot and faked that the *nesu's* seed grew inside me. Anhai became a priestess and gave birth in the temple. The priestesses delivered the baby and Kagemni brought them both to me. Then Anhai and I sacrificed a cosset to the goddess Meskhenet." She looked directly into his eyes. "After that we wrapped the lamb in royal cloth. The blood on the floor of my bedchambers was the proof I needed to say I had given birth. Kagemni then took the bundle to the priestesses, telling them Anhai's baby had died." She wiped a tear from her eye before continuing. "They would never question that the bundle was not a baby, since it was wrapped inside royal cloth. He then buried the baby on temple grounds, so as not to disgrace the royal household, since she was my handmaiden and her lover was married to a noblewoman." She sniffled.

"Oh, Mother, what are the gods going to do with you when you enter the afterlife?" He shook his head, showing sorrow for her.

She didn't answer. She just continued. "Then *wa* full moon later I found out I was also blessed by the goddess Meskhenet, with you." She lowered her head. "I slept with Userkare during my purification. King Teti was not your *abi*. I loved him as one loves their king, but Userkare was my friend. He always treated me with respect, unlike Teti." She paused. "And I was lonely when I entered my confinement." She swallowed hard to keep from crying. "Remember, son, I wasn't really with child. Other than servants, Userkare was the only person I saw throughout my confinement and purification."

"And what were your plans for me, Mother?"

"If you were born a girl, it would have secured my position and shown I could bear the king more children. And if I birthed a boy, Userkare was going to make you a great soldier and warrior. And he did!" Her voice was stern to hold back the tears. "But when King Teti ordered Mereruka to kill Kagemni, Anhai was with him. And she had Tetiankhkm sleeping inside a basket when they entered Kagemni's tomb.

Everyone thought the basket contained food and drink for the gods."

"Mereruka killed my brother?" She saw betrayal mirrored in his eyes.

"Yes, but he was your brother in name only." She sighed. "I was beside myself with fear. Because I knew Tetiankhkm was in the basket." She spoke slowly. "It was your father, Userkare, who eased my fears, reminding me you would now be the one to rule after King Teti. For you are the true *nesu*, being born from me. Your grandfather, the late King Unas, and myself are from pure royal blood, which is why Userkare had no problem stepping down and making you the king of Egypt." Except for her sniffling, silence permeated the room.

After a few moments, Pepi spoke. "So that is why he confided and chose advice from you, instead of Vizier Mereruka?"

"Yes, because our sole interest was putting you on the throne." She stood. This weight she had carried for so many years had been lifted. She felt lighter. Then she saw his face redden. He was quiet, so she extended her hands to reach for him. He looked so young. "Sit, my son. I am sorry that when my burden was lifted it was placed upon you." She saw his eyes dart from left to right. He looked mystified. A door opening broke the stillness. It was the scribe Hezi.

"Go! You have not had my permission to enter!" yelled Pepi. The door made a loud bang as it closed.

She noticed the veins on his neck protruding and she wondered if she had done the right thing.

FIFTY-EIGHT

LAND OF THE SAND DWELLERS
BATTLE, NORTHEAST OF EGYPT
2332 B.C., ANCIENT EGYPT

The soldiers were in position to fight the Asiatic Sand Dwellers. They all wore cloths of stripes entwined with roping upon their foreheads. The men were waiting for the sun god Ra to raise his golden orb against the horizon. They had sailed and arrived by boat, not wanting to arouse or alert the foreigners. These people had rebelled against Egypt before, so Userkare knew King Pepi wanted this battle to be an unexpected jolt to put an end to their rebellions. He wanted to be renowned as a strong king.

Userkare himself had fought many battles. So had the commander and head of the *Khenty She*, Weni. The plan was to split so the Sand Dwellers would not know which direction the battle was coming from. Pepi had ordered Userkare to take half of the troops to the front of the mountain range, while Weni had taken the other half to the back of the mountain range. Weni was strong and smart in battle, and he was younger than Userkare. So he wondered why Pepi had chosen to stay and fight with Weni instead of going into battle with him.

At least King Pepi had made sure all his troops had the finest weapons. They carried shields made of wood, while Weni, Pepi and his shields were made of leather.

Everyone carried either a sword or a copper-headed spear. And all the troops had a macehead or a dagger with a copper blade, used for hand-to-hand fighting, tucked inside their belt made of rope. Since they'd sailed, they had not brought their horses. They would have to sneak up on the Sand Dwellers. This was to be a hand-to-hand ground battle.

When the golden orb showed its tip above the horizon, Userkare raised his sword and with a long, high-pitched, wavering shrill shout, he ululated the command to charge.

*

On the other side of the mountain range, King Pepi and Weni sieged the Asiatic Sand Dwellers in their homes, piercing their hearts in the name of Ra as they woke. As the troops proceeded down the lanes and through the marketplace, you could hear the women crying in fear for their men and the children screaming in terror. There was much slaughter, and blood was spilled. When they had defeated their enemy, a third of these soldiers stayed to maintain control of the city. King Pepi and Weni took the rest of them and carried on the campaign to where Userkare was fighting.

FIFTY-NINE

LAND OF THE SAND DWELLERS
BATTLE, NORTHEAST OF EGYPT
2332 B.C., ANCIENT EGYPT

Sweat was dripping into Userkare's eyes, along with the dust of the desert. He could barely see, there seemed to be so many of them. The fighting had kicked up collossal amounts of sand, creating a dust storm, and he couldn't breathe. He inhaled the smell of death but kept turning left then right, killing anyone or anything that moved. As his weapon penetrated into more bodies, miniature specks of blood splattered all over his face. He turned and saw Egyptian soldiers rushing toward him. He was relieved to have reinforcements.

Bloodshed was all around him. Next to him he saw the head of a soldier fly from his body with one slice of the sword. He raised his sword in return, tripping over a dead Sand Dweller, and then felt a blade go through his back. It burned, piercing through him like fire. He fell to the ground. Bloodstained bodies were all around him.

Weakness overtook him. Userkare closed his eyes and he thought he wet himself. With all his strength, he inched his hand to the dampness. It felt thick. He knew it was blood. He opened his eyes and saw Pepi first. From his view he and Weni looked like giants. "Please help me."

"You know it is treason to sleep with a wife of the king, no less his queen," said Pepi. "I know everything about you." He spat out his next words. "My *abi*."

Clutching his leg, Userkare tried to rise but couldn't. With shortness of breath, he spoke. "You need to know I had King Teti poisoned for you. So you could rule Egypt." He gasped for air. "I wanted to be near you, to mold you from me as you became a man." He coughed. "I could only prepare you if I was co-regent, as you were preordained by the gods for greatness." He tried to raise his hand. "My son, help—"

Userkare was not aware that Pepi, had no knowledge of this. He also didn't know the rage that was about to burst from Pepi would have caused the Nile to flood. He squinted his eyes and saw him talking to Weni but could not hear what was being said. The dankness beneath him had spread down his legs and he no longer felt them. He no longer felt pain. He had trouble keeping his eyes open. Sweat was dripping into them, yet he felt cold.

"I said, do you have anything else to say before you enter the Two Halls of Truth, to be judged by Osiris on your way to the Underworld?" Pepi repeated.

With the last of the life force he had in him, Userkare lifted his head just above the ground and whispered, "Son, help—"

"Oh, I intend to. Anubis, the god of death, is here." And with that Userkare saw Pepi look over to Weni, who thrust his sword into Userkare's stomach not once but twice, showing his loyalty to the new king.

He spoke his final words to Weni. "I trusted you." Then he felt someone club him. His head cracked, then split. The last thing Userkare saw was his son's face splattered in miniscule deposits of blood, his blood, and the splattered face spitting on his body. The golden orb behind him was now high in the sky. He felt his *ka* leaving his body and he knew he was to begin his journey with Osiris into the Underworld.

SIXTY

2332 B.C., ANCIENT EGYPT

Queen Iput looked at the king's seal and reread the message she had received from Pepi: "We have landed safe and in victory. With the help of the powerful god Horus, Egypt has defeated the Asiatic Sand Dwellers." She had been keeping the message with her, next to her heart. Now she and Userkare could be married, and then, as queen mother, her first act of business would be to find Pepi a wife. A royal wife, a woman worthy of becoming queen. Her gaze was toward the courtyard, but she only saw the daydreams she beheld. She didn't realize how long she had been with her visions until a guard came to the door and announced her son's arrival. "King Pepi enters your chambers. Please bow before your king." She did, and the guard left them to be alone.

"Mother, please sit." He gave a slight nod to her out of respect, then took her hand, leading her to her favorite ebony chair, the one with carvings of gazelles on the legs. He took off his crown and placed it on the table where she applied her makeup. "We were victorious in war." He pounded his fist to his chest. Then he got down on one knee and placed his mother's hands into his. "But we lost men. Good men. And Userkare has left us. His *ka* is gone and his *ba* has begun its journey into the afterlife."

"*Aahh!*" She felt as if someone had ripped out her heart. Her eyes welled up like a dam ready to burst. Another person she loved, gone. "No, not another death," she mumbled. Her handmaidens and a guard rushed into the room, bowing slightly before responding.

Pepi shouted, "Please get the queen some water, and also bring us two cups of warm *henqet!*" He stood, raising his hand and dismissing the guard.

Iput felt feeble. Trying to get out of the chair, she fell onto the floor. She was having trouble breathing. The dam burst and she began sobbing uncontrollably. "We were to be married! Pepi, oh, my Pepi, what am I to do?" She had succumbed to ennui and despair, so he picked her up and laid her onto the bed.

The ladies in waiting returned with the water and warm *henqet*, and set them by her bedside table. He told them to fluff her pillows and help him prop her up before dismissing them. He held the cup of water to her lips. After a sip, she pushed the cup away. "Userkare," she wailed, "what am I to do without you?"

He sat on the bed, grabbing her upper arms to steady her. "Now, now, try to settle yourself. You still have your throne and you have me, your son."

In between gasps, she spoke. "I only have you for a short while. Now that you are *nesu* you must take a wife, to secure the great King Unas's lineage with an heir. Then she will take my place as queen." She was crying so hard she was fighting hiccups. "And… and, I won't even have my trusted friend to be with me in my oldness. He hasn't even built his pyramid." He handed her the cup of *henqet*. It was warm going down her throat. It soothed her hiccups but gave her little comfort.

Pepi downed his drink before speaking. "He doesn't need a pyramid; he was a co-regent of Egypt."

"He may have only ruled for *medshu* plus *senuj* full moons, but he was a king. And now he has no *akhu*, no pyramid, not even a mastaba." She drank until her cup was empty then wiped her eyes with her hand, trying to control the dam.

He took her cup. "Mother, he does not need a mastaba. I did not bring his body back. He is entombed within the sand of the desert, in the land of the Asiatic Sand Dwellers."

She stopped crying. The dam was suppressed. "Do you have no shame? It was Userkare who taught you how to hunt and fish and fight like a warrior."

"Userkare's body was ravaged. You would not have wanted to see him like this. It is best that he dwells within the sand." She noticed he seemed calm. "My chief commander, and head of the *Khenty She*, Weni, advises me now. He is a good man and always wins in battle. He trusts me, for I have royal blood. And I have my half-sister's husband, Mereruka, as my vizier. The throne is stable. Have no fear, Mother."

But she was afraid. All she had was fear. "Show some respect; he was your *abi*."

King Pepi backhanded his mother across the face. "How dare you insult my *abi* King Teti! Have you forgotten who you are speaking to?"

308

Startled, she got up off the bed and bowed before her son. "It was all for you. All this was for you. Because I love you and so you could be crowned king of Egypt, for royal blood runs within you." She looked up. His face was tense. He was pointing his finger at her, his body shaking.

"No, Mother, you did it all for you! And if you ever tell anyone what Userkare did, it will make for instability in my kingdom and rebels might want to try to overthrow my reign. I am facing a real fear." He closed his eyes. "Mother, do you realize my rule must remain steadfast?"

*

Queen Iput did not know how much time had passed as they proceeded toward the temple. Her son held her up. His arm around her waist was what kept her walking. Their sandals clicked on the slanting floor as they made their way to the gods and goddesses. The flaming linen, floating in the oil of the terra cotta bowls lining the walls, lighted the temple. Pepi opened the cedar wood doors. Upon entering the room, they saw the gilded wooden statue of a man with a falcon head. On top of its head was a round disk made of gold. Seeing this, they kneeled to the ground and prayed to the god to keep their secrets hidden within the tombs of the dead.

When they were done, they stood and looked into the eyes of Ra, which were inlaid with the intense color of the semi-precious stone aventurine. It was then Pepi finally spoke. "Even after praying to the gods, thanks to you, I have no relief. My *ka*, my soul, feels nothing."

With red and swollen eyes, Queen Iput responded. "Now you know how I feel. I am afraid we will be of little comfort to each other." In silence, she turned, leaving her son in the temple. Alone.

SIXTY-ONE

A.D. 1988, CAIRO, EGYPT

The banquet room at the hotel had a retro seventies look and feel to it. Soft lighting fixtures were underneath big shades, attached to long chains hung from the ceiling. The wallpaper was black with earth-tone colors of geometric symbols made of velvet, and more than one person touched the walls as they entered the room. The bar was made from a type of wood that resembled paneling. Mark thanked the bartender for his Manhattan, noticing the room wasn't the only thing retro, as so was the music. Elevator music is elevator music, no matter what country you're in.

Just like the reception the group had had when they first arrived, this was their final bash. An evening together, and after what had happened today, a time to unwind and discuss their findings. He tasted his drink. Very well made. He was immersed in drowning out the day's events with his cocktail and didn't notice Dr. Granite until he tapped him on the shoulder.

"Who else is here?" asked Tom.

"Everyone, except Dr. Ramsey. He's running late. He's

securing our findings with the antiquities minister. He's also making sure we can visit Pharaoh Djoser's pyramid tomorrow for our final day in Egypt. And of course Dr. Seldon won't be here."

"You seemed upset with what happened to Dr. Seldon today?" asked Tom.

Mark raised his drink, acknowledging Ian. "Not to change the subject, but there's Dr. Richards. Let's join the group."

Everyone said their hellos before Dr. Granite spoke to Dr. Richards. "What is going to happen to the papyrus now that we're leaving?"

"The papyrus is now resting on a layer of polyester netting, stretched onto an acid-free mount. The back is reinforced with a Japanese paper tab and wheat starch paste. I then enclosed it in a frame made of polycarbonate plates. It has been assigned an inventory number, which I placed within the plates for reference. I have it stored horizontally in a climate control, no light, environment drawer, and writing experts who work at the Cairo museum will continue the analysis, along with checking on it periodically," said Ian. "Oh, and one more thing. Mass spectrometry has dated the papyrus at roughly a little over 4,300 years old. I may be off by a few decades, but it's definitely from Dynasty Six."

"And the bones of the woman and baby are being sent to the John Hopkins Archaeology Museum," said Edmund, "for further study."

"Oh," said Tom. "When did you sneak in?"

"Just now," said Edmund. "Did you know the earliest mummies are called natural mummies, because they were left in the sun to dry?"

"I knew that," said Tom.

"I know the oldest mummy is a baby from Peru," said Mark. "The C.T. scan determined it died from a heart defect." There was a lull in the conversation. "I'm headed off to the bar to get a refill. Anyone care to join me?"

He couldn't help thinking about Cassie and wondered how she was coping with everything that had happened today. He ordered another drink, noticing Ian had followed him. "So tell me what Dr. Seldon had up on the screen," said Ian.

"Why? What did you see or hear?"

"Nothing, that's why I'm asking."

After Ian placed his drink order, Mark began. "Queen Neithhotep, King Narmer's wife, had a wine jug with symbolic pictures of the ceremony called Receiving of the South and North. This proves it represented the unification of Egypt in two ways. The figure of King Narmer wearing the *Pschent* or double crown of Egypt, and the two men holding lotus stalks entwined with papyrus representing Upper and Lower Egypt as one. It was written that the jug was made especially for the ceremony celebrating the unification of Egypt."

Ian looked intrigued, so Mark continued. "Then King Sekhemkhet, a Dynasty Three pharaoh, looted the wine jar from Queen Neithhotep's tomb. Later King Unas stole it from King Sekhemkhet's tomb, where it was dropped and broken. He gave a piece of it to Princess Iput. Once she became queen, it ended up in her tomb, where Dr. Seldon found the fragment."

"Whoa," said Ian, picking up their drinks and handing one to Mark.

"Yeah, that's what I thought too. Come on, we need to get back to the others."

Edmund and Tom also returned at the same time they did. "Sorry, everyone," said Dr. Ramsey. "Dr. Granite and I had to step away to take a call from the office of antiquities. Their team has been on an excavation in Kom-El-Ahmar. Or, as it is better known from ancient times, the city of Hierakonpolis. They found the ruins of a brewery. And it has been concluded that the brewery has been there since 3850 B.C." He went on. "While they were there, the equipment they used confirmed Egyptologist Günter Dreyer's find of tomb U.J. as being Scorpion's tomb."

"Oh, so the latest excavating equipment did help?" asked Ian.

Edmund smiled. "Yes, it did. Most of the excavators went to Kom-El-Ahmar—seems it's a madhouse over there."

"So what does this mean?" asked Ian.

"What it means is that Scorpion was before Narmer," said Edmund. "The consensus used to be that he and Narmer were the same person. We now know they were not. Scorpion's tomb was found in Hierakonpolis, or modern-day Kom El-Ahmar, in a different region from King Narmer's tomb, identified as B17 and B18—these two chambers are located in Umm el-Qa'ab, a region of Abydos."

Edmund's voice faded as Mark processed this. *So Scorpion and Narmer were not the same person. Huh.*

Edmund continued. "Dr. Günter Dreyer is the person who will be mainly recognized for the acceptance of Dynasty Zero, because of the proof yielded from his discoveries that the Scorpion King and Narmer were not the same person.

However, Dr. Seldon will be given acknowledgement for her findings, especially the etchings on the pottery shard, due to its authenticity, which immensely substantiates more evidence of a Dynasty Zero." Edmund smiled before he continued. "Seems our group choosing Saqqara to excavate really did help with the timeline theory."

Ian pulled Mark aside. "Are you okay? What about the spells in King Unas's tomb?"

"They only confirmed the red crown was used for the Ritual of Valor ceremony," he said. "Seems the spells also mentioned King Unas partaking in the Ritual of Valor as a symbolic ceremony. As we know, he was the last pharaoh of Dynasty Five and Egypt was already unified, so even after the unification, sometimes they still wore only one crown for ceremonial purposes." He sighed.

"The red crown, or *Deshret*, does represent Lower Egypt, where the Ritual of Valor ceremony started. And the white crown, or *Hedjet*, does indeed represent Upper Egypt, even back in Narmer's time. But it doesn't matter." He shrugged. "I'm the one who showed Dr. Seldon's findings to Dr. Ramsey and right now I'm worried about her." They rejoined the group.

"Dr. Granite," said Edmund. "Please bring everyone up to speed on the rest of the findings while I speak with Dr. McCormick."

Tom smiled and took a swig of his drink. "It has also been indicated that ancient Egypt's predynastic times started as early as 3850 B.C., not only because of the brewery, but they also found a carving of an elephant in a rock. This proves there were people in that time frame. After all, someone had to carve into the rock, which denotes that if Egypt had elephants, it had fertile land." He continued. "We believe the monsoon rains made the land fertile, because there is evidence of acacia wood being present in that time frame. The fertile lands brought the wandering nomads."

Tom spoke faster. "Once they quit wandering, the nomads turned into shepherds. Which we now know is the origin of the pharaoh's crook and flail, because they were originally husbandry tools for herding sheep. Over a seven hundred-year period, the rains quit and the 'red land' was first to become a desert. So the people moved to land nearer to the Nile, because after it flooded there were rich black deposits of silt, which was conducive for growing crops. The shepherds settled in Lower Egypt, or what was called the 'black land,' because of the black silt."

He took another drink of his cocktail before continuing. "Now when they left, the hunters came and settled in the 'red land,' which is Upper Egypt. This land was now a barren desert, but it separated them from neighboring countries and invading armies. It also was a source for precious metals and semi-precious stones. However, the hunters knew they also had to take control of the 'black land' over the shepherd kings, for their survival. They needed food. So after the fighting ceased, the unification was honored by sacrificing the shepherd kings' lambs to the gods."

There were some gasps, until Ian spoke. "You just said it was indicated it took seven hundred years for Egypt to go from shepherd kings ruling to when the hunters took over both lands?"

"Yes," said Dr. Granite.

"This is all starting to make sense," said Ian. "Some ancient Egyptian probably carved seven hundred into the belly of the lamb statue, knowing it was the final battle, because King Narmer won. It could have been his way of recording the length of time the shepherd kings ruled, because everyone at that battle would have known it was over. King Narmer would now rule both Upper and Lower Egypt."

He cleared his throat before continuing. "Don't you see? More proof that Dr. Seldon's theory is correct. The lamb statue represents the shepherd kings. It makes sense why the cosset Dr. Seldon found had *Sefekhu Shenet* written on its belly. The math checks out. So, 3850 B.C. minus seven hundred, the number on the belly of the lamb, equals 3150 B.C., which is in alignment to when King Narmer ruled."

Everyone nodded in agreement, but before anyone could speak, Mark and Edmund returned. "And now Dr. McCormick has his answer as to when the war ended," said Dr. Granite. "The pieces of this puzzle all fit into place. Queen Iput had the statue since she was a child. Remember the papyrus said Pharaoh Unas told his daughter it represented when they took control of Lower Egypt from the shepherd kings."

"I don't mean to interrupt," said Dr. Ramsey. "But something has come up and Dr. McCormick and I must leave Egypt tonight. Dr. Granite, I'm putting you in charge of tomorrow morning's tour of Djoser's tomb before it opens to the tourists. And then see to it the bus takes everyone directly from the pyramid to the airport. Please make sure everyone makes his or her flight. I'm sorry, but if everyone would excuse us—"

"Of course, Dr. Ramsey," interrupted Tom.

Edmund exited the room at a fast pace with Mark following. "Dr. Richards!" Mark's voice was elevated as he walked backwards out of the room. "Tell everyone what I told you. Remember, Queen Neithhotep and her wine jug. The Receiving of the South and North. And don't forget the good stuff. The looting, stealing and how it ended up in Queen Iput's tomb."

"Got it!" Ian yelled, giving Mark a thumbs-up.

"It's important to clear Cassie's name, her reputation." Mark's voice trailed off as Ian continued to nod.

After exiting the banquet room, Edmund stopped abruptly, causing Mark to bump into him. "I'm becoming more and more unsettled because everything is becoming tied to this papyrus." His voice became solemn. "I regret firing Dr. Seldon." He paused. "I probably jumped too quickly on this one. Ever since I arrived in Egypt I seem to be having regrets about some of the decisions I've made in my life." He looked down, and Mark knew his words were genuine.

"Well, all of us were interested in the story the papyrus was revealing."

"I know," said Edmund. "And that's why I'm taking you with me. Because I know, whether she wants to admit it or not, she trusts you. She'll talk to you. At the very least I owe her an apology—and to tell her that her findings have been accepted as part of the reason Dynasty Zero will be added to the ancient Egyptian timeline." A faint smile of hope was visible. "With you backing me up, she'll know it's true. I took my irritation and anger out on her when everyone was reading the papyrus."

Mark arched his brow. "Well, we need to get going and start packing."

"You're right," said Edmund. "But first I need to make a phone call. Egypt's antiquities minister told me if I needed anything during our stay to just ask."

"And what are you asking for?"

"A private jet." After Edmund told Mark to close his mouth, they proceeded to their rooms.

*

Cassie tilted her seat back and closed her eyes as the plane taxied down the runway. It was then that Mark popped into her thoughts. Was it because he had been so nice when she had had too much to drink?

She would definitely call him when she got back home. They may have settled their differences except for the timeline, which she could now prove. But she wanted to give him a piece of her mind for telling Dr. Ramsey about losing her baby. What business of his was it, anyways? She hoped Mark didn't think she had made this expedition a personal one like Edmund said and that's why he'd told him. As far as she was concerned, he had violated her trust in him, as if she didn't already have enough trust issues.

Her hand throbbed. She undid the bandage and saw a red line running past her wrist. She told herself as soon as she met her mother, they would go to an urgent care clinic before they went out to grab a bite to eat. She felt weak and emotionally drained. She closed her eyes to get some sleep because she knew once the plane landed, she had a lot to do.

SIXTY-TWO

Wow! Mark had expected the private jet to look like first class on a commercial flight, but this jet also had two small rooms in the back with beds where they could grab some shuteye. "Would you care for some dinner?" said the flight attendant. He looked at Edmund, who was rearranging his briefcase.

"Yes, say yes, let's eat before we try to get some sleep."

"Sure, whatever you have will be fine," said Mark.

"Would you care for some beer or wine with your meal?" said the very pretty auburn-haired flight attendant.

He once again looked Edmund's way. "Uh, Dr. Ramsey, do we care for some beer or wine with our meal?"

"You send me your enormous bar tab from the hotel's lounge and don't think twice, but now you ask me if it's okay to have a drink. Yes! Have her bring some beer. It will go great with the steak." Edmund was fumbling with his briefcase, still trying to get settled in.

Mark did a double take. "Steak?"

"I didn't get anything to eat or drink at the party," said Edmund.

Mark nodded to the flight attendant. "Yes, beer would be fine with our steak."

She smiled. "Thank you, sir. Would you like a glass with your beer?"

"Why not?" Mark's smile was glued to his face. "Seeing how we're doing everything first class." The flight on this private jet was much smoother than any commercial airline and he felt just fine. Plus, no one on board was smoking, so he would be able to enjoy this first-rate meal. "How do we know where to find Cassie when we land?"

"She'll be at the United Methodist Church, on Race Street."

"Oh, how do you know that?" Edmund was looking at him like he wanted to reprimand him for asking.

"Because it's the closest church to the Kreativ Museum." Mark sensed Edmund knew more but decided not to press him any further. "Anyways," said Edmund, "when did you start calling Dr. Seldon, Cassie?"

"Oh, wow, that's a story I'll need a couple of beers in me before I can tell you." The flight attendant brought two beers in chilled glasses and set them on the table between them. Mark handed Edmund his beer. He raised his glass in the air as if to toast, but just then she also put the biggest, juiciest steak down in front of him. He had not seen such a steak since leaving Chicago, and the only thoughts he had were of his food. "Miss," he raised his beer, "I'll have another one. Please!"

SIXTY-THREE

A.D. 1988, CINCINNATI, OHIO

The church had been declared an historic site in the late twentieth century. Built in the 1880s, it was one of the first German Methodist churches. It was a two and a half-storey stone structure with a front gable and a grand tympanum. The front had a Romanesque revival arch with small, circular windows and porches on both sides of the façade. It not only felt old world, it was. The offices were located in the back and the church was open during the day.

The interior had a senescent look to it with dark wood and dark pews. Even the pipe organ to the left of the altar was aged. Little light filtered through the sanctuary. This was the church where Reverend Westin used to be the minister and Susan felt comfortable inside its sanctuary.

She had been there most of the day in a state of torpor, entranced by the big, gold, ornate cross sitting on top of the altar. She was comfortable in her frayed jeans with the sparsely threaded knees and her dark blue turtleneck. She didn't feel the need to have to eat or drink. She had bathed—something she didn't feel compelled to do every day, because she was usually a miasma of sorrow. She had even tried to curl her long blondish-brown hair, parted down the middle, speckled in gray. She looked much older than her age, because of her lack of grooming. But she didn't care, because in her world she was always young and Cassie was always a child.

"In just a few more minutes my family will be here," she said aloud. Her right hand fidgeted along her right thigh. "I only have to wait a bit longer."

Cassie entered the church, taking a seat in the pew behind her. "It's me, Mama. I'm back."

Her heart started beating fast, yet outwardly she remained calm. She loved it when her daughter called her mama. She would always be her little girl. She felt Cassie's hand on her shoulder. "Mama, did you hear me?"

From behind, her daughter wrapped her arm around her shoulder. She enjoyed the fragile hug. Ever so softly, she spoke. "My little Cassie. You're back from Egypt. You are so much like him. You always thought the grass was greener on the other side. But you know it's not. It's just grass. Grass with weeds; the same weeds are on both sides of the fence. Because, after all, whether it is made out of fescues or Kentucky bluegrass, it's still made out of the same basic seeds." She sighed. "It only turns out better in some yards than others, because of the way it is nurtured and cared for; that's the only difference." She became silent, except for the fidgeting of her right hand against her right thigh.

"Mom, are you okay?"

"Everything I did, I did for you, you know," she said.

Cassie gripped her mother's shoulder. "Of course you did."

"In the end love does not bring you happiness, only sorrow." Her hand once again fidgeted against her leg. This was difficult, opening up. "That's why I did it, for you. So you would focus on a career and not a husband."

"Did what, Mom? What did you do?"

"You know he was weak. He would have done whatever his father wanted, and you were ready to follow him, no matter what. He felt unworthy of his minister father and saintly mother. He carried too much baggage. Like I do." She paused. "Without him, I knew you would become brilliant like your father. And I didn't want your future to be like your past."

"Who are you talking about? Chad?" She felt her daughter's grip tighten on her shoulder. "Why are you saying this now? After all these years?" Silence. "How would my future be like my past? I don't understand? Look at me, Mother!"

She kept her back to Cassie. "You would have been madly in love like I was. You would have done anything for him, just like me. And that's a dangerous thing." She kept rubbing her right thigh.

Cassie moved from her pew and sat at the end of the row next to her mother. "Look at me, Mama? What did you do? Answer me!"

"One Sunday, I asked Chad to take me to church. I told him I wanted to surprise his family, you know, so they would think I was really trying at this merging of our families. Although I didn't know why you still wanted Chad after Cassandra died. But I did it for your sake."

Susan's nerves fired inside her. "I arrived at the house after his parents had already left for church. His father was the minister, you know, and they had to leave earlier. I was wearing a black, long-sleeved dress and hat. I even put on a pair of lace gloves. I told Chad I was nervous and wanted to sit in the backseat. He opened the back door for me." She turned, looking into her daughter's eyes. "Imagine that, he held the door open for me. I almost didn't think I should do it after that. But then an ethereal feeling came over me. I thought of you. I only did it for you."

"Mama, I swear if you don't tell me right now what happened, I'll—"

"Settle, my little one. I got into the backseat. Chad thought when he turned the engine on I was fastening my seatbelt. But I wasn't. When he turned the engine on, I stabbed him in the back of his upper neck under his hair, with a double dose of your medicine. He yelled, and I had another needle ready, so I stabbed him again—another double dose of your medicine." She had her left hand in a fist, re-enacting the stabbing.

"He couldn't turn around. His body had begun to shake. He grabbed his chest, and when he did, I had the third needle ready and stabbed him. One… final… time. Then he went unconscious." She stopped for a moment, processing her words. "Then I put the empty syringes in my purse and got out of the car. All the windows were rolled up and the car was already running, so I pushed the button to shut the garage door and ran out before it closed on me."

"Oh my God! I'm going to be sick." Cassie put her hand to her mouth. She bent over, holding her stomach. "Chad didn't… commit suicide? You killed him?"

"I did it for you, and it worked." She was perturbed at her daughter and fidgeted some more, picking at her right thigh.

"You went on to college and focused on your career. And his family moved away."

"You made Chad your sacrificial lamb for the sake of me?" Cassie stood in the aisle. "Thank God Cassandra is with Chad, rather than with you or me, since I was a teenager and would have needed your help." She moved out into the aisle of the church, screaming. "It was my life, don't you see? And whatever I chose to do with it… it was my life! You didn't need to make Chad your sacrificial lamb. You already had one. I was your sacrificial lamb for your selfish need to keep your lover. Who probably never even loved you."

Susan was very tranquil and her speech was slow. "There was a time I thought he would marry me and come back to us. But in the end he didn't. And when you became pregnant, I wanted you to have a life, not a reflection of my life. Tell me, did your father ever tell you how good of an Egyptologist you really are?" She paused. "I'm sure that's why he took you to Egypt. He may not have been in love with me, but he must have loved you, or he wouldn't have cared. You look pale—sit down by me." She patted the end of the pew, but Cassie was just staring at her as if she was frozen in time.

"Is Dr. Ramsey my father?" she screamed. "Edmund Ramsey is my father!"

Susan stood with her hands behind her and walked to the aisle. When she did, blood exuded through the right leg of her jeans. She knew her daughter saw the blood when she grabbed her mouth, gagging. She watched Cassie turn and run past the pews, abruptly opening the doors of the church, tripping down the steps and fainting right into the arms of a handsome man around her age. Then the church doors swung closed.

*

Edmund saw Mark run up the steps just in time to catch Cassie as she fainted. "Let me help you lay her down." He noticed her hand. Even though it was wrapped, he could tell it was swollen. He looked at her arm and saw a red line running upwards. "Her wound is severely infected. She may be in a diabetic coma."

"Wound?" asked Mark. "That's the wound she had in Egypt. She refused to go to the doctor during the excavation. Wait, how do you know she's a diabetic?"

"Because I'm a diabetic." He saw Mark's confusion, but now wasn't the time for explanations. He noticed a woman on the street. "*Help!*" he yelled. "Call 911." Then he went inside the church looking for Susan.

She greeted him with extended arms. "Oh, Ed, you came. We can finally be married."

He noticed how unstable she looked and chose his words carefully. "Susan, I am... was... already married, and that was over thirty years ago. I am an old man now. Too old for this, and Cassie is all grown up. I cannot marry you." He was aware she now had a knife pointing at his chest. He didn't move, although his mind was racing. She was beyond disturbed. When had she gotten to this point? He noticed her pant leg had blood seeping through.

"You broke my heart and now it is time for me to break yours." She rearranged the knife in her hand, holding the blade higher. Her feral eyes were fixated on him. He reached his hands toward her to grab the knife, but they were sweaty, and in that split second he was too late. She stabbed herself savagely, dropping to the ground.

He kneeled down, trying to see through his tears. He had two people who might not live because of the decisions he had made in his life. He felt his wife would be ashamed of him if she were looking down from heaven. Inside his heartbeat was galloping. He started to weep; Edmund's voice was a whisper. "Mark, has help arrived? I found Susan." And with the next beat of his heart, paramedics busted through the church doors, along with the police.

SIXTY-FOUR

The hospital walls were a bland white. The nurses at the desk were busy and one looked overwhelmed. And a doctor's name was continuously being paged. Edmund's nostrils were inhaling the antiseptic sterile smells of the hospital and he was tired. He hadn't slept much last night, and now he was nervous. The closer he got to Cassie's room, the slower he seemed to walk. He was glad Mark was by his side.

When the paramedics had arrived, he had confessed he was Cassie's father and an old acquaintance of Susan's. He had listed his name as both of their emergency contacts, and when the hospital had called this morning, they told him Cassie had fainted from emotional trauma. The extra stress, along with her diabetes, had sent her into ketoacidosis, and she had an infection in her hand. She was severely dehydrated and had serious disturbances with the potassium levels in her blood. But she had not succumbed into a diabetic coma, and for that he was grateful.

He glanced at the clock on the wall. It was during afternoon visiting hours when he and Mark entered her hospital room. Cassie's bed was propped, she was awake and a doctor was speaking.

"For the infection in your hand," the doctor said, "the next few days we will have you on an intravenous corticosteroid. Also I'm changing your insulin dose. It should help with the light-headedness you've been having. And as a diabetic, my recommendation to you is that in the future, don't wait so long whenever you get any type of infection." She nodded. The doctor looked at Edmund. "Cassandra Seldon has excessive thirst and some fatigue, but nothing that can't be cured with a few days of bed rest." He turned back to Cassie. "And taking your insulin at regular intervals." He smiled at everyone then left.

"You can always call me with any questions about your insulin," said Edmund.

"You're a diabetic too?" she asked.

"Who's a diabetic?" Ian entered the room and stood by the foot of the bed next to Mark.

"We are." Edmund and Cassie spoke in unison.

"Did I miss something?" asked Ian.

"Did everyone get on the plane?" asked Edmund.

"Yes," said Ian. "Yesterday we checked out of the hotel, saw Djoser's pyramid, and then the bus took us to the airport. We landed at J.F.K. around 9:00a.m. our time this morning, and from there everyone took off on separate flights. I knew the three of you would be in Cincy, so I thought why not? So I took a detour to C.V.G."

"Cincy, what's a Cincy?" asked Mark.

"It's short for Cincinnati," said the nurse who had just entered the room. She was checking the equipment by the bed.

"By the way, why is the Cincinnati airport in Kentucky?" asked Ian.

Cassie answered. "The two cities are separated by the Ohio River. Ohio had the money and Kentucky had the land. Hence the name C.V.G. C is for Cincinnati, here in Ohio, and the VG is for Covington, which is in Kentucky."

The nurse frowned at her. "You're not supposed to talk while I take your vitals."

"Sorry," she said.

"Anyways," said Ian. "After I landed, I phoned Mark and he told me what hospital you were in, and, well, here I am."

"Thanks for coming, Ian," she said. "Oh, and Mark, I didn't get a chance to thank you for calling 911. And I also want to apologize to you. I thought you told Dr. Ramsey about my baby who died. But now I know Edmund always knew about Cassandra."

"Well," said Mark, "I stayed by your side, but I didn't call 911. A passerby helped us out." He paused. "And although I didn't tell Dr. Ramsey, I did tell Ian about your baby."

Edmund changed the subject. "I want you to know, Cassie; your mother is also in this hospital. Although she pointed a knife at me, she ended up stabbing herself. But lucky for her she missed her heart. The doctors stitched her up; however, she lost some blood, and they ended up giving her a transfusion."

"Why did they tell you about Susan?"

"I put myself down as both of your emergency contacts," said Edmund. "I also got her a lawyer. I spoke to him this morning and he thinks she probably won't stand trial for Chad's murder, due to the degringolade of her mental condition. She's going to be moved to the psyche ward and then evaluated." He moved closer to Cassie. "I want you to know I'm taking full financial responsibility for your mother. After the courts prove her unstable, I'm going to put her in one of Ohio's best mental institutions. I have been given recommendations in the Columbus area. I owe you that much."

"Thank you for taking that stress off me, but how did you meet my mother… and why did you leave her… um, us?"

"Because I was married." His tone was authoritarian, but then he softened his voice when he saw her eyes welling up. "You need to know, I always had some sort of contact with your mother while you were growing up."

"You mean Susan. She wasn't a good mother."

"Nor was I a good father." Edmund lowered his head. "Neither one of us did right by you. But I did buy the house you grew up in. It might have been small, but it was paid for. I didn't realize the neighborhood had deteriorated since you left home." He sat on the edge of the bed, extending his hand and waiting for Cassie to give him hers.

"Well, you're right about that. I feel I was deserted by you and Susan, physically and emotionally." She took his hand. "But, you're here now and trying to make amends. However, you need to know this won't be easy for me."

Edmund felt he needed to explain. "Once you graduated from the University of Memphis and were on your own… then I didn't have any more contact with Susan. You see, I used to teach at the Institute of Egyptian Art and Archaeology, which is part of the University of Memphis. It's where I met your mother." He reflected back. "After she became pregnant, I sent her money every month, and when the checks never came back, I knew she hadn't moved. But once I heard you were on your own, I stopped the checks and changed my phone number. I got tired of her calling for reasons that had nothing to do with you." He gazed downward, his conscience guilt-ridden.

"Then, when you became employed as an Egyptologist, with my connections… I was able to follow your career. When my wife died…" He paused. "Let's just say after her death, I realized how precious time is. It was then I knew I needed to get in touch with you." He took a handkerchief from his pocket and wiped his nose.

She adjusted herself on the bed. "I wish you had thought the right time was when I was born."

"I honestly didn't know she was this much out of touch with reality." Edmund felt exasperated. "I called her after I fired you." He stopped to contemplate on his next words. "She asked me to come to the church…" His voice trailed off; he cleared his throat. "I knew something was amiss, but I agreed because she said you would be there. Mark and I were able to arrive shortly after you because we flew non-commercial." He paused again. "So there you have it."

No one in the room spoke and Cassie was staring at him, so he felt he needed to go on. "I'm sorry I am making you feel so sad right now." His voice became apologetic. "I wish I had had these realizations years ago too. It's just… I didn't want to risk my wife finding out. It wasn't until after she died, I found out she knew about you all along." A tear streamed down his cheek. "I swear, Cassie, if I had known she knew, I would have been involved in your childhood."

She looked perplexed. "Then why didn't you get in contact with me right after your wife died, before the excavation?"

"And have you think that was the only reason why I chose you? Hell no!" He wiped his eyes with his handkerchief. "You're an expert in your field. And I knew you would be an invaluable asset in ending this timeline debate. I wanted success for you, so later there would be no doubt that I chose you because of the research and work you put into the timeline theory." He paused. "When you're feeling better and we're alone, then I'll answer all of your questions. And I hope at that time, you will find it in your heart to forgive me. I want to be a part of your life." He wanted to hug her. "After all, we're all we've got."

"Wait!" said Ian. "Dr. Ramsey's your father?" He pointed toward Edmund. "You fired your own daughter?"

"Yes, he did. Glad to see you're finally up to speed," said Mark.

Edmund ignored them; Cassie was speaking. "Yes, you're right, we're all we've got since I'm not ever going to have children again."

"Why?" said Ian. "You're still young."

"Due to my diabetes, I really don't want to risk it. Cassandra wasn't planned, but I do not want to go through another pregnancy."

"You can always adopt," said Ian.

"Oh, I already have, sort of, in my own way. I have four children I help support through a Christian sponsorship program."

"Wow, that's a lot of kids for someone who doesn't want to be a parent," said Ian. They all grinned.

"By the way," said Edmund, "if the museum does close, and you're looking for something to do, I can pull some strings and get you an associate professor's job for a term."

Mark interjected. "That might not be necessary. The Field Museum called me this morning, and it seems Dynasty Zero has generated a lot of attention, which has really helped both museums. So I put in for a grant to go on another excavation. And I highly doubt Kreativ Museum will be closing any time soon."

"So you'll be heading back to Chicago?" asked Ian.

"Only until my grant comes through. The excavation is to further research the remnants found in the city of Thonis-Heracleion."

Edmund saw Cassie perk up. "The lost kingdom of Cleopatra?"

"Yes," said Mark. "The city is submerged in Egypt's Aboukir Bay, in Alexandria. Seeing as it's Cleopatra's city, I could certainly use an Egyptologist." He raised his brows and nodded. "Especially one that is good at proving theories. Think I'll find anyone interested?"

She smiled. "You just might at that."

"Good," he said. "And if both of our museums make it a joint effort like we did with Dynasty Zero, we can share the expenses."

"And the credit," said Edmund. "This would ensure the solvency of the Kreativ Museum and add to the already-well-noted Field Museum." He noticed they were all smiling. "They say what caused the city to sink was the liquefaction of the soil. Pressure from buildings, along with flooding, can cause the soil to compress, forcing the expulsion of water within the clay. This could have happened due to an earthquake, or a tidal wave." He shrugged.

"Looks like you'll be needing Dr. Granite," said Ian.

"And you too," said Mark.

"I doubt any papyri survived beneath the Mediterranean."

Mark smiled. "Are you forgetting? If I receive this grant, well, you do have the latest equipment."

"Do any of you know how to scuba dive?" asked Edmund.

They all shook their heads no. "Do you?" asked Ian.

"As a matter of fact, I do. I am now officially retired, but I would love to come along... at my own expense, of course, to lend my expertise, whether it be excavating artifacts or helping all of you learn how to scuba dive."

"Is there anything you haven't done?" asked Cassie.

"I haven't told you how proud I was the day I heard you had become an Egyptologist." Edmund put his hand into his pant pocket. "Speaking of artifacts..." He pulled out an airtight baggie containing the statue of the baby lamb. Everyone gasped. He put his hand into the air. "Don't get too excited. It's on loan from Egypt's antiquities minister. And I'm putting it into your care." His eyes locked on to hers. "With Mark's good news, you'll be able to exhibit your favorite artifact, along with your other findings. People will come to the Kreativ Museum to see the artifacts which helped create Dynasty Zero."

Her voice was a whisper. "The cosset. Thank you." He leaned in to hand it to her and felt her arms around his neck. He knew his wife would be proud of him in this moment.

The nurse re-entered the room and told them they all needed to leave. Visiting hours would be over in ten minutes. "Well, you heard her," said Ian. "We have to let you rest."

Cassie nodded. "Okay, but before you go, did everyone part on good terms?"

"I hope so—I already spoke to Dr. Granite and he seemed to think so," said Mark.

"Oh, I almost forgot," said Ian. "Megan, the radiologist, showed after the two of you left." He pointed to Edmund and Mark. "And I had many, many drinks with her. Seems after several drinks, well… she wants me to contribute to her biological clock."

"Wait… what? She wants you to father her baby?" asked Mark.

"Don't get too excited, I haven't turned. It would just be… let's say, a donation done in a fertility clinic. It's a way for me to have a child. And next to the three of you, I'm not so screwed up after all." Everyone laughed.

"Well, I think you would make a great dad," said Cassie.

"We'd better go before the nurse comes in again," said Edmund. The three of them said their goodbyes and left.

*

Darkness approached outside the hospital window. Cassie felt tired but not drowsy, so she turned on the television and flipped through the channels, stopping at a major national news network when she heard her name. "…Cassandra Seldon's findings. An etched piece of a pottery shard found in Queen Iput's tomb. Given the provenance of this discovery, she has given another piece of evidence to Dr. Günter Dreyer's ratification of Dynasty Zero. Her conclusive evidence is more proof it did exist. And upon further review, the head of the Egyptian antiquities department has officially proclaimed Dynasty Zero is to be added to the Egyptian timeline."

She flipped to a cable news channel. They had a picture of Dr. Günter Dreyer, her father, Dr. Ramsey and an old photo of herself up on a split screen. At one point in time her mother must have given this picture to Edmund. She turned up the volume. "Seems it was easier to call it Dynasty Zero than to change all the numbers on the existing dynasties," the broadcaster said in jest. "Otherwise you would have to not only renumber, but then have to try to remember that King Tut was not of Dynasty Eighteen but now Dynasty Nineteen. That really would be confusing. It is much simpler to keep King Tut in Dynasty Eighteen and just record this new dynasty as Zero."

Cassie put her hand to her mouth and changed to a local news channel; *The World News* was wrapping up. "Dynasty Zero denotes the years 3150–3050 B.C." The newscaster continued. "Also from the excavation of the renowned archaeologist/Egyptologist, Dr. Edmund Ramsey, a thirty-two-year-old Egyptologist, Dr. Cassandra Seldon, has been given a footnote in Dr. Günter Dreyer's recognition of Dynasty Zero."

She couldn't believe what she was seeing and hearing. This was only the beginning. She would have papers to write, lectures to give, maybe even an interview or two. Her heart was beating like a drum. She finally felt she was qualified and worthy of all these accolades. Years of composing reports, outlining hypotheses, sketching, studying, probing, brushing and detailing from her amateur digging years as a curious student. And now she finally had the professional validation she'd been seeking.

She remembered something one of her college professors had said. Most discoveries are sitting there, right before your eyes, waiting for you to find them. And so it was in her quest to find Dynasty Zero, she had found her father. He had been there all along, right before her, waiting. The hole within her heart was beginning to fill, and for the first time in a long time she was happy.

She then thought about an ancient Egyptian saying: "Whatever you write down comes into being, if not in this life, then in the next." She picked up a notepad and pen off of the bedside table. She wrote: "Bringing the past into the present, ensures our future."

SIXTY-FIVE

Cassie strolled up the incline past the tree. It was bursting with dark brown buckeye nuts. She stopped at the top and smoothed her white cami. Over it she wore a navy blue blazer with a pair of jeans tucked into her hiking boots. As she approached the grave, the clouds released a light mist of rain, but she scarcely noticed as she read the headstone: "God took you up to heaven to dwell; you will always be in our hearts; you were a son that pleased us well."

She lightly touched the arch of the gravestone. Her voice was barely audible as she spoke. "I am sorry, so, so sorry, Chad, that Susan did this, but justice will finally be given to you. My mother will be locked up, institutionalized until she meets her death. And I'm not so sure you or Cassandra will ever see her. I don't really know if heaven is in her future, but because I know you, I know... if you did see her, you would forgive her." Her eyes welled with tears. She took a tissue out of her tote, ever so gently wiping them.

"I want you to know I will always love you and your death was not in vain." She sniffled. She opened her tote again, taking out Cassandra's baby blanket, the blue flannel one with the pink fluffy lambs and white sateen edging. She knew Chad was in heaven being a great father to Cassandra. She was just sorry it didn't happen in this world. She wiped away more tears.

The mist turned into a sprinkle. She turned to the next headstone, placing the baby blanket at the base of the stone. Kneeling on the blue flannel blanket, she ran her fingers along the lamb etched into the stone above the engraving that read, "Although your days on earth were few, the lives you touched will always love you."

She heard thunder. Then a steady stream of rain began. She looked upwards toward heaven, then at the headstone, speaking aloud. "Cassandra, please, please forgive me. I should have woken up that night. Oh, how I have replayed that day over and over in my mind until I have nearly gone crazy. But I ask for your forgiveness because I know you are now in God's protection."

She sighed, looking out into the darkness. "God, please be with every baby who has ever died from S.I.D.S. or S.U.D.C. No, wait. Please take all the babies who have died before their time into your protected care. Please take care of Anhai and Iput's son. And please take care of Chad... and me. I don't want to go crazy like my mother. And please, oh, please, forgive my mother." Lightning flashed; her tears turned into sobs. She cried throughout the storm and darkness.

*

Some time later, when her tears had passed, the rain and darkness had also faded. She propped herself up against Cassandra's headstone, thinking about why she became an Egyptologist. She remembered Mark telling her something on the plane—to bring to light the process of preservation against time.

Anhai gave up her baby to preserve her viability. The princess would hold her in high esteem for doing this, and in time, by becoming a priestess, so would the people. Iput wanted to preserve herself as queen, for she was of royal blood. And as time went on, she gave her son, Pepi, everything she valued in life. And Cassie, since losing Cassandra, had had to make a new life to preserve her existence. She now understood how precious time was and how it was not always a given.

The sun peeked out from behind the clouds, and for the first time since Cassandra's death she felt at peace. She would no longer cry for the loss of her motherhood. She now understood what she had always told herself. *For every baby or child God takes to heaven, there is a mother and father waiting to nurture them, because they were taken from their children on earth before their time.* She didn't want any more children. Ever. But she felt a sense of responsibility to the children who were still here on earth, so she would continue giving through the Christian sponsorship program that Chad's mother had suggested.

And Egyptology was about bringing the past into the present to ensure the future. That was why she had become an Egyptologist. And now, by making peace with her past, she could overcome the burdens and pains of her present, ensuring her future. Not only in this life but also in the next. She found herself smiling, realizing how the meaning of her profession was also the meaning for her personal life. And she did not fear death any longer. For she knew Cassandra and Chad would be waiting. And in death she would once again become a mother to babies above who didn't have theirs anymore.

She stood, shaking Cassandra's baby blanket. It was damp and had some mud on it, but it didn't matter now. It was no longer a shrine to her baby. It was her baby's blanket. She shoved it into her tote, pulling out an airtight baggie full of dried blue lotus flowers. She opened the bag and gently sprinkled them around Cassandra's grave. She scattered the remaining few along the base of Chad's headstone.

Cassandra would have been sixteen years old today—the same age Cassie was when she gave birth to her. She took out a pair of leather gloves and put them on before pulling out the storage bag that contained the ancient statue of the cosset. She placed it on top of the headstone. Deep in thought for a moment, she contemplated if she was tempting fate by doing this, so she said a prayer for Cassandra and Tetiankhkm's souls. And then, ever so delicately, she picked up the cosset, placed it back into the airtight bag and returned it to her tote. Rummaging through it, she pulled out the little stuffed lamb her baby had loved. She decided to leave it on top of the headstone, symbolizing the 'Death of the Cosset,' the loss of her little lamb. She said another quick prayer for her mother and herself.

Strolling downward, passing the tree bursting with buckeyes, she spotted Mark. He was leaning against the trunk of her car. She smiled and hurried down the muddy incline toward him, trying not to fall. "How did you get here?" She was enthusiastic.

"Taxi. Dr. Ramsey, well, Edmund, told me he brought you home after you were discharged this morning. He mentioned you said you wanted… well, needed to come here."

She smiled. "Don't you have to get back… to work?"

"Vacation days." He smiled back.

He looked so good leaning against the trunk of her car. His green eyes lit through his glasses when he smiled and he looked rather handsome in his leather jacket. "Do you want to drive? You need to know how to get around in this city."

"Sure, men are better drivers anyways," he said in jest. "Don't look at me like that. Not today. That can be the subject for our next debate." They both grinned. "Hey, I was thinking since I'm in town, maybe we could grab a bite to eat. I feel I owe you a meal after helping you get drunk the last time. And I also want to bring you up to speed on what happened in Egypt after you were forced to leave so abruptly."

"As in like a date?" she asked.

"Yes. As in like a date," he repeated. "I really want to take you to dinner and get to know you better."

She could sense he was sincere. And as she put her hands into his, he placed his lips onto hers. Coming out of their kiss, they got into the car. Cassie looked on as Mark adjusted the driver's seat before she spoke. "And I want to get to know you well enough to show you my closet."

"Well, I think that may be happening sooner, rather than later. You look like you've been out in the rain. Your clothes are all wet." The two of them laughed as Mark pulled away from the curb, and Cassie looked out the window.

The hole in her heart was filling with the peace she felt within this cemetery, within the ancient story and within herself. The sky was calm. She was calm. All was right in life.

EPILOGUE

The stars were shimmering amongst the night sky as the silver disc rose above Queen Iput's pyramid. The scribe Hezi knew he had to come when Pepi told him his mother, the queen, was dead. He said she fell in her tomb and hit her head. Hezi knew that was not the truth, but he was not going to accuse the *nesu* of murder. However, the queen's ending, he did not want to know. He thought it strange when Pepi began asking him questions about the goddess Maat. He said it was because he had unsealed King Unas's tomb and saw images of Maat engraved on the walls. He knew his mother would want the same goddess her *abi* had in his tomb.

Hezi knew much about Maat. All scribes did; they were taught in school to follow the teachings of Maat in their work. They were also taught it would do them well to follow the goddess's teachings in their private lives. He entered the tomb and saw Queen Iput's body still lying on the slab. Her burial process was to start at sunrise, so he knew he only had tonight.

He bowed before his queen. He saw her *ka* had left her body and he knew her *ba* had also ascended into the afterlife. He said a prayer to Maat, asking that her *akhu* would live amongst the gods and goddesses. Looking at the queen he respected, he began speaking. "Your royal highness, because of my love and esteem for you, I bury your secret, forever, with you, for only the gods and goddesses to see."

Then he held his fist to his heart. "For the betterment of Egypt." And with that he left the second papyrus written in red ink, the one that held the truth, inside her tomb. The truth would be buried with her—hidden within a large vase.

ACKNOWLEDGMENTS

The author would like to start off by thanking God. After surviving cancer twice and knowing how time is not always a given, I decided I needed to get my ideas together and finish my book. However, I was not sure how to go about this. So, I prayed often, asking God, "I know what I want to write, but how do I write it?" After organizing hundreds of ideas and creating a twenty-page outline, God answered... one word at a time.

I would like to thank everyone at Matador Publishing, who were consistent in helping me navigate through this process, offering sound advice. They are the ones credited for turning this manuscript into a book.

To my husband Rick, who when trying to print a form, discovered my book. The printer was out of paper and I was out of time. So after he purchased paper, and expecting to print a one-page form, out came a novel, then the form to follow. Enormous thanks for reading my story several times and letting me know what word, phrase or characters actions didn't work, as well as what did.

Thank you to my mother for expanding my world outside of Detroit and the United States. Much love to my daughters,

Lyndsey, Lauren and Alexis, for their boundless enthusiasm for life, finding their place in the sun and forever shining.

And to all of my family members and friends, tremendous thanks for being the wonderful people who fill my life. Thank you for taking the time to read my book.

Much love to all of you!

GLOSSARY

Abi:	Father.
Akhu:	An immortal soul.
Ankh:	Symbol known as the key of life, represented life.
Anubis:	God of death. Depicted as a wolf- or jackal-headed man.
Apep:	God of darkness. Depicted as a snake.
Ba:	Ancient Egyptians believed this was a person's personality. It could live on when the person died.
Deshret:	Red crown representing Lower Egypt.
Fenugreek:	A white-flowered herbaceous plant.
Hathor:	Goddess of beauty, love, sexuality and protection. Depicted as a woman wearing a headdress of cow horns and a sun disk.
Hedjet:	White crown representing Upper Egypt.
Henqet:	Egyptian beer. Usually served warm.
Hierakonpolis:	City in ancient Egypt. The modern-day city of Kom El-Ahmar, or Kom Al-Ahmar.
Hieroglyphs:	A formal form of ancient Egyptian writing.
Horus:	God of protection. Depicted as a falcon-

headed man wearing the *pschent* crown. The all-seeing eye.

Isis: Goddess of the afterlife. Depicted as a woman wearing a throne-like hieroglyph on her head.

Jfedu: The number four.

Jfedu cubits: An ancient measurement representing cubits. Four cubits equaled six feet.

Ka: Ancient Egyptians believed this was the life force of the body, a person's soul.

Kalasiris: A linen sheath worn by women.

Khemet: The number three.

Khenty She: An elite army of chosen men from the Egyptian army.

Kreativ: A German word for creative. Kreativ Museum means Creative Museum.

Maat: Goddess of truth, morality and justice. Depicted as a woman with an ostrich feather in her hair.

Mastaba: Tomb with a flat roof and sloping sides.

Medshu: The number ten, often represented with a symbol of a yoke.

Meskhenet: Goddess of fertility, childbirth and a person's fate. Depicted as a woman with a cow's uterus on her head.

Natron: A mixture of baking soda and salt. Used for embalming.

Nekhbet: Goddess of protection. Depicted as a bird with her wings spread, one upward and one downward.

Nesu:	King.
Nu:	Name of the cosmic ocean. Where creation began.
Nut:	Goddess of the sky, stars and cosmos. Depicted as a woman wearing a waterpot on her head and holding an *ankh*.
Opening of the Mouth Ceremony:	A symbolic opening of a mummy's mouth from a statue representing the deceased, so they could breathe and speak in the afterlife.
Opening of the Year Ceremony:	Held when the Nile began to flood, to ensure fertility of the farmlands for another year. Did not have an exact date.
Osiris:	God of life, death, afterlife, the underworld and resurrection. Depicted as a green-skinned man, which represented rebirth. Wearing a pharaoh's beard, with two ostrich feathers on each side of his head, mummified at the legs, holding a crook and flail.
Papyrus:	A thin, paper-like material made from the pith (soft, spongy tissue), of the papyrus plant once abundant along the Nile Delta of Egypt. Used as paper for writing. Papyri for plural.
Peseshkaf:	Spoon blade used in Opening of the Mouth Ceremonies.
Pharaoh:	Present-day term to describe the rulers of ancient Egypt.
Pschent:	Crown representing the combination of Upper and Lower Egypt's individual

crowns to unify the lands. Used in present time when describing the crowns.

Pyramid Texts: Spells carved into Old Kingdom pyramid walls to help a deceased spirit transfer into a new life.

Ra: God of creation, life and the sun. Depicted as a male with a falcon head wearing a golden orb, representing the sun. Pharaoh's god.

Receiving of the South and North Ceremony: A ceremony honoring the unification of Upper and Lower Egypt.

Ritual of Valor Ceremony: A ceremony where the king wears the deshret crown and has his royal powers renewed.

Saqqara: Ancient Egyptian burial ground.

Sarcophagus: A stone box receptacle for a corpse.

Sed Festival: A festival representing a king's right to rule.

Schenti: Kilt or skirt made of cloth or leather, worn by men.

Sefekhu: The number seven.

Sefekhu Shenet: The number seven hundred.

Sekhemti: Same as the *pschent* crown. Used in ancient Egyptian time when describing the crowns.

Senuj: The number two.

Senuj fingers: An ancient measurement representing two fingers.

Senuj palms: An ancient measurement representing two hands.

Serekh: A rectangle symbol representing the façade

of the palace. Enclosed was the king's name. This predated cartouches.

Shard: A broken piece of pottery.

Shedeh: A favorite Egyptian drink made from pomegranates and grapes. When mixed with wine it would hide the taste of poison, which was a mixture of opium and hemlock. Cleopatra and Socrates used this mixture to end their lives.

Shenet: The number one hundred, often represented as a coiled rope.

Sjsu: The number six.

Sobek: God of water, marshes and the Nile. Depicted as a male with the head of a crocodile.

Syenite: Rock made out of feldspar.

Thonis-Heracleion: Ancient Egyptian city referred to as the Lost Kingdom of Cleopatra.

Uraeus: A cobra head ornament sometimes found on ancient Egyptians crowns, worn by royalty.

Vizier: Advisor to the royal family, especially the pharaoh.

Wa: The number one.

Wadjet: Goddess of protection. Depicted as a snake-headed woman or as a cobra. The all-seeing eye.

Wesekh: A beaded collar worn around the neck.

CPSIA information can be obtained
at www.ICGtesting.com
Printed in the USA
BVHW080312011220
594589BV00038B/1732